The Hawk and the Wolf

Britain, the Island of the Mighty, stands on the brink of war with the Roman Empire. Excalibur is lost—the sword forged by the gods in the dawn of days, which has been passed down through the generations of High Kings. Can Britain stand without the help of the gods? Young prince Emrys, nicknamed Merlin, knows his destiny is to find the lost sword of power, for the gods have given him a special gift to see into the heart of the world. He knows the rebel goddess Morgana will kill him to take Excalibur and become Queen of the Island of the Mighty, with a promise of days dark and bloody. In this fast-paced and violent tale, the world seems poised upon the brink of two possibilities: darkness and death . . . or the age of Arthur.

"Gifted storytelling, erudite scholarship, and a deep sense of wonder combine in this fantastic tale of adventure through a time when mystery and magic still walked upon the earth" (Dr. Flint J. Armstrong)

"Drawing simultaneously from history and legend, Mark Adderley skillfully weaves realistic detail into the Arthurian mythos. His characters inhabit a very tangible ancient world, where magic must compete with the mud and smoke of the everyday. He gives us a young, struggling Merlin whose travels around the British Isles provide us tantalizing glimpses of the mature wizard he'll become. The result should prove satisfying for both scholars of Arthuriana and lovers of fantasy literature." (Nathaniel Williams, AboutSF, University of Kansas)

"A worthy addition to the Arthurian Canon" (Bill Tolliver, *Renditions of Camelot*)

Coming Soon from WestBank Publications:

The Hawk and the Cup

THE HAWK AND THE WOLF

Book One
The Matter of Britain

To Jack,
Best Wishes,
Mark A[...]
9/9/10

Mark Adderley

WestBank

Publishing

The Hawk and the Wolf
2nd edition

Published by WestBank Publishing

For Information Address:
4408 Bayou Des Familles
Marrero, LA 70072

Cover Art by Floyd Alsbach

Printed in the United States of America

To Adrianne

I

That evening always stood out in Emrys' memory, because that was the night his grandfather's guest turned into a serpent.

Rhydderch, king of Cambria, sat with his youthful guest, the orange light from the hearth suffusing their faces as they talked politics. Politics bored Emrys. Even in his later, and remarkable days, when he had been the advisor to many kings, politics would always bore him. They were a distraction from his real interests—the ways of birds and trees, history, tradition, poetry, the living ghosts that the bards sang about on long winter evenings. But Rhydderch was talking politics with his guest, because his guest was Coroticos, son of the High King of Britain.

Chief Dragon of the Island of the Mighty. That was the ancient title of the High Kings, since the time of Brutus the Trojan. Perhaps it was his reflection upon the High King's title that caused what happened next. For it was as Emrys pondered the grandeur of such a title that the transformation began.

First of all, Coroticos' nose and chin merged and stretched into an elongated snout. The hue of his skin darkened to a deep crimson, like a fierce sunset or heart's blood. It shone, like a serpent's scales. Great bat-like wings unfurled, catching and hurling back at it the hearth's light, and casting huge and menacing shadows on the wall behind him. The dragon raised one terrible claw, and Emrys saw clutched in it a sword of great beauty—*the* sword, Excalibur. Emrys gaped. He looked about the hall. Only the son of the High King was affected, and everyone else was behaving normally, as if they had not noticed their prince's metamorphosis. Emrys rubbed his eyes.

Coroticos was himself again. A remarkable man, but a man.

The hall swam about Emrys, and he put out a hand to the table to steady himself. Gradually, the world returned to normal, and Emrys sagged, panting over the picked-at food before him.

"How fares my lord the prince?" came a voice. Emrys looked up. There was an expression of concern on the face of Cathbhad, bard to his grandfather.

"Thank you, Cathbhad," he replied. "I was giddy for a moment, that's all."

"No more but even so?"

"No more."

Cathbhad peered at him closely. He seemed to be staring not at Emrys, not into his eyes, but at his forehead. Then, as if covering up a blunder, he reached up and with a self-conscious motion swept aside a stray few strands of Emrys' hair.

Emrys and the bard turned again to look at the king of Cambria and the prince of Britain, sitting together at their repast. But Emrys was wondering at the strange vision that had shaken him so; and he wondered if it would visit him again.

But all thoughts of dragons and visions were soon swept from Emrys' mind, for it was at that moment that he saw Boudi approach: Boudi, who wore her beauty like a mystery about her, and now lowered herself onto the trestle beside Emrys, saying to Cathbhad, "Will you not sing, my lord Cathbhad?"

"For you, my lady Boudicea," replied Cathbhad, "I shall sing anything."

"Sing of the sword of power," said Boudi. "Sing of Excalibur."

Cathbhad sighed deeply. "That is a tale of sadness, lady," he said, "but, since I have promised, I may not say you nay."

Cathbhad stepped forward, taking his harp reverently from its case. Emrys leaned forward. This was always his favourite part of the festivities. Beside him, he was aware of Boudi, regarding him out of the corner of her eye. Her eyes, he knew, never left him, and his eye delighted in nothing so much as her. But he wanted to hear the tale.

Cathbhad began to speak. At first, no one paid him any mind, and continued their own conversations; but after a while, one by one, they fell silent. Cathbhad's words became alive, and walked up and down in their minds and hearts.

Then they saw Brutus, dead to the world for over a thousand years, standing in the prow of his ship as he crossed the sea from Benwick. He did not look behind him, and he never had. He had been driven from the land of his birth, and had sought a new home throughout the southern seas; and the gods had brought him at last here, to a northern land called Albion. At his side was Excalibur, the sword of kings, handed to him by Argante, the Lady of the Lake. With Excalibur, Brutus would bring low all enemies, and would subdue Albion to him, changing even its name until it resembled his own: Britain, the Island of the Mighty.

Cathbhad plucked the strings of his harp, and the quality of his voice changed. He chanted, and the word-magic deepened. Men saw the bright blade in their minds, light pouring down it like an amorous liquid, fire flashing from its point. The hilt was bound with leather, the quillions were gold, red the stone set in the pommel. Cathbhad sang, and the fingers of the men of the warband twitched, for they felt the perfect balance of the sword, felt the joy of a perfect swing. The blade seemed to carry itself forward, to be eager to cut and slash, to drive back the enemies of the Island of the Mighty. The giants who lived in Albion threw themselves at the first Britons, but they drove them back, and Gogmagog, their chief, plunged from the cliff and dashed himself to pieces on the rocks; a wave crashed, and there was nothing left. Brutus and Excalibur had prevailed, and for a thousand years, no one would challenge the supremacy of the Britons.

Cathbhad drove his fingers over the harp strings in one last chord, and suddenly they were all back in Rhydderch's hall in Caermyrddin. Servants moved between the tables, conversation resumed, knife fell into meat. Emrys drew a deep breath.

Boudi leaned closer. Her proximity to Emrys was like a piquant aroma, and it stirred him deeply, even more deeply than the tale. She said, in her deep voice, smooth as samite, "Emrys, I have a dream."

"What dream is that?" he asked. Emrys had dreams too—strange dreams he could not fathom. But he kept them close in his heart, as he did many things, and not even Boudi knew of them.

9

"I have a dream," said Boudi, and indeed her voice sounded as if it came from another world, "that one day the Island of the Mighty will be mighty in more than just name."

"What do you mean?"

She looked at him with a little crease between her brows. "Don't be stupid," she said. "I hate it when you're stupid. It makes me think that everyone else is right about you, and I'm wrong. And I know I'm never wrong."

"Boudi," smiled Emrys. "I will never be stupid, because I don't want you to hate me."

"Very well," replied Boudi. "I promise I shan't hate you."

"But what do you mean? Britain *is* mighty. How could you make Britain mighty when it's already mighty?"

Boudi didn't answer at once. There was a knife on the table in front of her and, very carefully, she picked it up and wiped the grease from it so that it flashed like a mirror. And there was her face, as beautiful and wild as a wolf's, but sliced in half by the edge of the knife. She said, "The Romans rule the world, but one day, it will be the Britons who are greatest."

"The Romans couldn't conquer us," argued Emrys, but he spoke softly. He was fascinated by Boudi's face, by the curve of her lip and the flare of her nostril, by the perfect smoothness and whiteness of her cheek; by the fire that was in her eyes.

"Since they failed to conquer us," said Boudi quietly, "they have conquered many other realms. And they will be back. My father says so."

Emrys was silent for a while. He felt a prickling on the back of his scalp, and the slightest twitch in the shoulder, as if some invisible hand were impelling him . . . where? "It must be Excalibur," he said at length. "Only a High King wielding Excalibur can do as you wish."

"But Excalibur is lost," remarked Boudi. "The High King will have to succeed on his own merits." She turned to look at him. There was fire in her countenance, and her lips burned as they formed words. "Or perhaps not the High King. If the High King cannot rise to greatness, maybe others can. The greatness is in our blood, not in the metal of a sword."

Emrys shrugged. "But what can we do?"

Boudi looked down. "Nothing now," she said. "Nothing now." Again, she gazed intently at the knife, as if it were a mighty weapon and she a great warrior. "But soon," she murmured.

And Emrys knew that she would be the great love of his life.

* * *

The next day, Coroticos left, and Boudi returned home with her father, Cydwelli. It was a morning of mist and croaking ravens in spiny winter trees, and Emrys passed with fearful glances the yew tree that stood in the courtyard of his grandfather's castle and, finding a tree that grew near the palisade, climbed to the top of it to look down at the departing household. There were a few warriors, and a closed cart for the women. Boudi watched him silently from among the women. She did not smile, nor wave, but from her heart, she bade him farewell for the moment; and his heart understood.

For a moment, and quite suddenly, the mist seemed to rise up all about him. Not a dark mist, but one suffused with light. Emrys clutched at his heart. He bowed his head, and his other hand groped for the branch. There were shapes in the mist, shapes all around him, but there, where Boudi had been a moment before, stood a wolf, its jaws slimed with gore. The wolf lifted its head and opened those bloody jaws, and emitted a mournful sound, a howl of piercing agony. Something stirred near Emrys, and he saw a hawk, its wings spread, glide down to stand in the shadow of the wolf.

Then, in a twinkling, the vision had gone. The mist retreated into the ground, and Emrys sat among the labyrinthine branches of the old yew, looking down on Boudi as she sat in the cart among the other women. She was frowning, as if she had seen something of what Emrys had seen. But now the farewells had been concluded, and Cydwelli had mounted his horse. A horn sounded, and the cavalcade began to move off through the gates.

Emrys clambered down the bole. He still felt weak in the knees after his odd waking dream, but he dashed across the courtyard, and climbed to the top of the wooden stockade. He was in time to see the last of the cavalcade as it rolled along the narrow road. Soon, the mists had swallowed it, and left Emrys alone.

Alone. Emrys looked to the left and right. The sentries were not near him. He seemed to spend a lot of his time alone. The other children of the fortress avoided him when they could. He did not think they disliked him; but they thought him different, somehow.

But there was one person who would listen to him, other than Boudi.

Stirred into action, Emrys dashed down the ladder that was set up against the battlements. The courtyard was a busy place at mid-morning, crisscrossed by various people on errands from one place to another. The aroma of wood smoke mingled with that of pigs that rose from the nearby sty. Emrys turned to the left and passed out through the gates into the road that Boudi and her father's household had so recently taken. But he did not stay on the path. Instead, after a few paces, he plunged into the forest.

Presently, he heard the merry chatter of a stream, and followed it against the current. It was narrow and brown, and he could have stepped across it, but the banks were muddy from the recent rains, and the ground slick with wet autumnal leaves. Emrys' breath steamed as he plodded along, the wind in the branches above him, and the rattle of magpies coming to him from all around.

When he had followed the stream for perhaps ten minutes, he came to a place where the ground rose steeply, and hazels stood about a moss-grown rock. It was out of this rock that the stream issued, spouting from a fissure with joyous abandon. A small bronze plaque had been fixed above it, into which was etched a picture of Tylweth, with waters churning all around her. It was said that the spring had originally been harmful, but that the goddess had hurled her magical powers against it. The spring had risen and over-whelmed her, but thereafter the river was sweet and healthful. Emrys cupped his hand in the icy water and raised it to his lips, breathing a quick word to the goddess of poetry.

Beside the spring was a small bothie made of wattle-and-daub leaning against the face of the rock. A bull's hide stretched across the doorway, and Cathbhad sat outside, strumming upon his harp in an apparently absent-minded fashion. On seeing Emrys, however, he ceased at once, and narrowed his eyes, as if he saw something that puzzled him deeply.

"Good health and long days attend you, Cathbhad," said Emrys.

"And you, Prince Emrys," returned the bard. His brow was still dark, but with an effort he cleared it.

"What are you doing?" asked Emrys.

Cathbhad set aside his harp. "I was composing a eulogy in praise of your grandfather," he said, "but now I am talking to you. But you, my prince," he added, peering closely at Emrys, "what brings you so far from the fortress of your grandfather?"

"I want to know things," said Emrys.

"What, exactly?"

"Everything," replied Emrys. "Everything you can tell me."

"That would take many moons," answered the bard. "It took me all my life to learn what I know, and I have traveled to many lands, to Eirin and Gaul and Benwick, and even beyond. And I was young when I started." He looked piercingly at Emrys as he said this. "Why don't you sit down?"

Emrys sat beside him, on a rock. His hands were between his knees, fidgeting as if he were nervous. "Then tell me about Excalibur," he said.

Cathbhad smiled. "Would you wield it in battle, for the love of the beauteous Boudicea?" he said. Emrys squirmed and looked at the ground between his feet. "A perilous desire, that. It is the sword of kings, and only a High King may wield it."

"How was it lost?"

Cathbhad sighed. "No two storytellers agree on that," he said. "Some say that Belinos, bosom-companion of King Cassivelaunos, took it with him in the ship *Prydwen*. No man can say whither he went, but the legends speak of a hidden place, protected by strong magic, where the *Prydwen* is said to rest. Others claim that Morgana, great enemy of the Britons, knowing Excalibur to be separated from the High King, attacked and murdered Belinos and took the sword to her realm of Annwn. Still others attest that the sword sank with the ship."

"How can one be certain?"

"There is no certainty beneath the moon," replied Cathbhad. "The finding of Excalibur will be the task of many lifetimes of men, if it can be found at all."

"What do you think?"

13

Cathbhad considered the question for a moment. At length, he took up his harp, struck a chord, and sang softly:

"Bright was the blade   of Brutus the brave

Loyallest of lords,   beloved of men,

Forged by fäerie   in the freshness   of the first day

Sundered from men   the sword of kings

Through stone,   over sea,   under sod,

Unseen by eyes,   Excalibur of old,

Fear-maker in foes,   ancient heirloom.

The brand abides   the best of all Britain

To raise from the rock   and reign over all."

The chanting ceased, and Cathbhad said to Emrys, "I believe it is in Annwn. But that place is wrapped around with Morgana's art. It is no place you could just saunter into."

"How can I get there?"

Cathbhad smiled indulgently, and patted Emrys on the shoulder. "It is the wise men of Ynys Mon that would know. Seek this knowledge in Ynys Mon. But go not unless you first say farewell to your mother. It would break her heart that you had gone without seeing her first."

"I will do it," said Emrys, standing. "I will say farewell to my mother first, and then I shall go to Ynys Mon, and I shall find Excalibur for the High King, and Britain shall be mighty once more, as it was in the days of Brutus."

"It is a noble aim, Emrys of the high mind," replied Cathbhad. "But stay awhile. Is there nothing else you wish to tell me?"

"I can think of nothing," replied Emrys.

Cathbhad was peering intently into his face. "Then nothing unusual has happened? You have seen nothing out of the ordinary?"

Emrys thought of the wolf and the hawk, but he spoke not of it. That was a thing he felt disinclined to share, at the moment. "Nothing," he repeated.

"Go then," said Cathbhad, "and good fortune attend your journey. But remember to say farewell to your mother first."

"I shall remember," said Emrys, starting off back down the course of the stream.

* * *

Emrys found his mother in the women's quarters. This building stood apart from the hall, in the shelter of the fortress' outer wall. It was spacious and airy within, but Viviane, a member of the royal family, possessed her own chamber. Emrys strode directly up to the door to her chamber and pushed it open. It was light within. The windows were open, so that a breeze flowed through the chamber, but coals glowed in a brazier in the centre of the room. Curtains had been drawn across the enclosure where Viviane's bed stood, and she herself sat upon a small seat with bronze arm-rests in front of one of the open windows.

Emrys thought that she was the most beautiful woman in the world, save for Boudi, of course. Her dress was of deep blue, like the sky on a summer evening, and she wore a plaid shawl over her shoulders. Her hair was black, so black it was almost blue, and she wore it braided and tied behind her head. Her cheekbones were high, her eyes dark and deep, and she looked inquisitively at her son as he entered. She held up one hand regally, and re-turned her attention to the report that the steward was making. He finished, and bowed before her, then she dismissed him and, at last, turned to Emrys.

Emrys did not speak at first. He put a knuckle to his mouth, and paced up and down a few times, as was his wont when on the brink of doing some-thing difficult. At last, he spoke. "I have come to say farewell, mother," he said.

"Where are you going, my son?" she asked.

"I have a long journey," he replied. "It's to Ynys Mon that I must go."

"And why is it you must undertake such a journey?"

Emrys paused again. "It is the beginning of my quest, madam," he said. "I must find the sword of kings, Excalibur, and restore the High King of the Island of the Mighty to his former greatness. Will you not give me your blessing ere I depart?"

"My blessing goes with you wherever you go," answered Viviane. "But will you not stay with me a little while longer yet?"

"My business cries haste upon me," replied Emrys. "This is no light matter."

"No," agreed Viviane, "but it is a matter of many years, and a little delay at the outset will not greatly disadvantage you. Will you not abide here a while longer?"

"Madam," insisted Emrys, "how long would you have me stay here and gather moss?"

"Well," said Viviane, "at least until you are nine, though I think that you should perhaps gain the strength to carry the sword that is your quest's object."

Emrys had nothing to say to this and, in some frustration, beat a hasty retreat from his mother's chamber.

II

Shortly afterwards, a great storm swept through the mountains of Cambria. The sky darkened, dogs cowered in corners, and horses whinnied in the stables. Many men refused to go out of doors. Lightning split the sky, deep thunder rolled above the clouds. Emrys watched in fascination from the doorway of the great hall, fearing for his life even while he gaped on in amazement. At the height of the storm, a huge brand of lightning flashed from the clouds and struck the old yew tree. Sparks and flames burst in all directions.

Emrys gasped. For the split second that the lightning lit the heavens, it seemed to him that he had seen, as clear as if it were truly there, a windswept hill; and upon the hill, a man was being put to death upon a tree. His blood streamed down the sides of the hill and, it seemed to Emrys, ran in great cataracts to every corner of the world.

The next morning, the yew was dead, smouldering and black. No one cared to cut it down, and so it stood there, a monument to the worst storm most men could remember. It had been an ancient tree, and had stood on that spot, they said, since the time of Camber, the first king of Cambria. It saddened Emrys that a link with the ancient past should be lost; but the yew had frightened him somewhat. Even now, in its shattered and blackened death, he felt a shadow upon his soul as he passed it by.

* * *

The next few years were frustrating for Emrys. He saw Excalibur in his dreams all the time, glimpsed through clear water, or buried deep in the earth, or in the hands of a young man with golden hair. And when Boudi visited, which was not as frequently as he would have liked, she too talked of the sword of kings, and of the power over his enemies that the Chief Dragon of the Island of the Mighty would have if he wielded the sword that was his hereditary right.

Emrys' soul itched to leave Caermyrddin behind him, and search through the mountains of Cambria for the hiding place of the *Prydwen*. But the walls of his grandfather's fortress seemed comforting to him, the outside world a wild place of wind and ice, and he did not leave.

He resorted frequently to Cathbhad, but he knew no more than rumours about the missing sword of kings, and Emrys was never sure whether he was listening to history or legend. On one occasion, he asked the bard directly. Cathbhad had been teaching him a song about Bran the Blessed, and when Emrys asked, he paused over his harp, and stared out through the trees at the sky. It was early spring, and though the air was cool, the trees were beginning to bud.

"Legend or history?" he said. "Is there a difference? What I am teaching you now is the legend of Bran the Blessed and the Cauldron of Garanhir; and the story is his history."

"What I mean," insisted Emrys, "is, how can we tell what really happened and what people just made up afterwards?"

"Made up? Do you mean lies? If you do, think no more on it. I was taught this tale by Gwelydd, the Archdruid of Afallach; he was taught by another. We each tell the tale in our own way, but it is the same tale."

"In your own way?" Emrys was dubious.

"Yes, we use our own words, but the stories are the same. This is not a new lesson to you, little hawk."

"But how do you know what Bran said? How do you know what words *he* used?"

"Well," said Cathbhad, considering, "he must have used the words that caused the things to happen that the story relates."

Emrys was still not satisfied. He drew his knees up to his chin, and bound them about with his arms. A cuckoo was singing its plaintive song somewhere in the depths of the forrest. "Take us, for example," said Emrys. "Just now, you said, 'Bran spoke words that caused something to happen.' What you meant was, you know what Bran said because of what happened; the events tell us what the words must have been. Is that right?" Cathbhad nodded. "But if someone were to tell the story of us sitting here talking, how would they know exactly what you said, or what you meant? I know what course our conversation has taken, but even now, I'm not sure I can remember the exact words you used."

"What is a word, little hawk?"

"What is a word?" repeated Emrys, surprised. "Well, it's . . . a sound, with a meaning."

"So, when the cuckoo, who sits even now not far hence, sings his note in the forests of spring, is that a word? His note has a meaning; it means, *Spring is here—rejoice!*"

Emrys bit his knuckle, then said, "But the cuckoo does not mean this. He does not intend you to understand that. Do you mean to say that meaning is in ears, not tongues?"

"No, for that is foolishness—there would be no discourse then, but every man would be in a prison of self-reflection. But the cuckoo knows that it is spring. His notes are a spontaneous overflow of the joy he feels."

Emrys was silent. The cuckoo cried out its double note again, but somehow it did not sound so forlorn as it had earlier. And Emrys looked around, and he saw the buds bursting out on the trees all around him, and the bright splash of white and pink where some wood anemones spread open their petals for joy. The world spoke, in words beyond hearing.

Cathbhad reached the conclusion for him. "Storytellers are translators all. We translate experience into stories, and sometimes, we have to translate words from one language into another. Perfect accuracy is less important than being able to stir our listeners. When the hall falls silent, and Bran the Blessed or Brutus the Trojan walks in the hearts of my listeners—*that* is truth."

Emrys did not speak for a while. Cathbhad strummed the strings of his harp, and began to pick out a slow melody. Somehow, the notes of the cuckoo became bound with his notes, a part of the song. Nature and artifice met and mingled. And Emrys thought. He thought about Excalibur, and Belinos, and the ship *Prydwen*, and its mysterious resting place; and he thought about generations of storytellers, and their words, and suddenly Emrys felt as if it would be a very long time indeed before he could hope to restore the sword to the High King.

When he finally went back to Caermyrddin, he made his way slowly along the path, and his face was turned downwards. He felt overwhelmed, hopeless. It was as if he stood upon the edge of a dark abyss. There was only one way to find out what was at the bottom, and his whole being recoiled from that in horror.

It was raining by the time he got back to his grandfather's fortress.

* * *

Emrys was long going to sleep that night. A wind had sprung up at nightfall, and it rattled the shutters of the high windows of the hall. A stripe of silver moonlight fell across Emrys' legs, and across the face of his uncle, Grwhyr, who slept on the pallet next to his. He was thinking of the wise ones of Ynys Mon. In his mind he pictured them all tall, with long silver beards and flowing white robes. They were garlanded with oak leaves, and carried weighty oaken staffs. But when at last Emrys did sleep, he dreamed of something wholly different.

He dreamed of a dragon, mighty to behold, with scales of bronze, dark and hard. Its eyes were like gledes dropped from a blacksmith's forge, and its wings, batlike, cast shadows over fields and vales and hills. It swooped and dove, and came at last to rest upon the crest of a hill, in the shade of an ash tree. Its chest rose and fell, as if it found breathing laboursome. Then, quite suddenly, the dragon arched its neck. Its wings darted outwards. Its tail thrashed, and its chest convulsed. It rolled over onto its side, writhing and struggling, as if with some invisible foe, vaster and mightier than itself. Its claws slashed the air, its jaws opened wide, its forked tongue flickered between the sword-like teeth.

Then, all at once, a rent opened up in its breast. The scales popped apart, and a deep wound appeared. There was no blood, only a gaping breach in the armour of the dragon, black as the dunnest night. The split expanded, expanded over its shoulder and between its forepaws. The wings spread and quivered, the tail curled about the tree in its anguish. The dragon emitted a piercing scream that shook the tree and the hill, and chilled the

20

blood of men working in the farthest reaches of the kingdom. Then it sank, lifeless, to the ground.

After a moment, the dragon stirred again, and lifted its head. Beside it, another head rose from the pile of bronze scales. A tail flicked, a wing stirred like a sail catching the breeze. There were two dragons now, smaller than the one Emrys had been watching. Instantly, one of the dragons snapped at the other. They began circling, each looking for the swiftest way to finish off its adversary. So intent were they upon this combat, they saw not an eagle stooping out of the sky. The eagle landed with a sound like thunder upon one of the dragons, its talons outstretched. The dragon rolled over two or three times, its neck broken, then lay still, twitching ever less and less. The surviving dragon took to the air and struggled with the eagle, but in vain. The remorseless talons of the bird throttled the life out of the dragon, and it too sank to the ground beside its brother, its eye dulling, its chest heaving in one final shuddering breath. Then it was dead, and the eagle began to feast.

Emrys awoke with a cry. The hall was dark, and Emrys trembled with fear, although all about him were the sounds of his grandfather's slumbering warriors. He could see a faint red glow, the embers of the fire; it reminded him of the dragon's eye.

There was a noise beside him. His uncle Grwhyr had been awoken by his outcry.

"Uncle," breathed Emrys, "I have dreamed a dream."

Grwhyr sighed. "What dream, small one?"

Emrys related the events of his dream. "What can it mean?" he asked.

"That you ate less than you could wish tonight. Go back to sleep," advised Grwhyr, "and eat a hearty breakfast."

Emrys settled down, and was soon snoring softly; but Grwhyr lay awake long that night, for his soul was troubled by what he had heard.

* * *

Emrys had all but forgotten the dream later in the day, when one of the servants hurried up to him with the news that a small hawk was trapped among the rafters of the hall, and unable to escape through the louvre. "I thought you might like to know sir, seeing as you like birds so much," said the servant, smiling and dropping a curtsey. She was carrying a towel, with which she had been intending to clean some of the pots, but Emrys took it and charged her to bring a large box. Then he raced off to the hall.

If there was one thing that captured Emrys' attention, it was birds, especially birds of prey. The stooping of an eagle, the hovering of a kestrel, the fatal and swooping flight of a sparrowhawk filled him with wonder. He admired the curving scimitars of their beaks, the lordly command of their far-seeing eyes, the poniard-sharpness of their talons. Reaching the hall, he first checked that it was empty of humans—his grandfather gave him the distinct feeling that he disapproved of everything he did—and then scanned the shadowy vault of the ceiling for the bird in question.

Emrys' eyes adjusted slowly to the darkness of the sloping ceiling. It took him a moment to find what he sought—his eyes were as sharp as a hawk's, but now that he saw the bird, he saw that it was the smallest of birds of prey, a tiercel merlin, glaring at him with the incensed eye of its kind.

Emrys fastened the towel to his belt, reached up to one of the pillars that supported the rafters, and hauled himself upwards. He found footholds easily, for the pillar was carved into fantastic curving shapes. In a moment, he was among the rafters, and creeping along one of them, his feet dangling in mid-air twenty feet above his grandfather's throne.

At that moment, there was a flurry of noise from below. Emrys looked down towards the doors, and saw that his grandfather had entered, with a number of his counselors. Cydwelli, lord of Dinas Morfan and father of Boudi, was there too.

Rhydderch seated himself upon his throne, and motioned Cydwelli to remain standing. "So," he said, "if King Tenvantios is as sick as you say, who is to be High King after him? This is still to decide." His voice echoed in the large and empty chamber. Emrys turned his attention back to the merlin. It was perhaps ten feet away from him, directly above Boudi's father, and it regarded him out of the shadows with a bad-tempered eye. Stealthily, Emrys untied the towel from his belt, and edged closer.

Down below, Cydwelli said, "There is to be a council in Lundein to determine that, my liege."

Emrys heard what his grandfather's liegeman said, but paid little heed. The affairs of kings held no interest for him: birds had been around before there were kings, and would remain long after them. They were permanent, whilst kings came and went. That was why he had hastened into the hall after the merlin. He had often caught doves and pigeons there. Once, he was sure, he had even spoken with another bird of this type, a merlin. Emrys frowned, remembering. It was like speaking, but he did not think he had moved his lips. They had just seemed to understand each other. It was hard to say. Often, since that moment on the palisade looking down upon Boudi, Emrys had seen things that were not there, heard things nobody said. Sometimes, what he had seen and heard had become true later. Sometimes, he hardly knew what was true and what false.

Cydwelli was still speaking of the dispute over the succession. "As your lordship might expect, the main contenders are Cymbeline and Coroticos. To all appearances, they are friends, but . . . "

Rhydderch nodded sagely. "The Island of the Mighty must be united under a single High King."

Cydwelli nodded his agreement. "There are precedents, of course: Belin and Brennios led Britain to great victories. They shared power well, and the kingdom throve."

"Aye," agreed Rhydderch, "but there are other precedents as well: Porrex and Ferrex brought the realm to the edge of ruin with their quarreling. But the world has fallen since the times of Brennios and Belin. Those were years of gold; now we live in years of bronze, or iron. The virtues of old have rusted: kings and statesmen have become mere politicians. I fear for our island. I fear the Eagles who lurk with jealous eyes beyond the Narrow Sea. Once before, they came to these shores, and it was not willingly that Julius left with his many spears."

The talk of eagles caught the attention of Emrys for a moment, and he listened for a while; but then he realized that they were talking of the Roman legions, which carried eagle standards into battle, not of real birds, and he gave his attention to the merlin once more. The true method for catching

23

such a beast was to throw a large, light cloth over it, and then safely bundle it up until it could be placed in a box large enough for it to stand upright. One had to take special care not to damage its feathers, and to avoid scratches from the talons. Emrys' eyes gleamed. He braced his knees on the rafter, and readied the towel in both hands.

"There is much to fear from Rome," agreed Cydwelli, below. "More than half the world submits to the Eagles. But they are much weakened now. Is not Tiberius old and bedridden? And he has spent his days not with his generals, but with women and small boys. And who will succeed him? Gaius Caligula is little more than a boy. And is he one to wrest the Island of the Mighty from the heirs of Brutus?"

"It is long," said Rhydderch slowly, "since the Romans were ruled by a strong emperor—Andraste be praised—but the strength of the legions has not waned."

The merlin cocked its head on one side and regarded Emrys directly. Emrys' brow furrowed. Laying the towel down across the rafter, he reached out with his hand. The tiercel bobbed its head once, then stepped onto his finger. They regarded each other for a moment, and Emrys felt like a subject before his sovereign.

At a commotion down below, Emrys bent his eyes down for a moment. New people had filed into the hall, and servants began setting tables and sideboards. Others were bringing in platters of food, and Emrys' nostrils twitched at the sweet aroma that rose towards the ceiling.

"Eat," advised Rhydderch, spreading his hands to the feast. "Your journey has been long, and pressing as your business was, now it is dispatched, and you needs must take sustenance. My lord of Dinas Morfan, is not this your daughter?"

"It is, my lord," responded the other; and Emrys looked in surprise down towards the dais. There stood Boudi. It was almost a year since he had seen her, and she had grown in beauty in the meantime. Her hair flamed crimson, and she held herself with a mature poise that surprised Emrys. She was fire. She was air. She was nothing corporeal, for her beauty struck Emrys to the soul, and it seemed for a count of ten, that nothing moved, nothing made a sound. Emrys contemplated her in silence, and knew her to be all that he was not: he was thought, she action; he talked, she turned words into achievements.

Then the moment was over, and everybody's speech returned to Emrys' consciousness. Slowly, Boudi turned her eyes upwards to the rafter, and she looked directly into Emrys' eyes. He felt his heart stop, and then resume, faster than before. Then things began to change.

It was the wolf again, its jaws open and slavering. Where the floor had been strewn with rushes, now it was ankle-deep in blood, and the stench of it clutched Emrys' throat. Now the wolf had vanished, and Emrys beheld a woman of surpassing beauty, streaked with blood, a dripping sword in one hand, a shield on the other arm. Bodies of slain men surrounded her, some unclothed, some in armour and scarlet tunics: swords, spears, bits of twisted armour, all lay around her in an unholy mess, and she exulted, she opened her throat in a great ululation to the god of war, spreading her arms wide, magnificent and terrifying.

Emrys cried out. He lost his grip on the rafter and plunged through the air of the great hall. The merlin released his hand and soared out through the louvre. There was an outcry from those in the hall: servants and nobles turned their eyes upwards as Emrys, grandson of the king of Cambria, plummeted towards the stone floor of the great hall. Only Cydwelli acted. He took two steps forward and held out his arms. Emrys struck him full force, and both of them tumbled over and over, coming to a rest, a tangle of arms and legs, a foot away from the fire. There was silence for long moments in the hall, then Cydwelli gasped and started to move his aching limbs. Emrys was limp. Quick as lightning, Cydwelli disentangled himself and examined the boy.

"He does not appear hurt," he said. "Is not this your grandson, sire?"

"Aye, he is so," answered Rhydderch, but he blushed to acknowledge Emrys. "I owe you a great debt, my lord of Dinas Morfan."

But Cydwelli shook his head. "Nay, such is the service a good king is owed by his faithful servant."

A groan escaped from Emrys' lips. All turned to regard him. His lips moved, and words came, faintly. "Beware the she-wolf," he said, "beware! She walks in blood."

Rhydderch turned his face away. "Thus does he ever speak," he said. "The boy is a wittol—he would rather roam through the forests than learn arms like a man in his grandfather's hall."

"No bones are broken," observed Cydwelli, examining Emrys' limbs and moving each joint in turn.

"The sword," muttered Emrys, "the sword . . . what was lost must be found. The king without a sword . . . the land without a king!"

Cydwelli wore an expression of surprise and, perhaps, the beginnings of fear, but his daughter had moved closer and was regarding the unconscious boy with interest. "He speaks often this way, you say?" she asked.

"He is witless, to my eternal shame," answered the king.

"I knew not of . . . " Cydwelli had been going to say that he had not known that Rhydderch's daughter had a husband, but then he realized the true reason for the king's shame and added instead: "I know of nothing else I can do for him, but he does not seem hurt." He looked up again. "He should be laid in a bed," he advised.

Servants moved forward to take up Emrys' limp form. They carried him from the hall and, after a moment, Boudicea followed them. Rhydderch gestured to the sideboard, and Cydwelli joined him for his noonday meal.

III

Emrys felt as if he were swimming through a long, grey tunnel into sunlight. When he broke the surface, he could hear voices, but still could see nothing. The voices, indistinct at first, resolved themselves into those of his grandfather and his mother.

"I could wish," said the voice of his mother, "that you would treat the boy with more kindness."

"I could wish," answered Rhydderch, "that he would behave more like the grandson of the king of Cambria, and not some addle-pated girl."

"Emrys is different from other children," said Viviane defensively. "He sees further than others, he thinks more deeply, and he feels the agony of the world in his blood. He is more mature than the other boys—he always has been. That is why he seems strange. He cannot be treated like the other children, and you cannot expect of him what you expect of the others. He will not be king—others stand before him in the succession, many others. Grwhyr will be king of Cambria after you—you need not fear that my Emrys will ever aspire to kingship. Why treat him thus?"

There was an icy pause. "Who is the lad's father, lady?" asked Rhydderch pointedly.

"I cannot say." Viviane's voice was like shattered ice. "We have discussed this before now, and my answer has not changed. But he is certainly my son. He quickened in my womb, and suckled at my breast. Through me, your blood runs in his veins."

"Aye, that's certain, lady," interjected Rhydderch, "but with whose blood is it mingled?"

"You shall never know."

"Then do not expect me to treat him as my own until I know exactly who he is. The boy is witless, madam. I shall treat him as well as the witless should be treated." There came to Emrys' ears the sound of rustling clothes, and his grandfather's footsteps receding. But Emrys could feel his mother's presence very keenly. There she stood in his mind's eye, wringing her hands, her shoulders tense beneath the plaid shawl. He opened his eyes, and found her exactly as his mind had seen her. She stepped forward with a kindly smile, and placed her hand on his forehead.

"Rest, small one," she said. "Are you well?"

"Well enough, madam," replied Emrys. He hesitated. "Madam," he said, "who is my father?"

Viviane's brow clouded over. "One of whom your grandfather would disapprove," she answered. For a moment, they regarded each other, mother and son; but Viviane's expression changed suddenly, with a little shock, and then it seemed that they spoke between themselves as equals. Viviane said, "I never saw your father. He came to me in the darkness of night, and lay with me, but I never saw his face." She squeezed her eyes shut a moment, and when she opened them, a pair of tears flowed from them and down her cheeks. "In truth, my son, I cannot say who your father is, for to my shame I never saw his face. But his company lifted my heart, and made my blood sing for joy, and my resistance was as a reed before a tempest, for it seemed that to lie with him was the only important thing, the only joy in the world."

Emrys reached out and took his mother's hand. As he did so, for the briefest moment, he saw the shadow of a man, a man who moved towards her bed with a limp. Viviane reached out and smoothed his hair, and the vision dissolved.

"Be at peace, mother," said Emrys. "I will find him."

"How?" she asked, sitting upon the edge of the bed and turning her face away from him. "There is no clue, none whatsoever."

"I know it will not always be a mystery to me, madam," said Emrys, "so be content; and there is no shame in my parentage, that I know."

Viviane turned and squeezed his hand. Then she gently eased him down upon the bed and tucked the covers in around his chin. "Sleep now," she said, and left; and a few moments later, he did.

* * *

King Tenvantios did in fact die shortly thereafter, and Coroticos and Cymbeline shared the throne between them. For a few months, Rhydderch and his nobles were tense. Rhydderch summoned council after council, and they locked the doors against all who would enter the hall. Smoke rose from the louvre towards the heavens, and from within came the low rumble of elderly men in earnest conversation. But it became apparent that the alarm was unwarranted, for the twins reigned for a while in peace. There was no power vacuum. There was no civil war. The Romans stayed where they were. The nobles of Britain forgot that they had been worried about the succession.

It was at the time of the Beltane feast, some years after the twins' accession, when Emrys and Boudicea met again. The nobles of Cambria were gathering in Caermyrddin for their annual council. One by one, they arrived at Rhydderch's fortress. Cydwelli was one of the first.

Emrys was practising with sword and shield. His grandfather insisted that he at least attempt to learn the rudiments of warfare, and Grwhyr was running him and several other boys—all two or three years younger than Emrys—through their paces. The sword felt clumsy in Emrys' hand; all the weight was distributed awkwardly.

He wondered for a moment how Excalibur would feel in his hand. Its balance would be perfect—it had been forged by the gods. But this sword felt awkward in his hand. It made him despair of his quest. Why seek a thing he could not even use?

"Let the weight of the sword carry through your swing," Grwhyr advised them, breaking in on his ruminations. They were sweaty and panting from the exertion, but they were all willing to do more—all, that is, save Emrys. He was watching a kestrel hovering over the spur of flat land in the crook of the river. "A sword," Grwhyr went on, "is really best as a stabbing weapon, but a sideways blow to the head is a good way of finishing your foe quickly."

"May I show them?" came a deep, female voice. All eyes turned, and there she stood: it seemed that the whole world bowed before her. The trees inclined their tops to her, the beasts of the forest and the air stopped to pay their respects, the boys at practice regarded her with hushed awe. Boudicea was, Emrys saw, a grown woman, deep-bosomed and long-limbed. She wore a torc about her left arm, and held a sword in the other hand. Her teeth were straight and white, her lips faintly smiling. Her eyes were fixed on Emrys.

"My lady Boudicea," said Grwhyr, "as you wish."

She took a shield from one of the boys, and swung the sword once left, once right. The air hissed. "Emrys," she said.

Emrys put his shield before him and hefted his sword. He faced her, knees bent, as he had been taught. For a moment, they regarded each other, each taking small, sidelong paces. Then Emrys attacked.

His sword sliced through the air and came whistling towards her head. She fended it off with her shield, but made no counter-attack. Emrys recovered, and watched for a moment. Her shield was low—he might get her left shoulder. Once more, he swung at her, but the iron rang on the wood with a noise that echoed from the trees and sky. Emrys retreated a pace, looking for another opening.

Boudicea dropped her shield. Emrys lunged, springing on his left foot, his right knee bent. Boudicea jumped one pace backwards: the point of Emrys' sword was inches from her flat stomach. Emrys took a small pace forward with his left leg and lunged again. This time, Boudicea took one step to her right, and lashed out at him, with her shield, and not with her sword. Her shield hit his square on. The noise felt as if everyone's eardrums had simultaneously burst. But Emrys was off-balance. He toppled sideways to the turf, dropping his sword. In a flash, Boudicea had straddled him, her sword-point at his throat.

There was silence for a moment, then one of the boys, Gwern by name, said, "It's easy to defeat Emrys. He has no wits." And he stepped forward, his shield before his body, his sword held in readiness.

Boudicea stepped away from Emrys, who scrambled out of the way quickly. Gwern's sword flashed out, but Boudi's shield knocked it easily, almost contemptuously aside. They circled a moment, then came another attack, this time at the head. Boudicea held the shield up and the sword edge rebounded with an ear-shattering crack. Another pause, the combatants watching each other warily over the edges of their shields, then Gwern lashed out one more time. Boudicea stepped aside so that Gwern's sword almost hit the grass. She placed a foot on the blade and drove it down into the earth, trapping Gwern's fingers under the hilt. She pressed the point of her sword to his throat and said, "Was that easy?"

Gwern looked at her as if his world suddenly had meaning.

* * *

Emrys did not see Boudicea for the rest of the day. At the feast that night, she was surrounded by the boys of Caermyrddin. Emrys sulked. He left the feast and sought solitude in the darkness outside. It was a chilly night, and he could see beyond the torchlight of the courtyard the vague shapes of the guards pacing the palisades. He climbed the steps to the stockade, and looked out into the forest. An owl hooted nearby, and he reflected for a moment upon his plans to train a hawk for night-time hunting. To his knowledge, it had never been done before.

But he could not think long about his plans without his mind returning to Boudicea. He yearned for her. His life, he thought, would be complete if he were only joined to her. Then it wouldn't matter how poorly he handled a sword—she would do that for him.

He became aware that someone had joined him and, still as a statue, was watching him from not many yards away in silence. He turned, and found himself caught in the gaze of a pair of green eyes.

"I have sought you long," she said. "Why did you leave the feast?"

"I wished to be by myself," replied Emrys.

Boudicea moved closer. "I have longed for your company all evening," she said, "but all I have had is the conversation of idiots."

"I am an idiot," observed Emrys. "Ask my grandfather." She was close enough now that, if Emrys had reached out with a hand, he could have touched hers.

"You are not an idiot," Boudicea observed. "Your skills are different from theirs. Any man can follow a king with a spear in his hand. Not every man can do what you can do."

"What do you mean?"

Boudicea moved closer again; her closeness made Emrys feel warm from the crown of his head to the tips of his toes and fingers. She reached

31

out and took his hand in hers, and said, "Do you remember that day when you were chasing a merlin among the rafters of the great hall?" Emrys nodded. "Well, you were delirious, and kept muttering things. You spoke of a she-wolf, and of a sword. Don't you see it, Emrys? You can't hide it for ever—you have the Sight!"

"The Sight!"

"Yes," agreed Boudicea. "You see things that have not yet come to pass, do you not?" Emrys did not answer, and Boudicea went on, "This you know is true. You must ignore it no longer. The gods have placed a geis, a destiny, upon you. You cannot avoid it." She took his hand, and placed it firmly upon her stomach. Emrys regarded her with wonderment for a moment, then their faces closed together, their lips sought each other out. Emrys pulled her body against his own and kissed her with all the passion that had been building for the years he had known her.

They parted, and Emrys looked at her curiously. "I love you, Boudi," he said. "I always have. But why do you choose me? There are other men at Caermyrddin, men of more kingly skills."

"Please don't call me Boudi," she answered. "That's a child's name. But don't you see? There are no men like you here. I can cast a spear as well as any man, I can shoot a bow, I can drive a chariot, and you have seen me fight with sword and shield. But no one else can do what you can do, my hawk."

Emrys kissed her again, and this time it was long before they parted.

"Will you be mine for ever?" asked Emrys.

"I am you, and you are me," she responded. "Nothing can come between us. Nothing." She kissed him again, and her lips were like the whisper of a warm breeze at midsummer. "Whatever you hear of me, remember that you and I are one, and always will be."

She pulled his face down to hers, and they kissed with passion, with ferocity, as if they had but seconds to live. They parted. "Come," said Boudicea. "I know of a secret place."

Together, they stole away from the stockade, hand in hand, seeking together a secret place for themselves, where no one would find them; and it was long ere they returned to the feast.

The council, with the attendant festivities and rituals, lasted a week, and then Boudicea returned to her home. When she had gone, Emrys hurried into the little collection of wattle-and-daub shacks that constituted the township of Caermyrddin, and found a small smithy where a man, black with smoke from his trade, was making small bronze statues. Emrys emptied his purse to purchase a pair, a roughly-fashioned hawk and a wolf, and then he entered the forest.

It was not long before he came to Cathbhad's hut. There bubbled the spring, and there was the bronze plaque of Tylweth. Emrys took the figurines and cast them into the spring. They disappeared without a trace, and he stood facing the image of Tylweth, as he had seen the druids do at the rituals of Beltane, with his hands extended, palms upwards.

He did not know what to ask Tylweth for, and he suspected that the gods did not want to be bothered with the affairs of humans, especially an affair so small as his own.

"Tylweth," he said, "I hope you like the hawk and the wolf." He hesitated. "Do I have the Sight?" he asked after a while. It seemed the more important thing of the two that were on his mind. But ever he recalled the soft touch of Boudicea's lips upon his, her arms about him, her body beneath his own.

He heard a noise behind him, and turned to see Cathbhad's approach. "Peace and long days be with you," he said.

"And with you, little hawk," answered Cathbhad. "What business brings you hither so early in the day?"

"Cathbhad," began Emrys, and then hesitated. It began to sound stupid, presumptuous. He steeled himself and blurted out: "Cathbhad, do I have the Sight?"

"Yes," nodded the bard. "Yes, you do. I have myself seen the Mark upon you. I saw it at your birth. I believe, on that occasion, it saved your life. It is more visible when you have recently had one of your visions, as you had on that occasion when you came to me asking about Excalibur. But for all who can see, it is evident all of the time."

"What must I do?"

"That is what you must find out," answered the bard.

"Shouldn't I become an advisor to a king, or something like that?"

"The matter is dark to me," said Cathbhad, "but it will not long remain so to you."

"How can I use it?"

Cathbhad sat down. His harp was to hand, but he made no effort to pick it up, gazing instead into the bubbling waters of the sacred spring. "I do not believe that you can," he said. "It will use you. The Sight is the gift of the gods, particularly Argante. She knows what she wants, and will tell you when she needs you."

"Should I tell the others?"

Cathbhad shook his head. "Probably not," he said. "It is a seer's family who is least likely to believe him. Yours is a lonely flight, little hawk, with none to keep you company in the long hours on the wing."

Emrys remained silent. He was thinking of the wolf, at the bottom of Tylweth's spring.

* * *

Emrys stayed with Cathbhad that afternoon, and returned to the fort when the night was drawing its blue cloak about the huddled buildings. He entered the hall and was immediately surrounded by the golden light and aroma of wood smoke. Flute music came from somewhere. Emrys saw the knot of boys with whom he had been practising sword a few days earlier, and he walked past them on his way to the table. As he did so, he heard Boudicea's name, and stopped.

"It is a great shame," Gwern was saying, "for she is young, and he is old. What does it profit an old man to marry a young girl like that? He can hope for no comfort from her. It is for us to enjoy the young women."

"What are you talking about?" asked Emrys, jumping in on their conversation, the pit of his stomach suddenly hollow.

34

"That girl who was staying here," answered Gwern, "Boudicea. She is to be married to Prasutagos, Duke of the Eicenni, who is thrice her age. What a waste!"

Emrys stood for a moment like a man wounded to the death, coldness growing through his gut. Then he turned sharply and left the feast.

He ate nothing at all that night.

IV

It was a particularly wet spring that year, and Emrys moped about Caermyrddin, his soul as grey as the sky. "Whatever you hear of me, remember that you and I are one, and always will be." Emrys heard Boudicea's words in his mind frequently. He heard her voice, felt her warmth, when he closed his eyes. Now he knew what she had meant. She had known, even as they had made love, that she had been contracted to another. But how could he have faith in her, how remain true? How could they be one, when her body belonged to Prasutagos, and when she was so many miles away from him? The moments they had seized together were nothing but a memory, now. Eicenniawn was north of Lundein, between the rivers of Thames and Glein. The rivers of her homeland, the Wysg and the Trybrwyt, flowed far from her now.

He shunned the company of others even more during those weeks, wandering through the forest, often with the icy rain dripping down his back and mud squelching beneath his boots. The paths were known to him, threading between the hills and trees, often crossing, looping back on themselves, bringing him to half-familiar places, to glens wholly unknown or to glades he knew but did not wish to see. At first, he grew in knowledge of these pathways, but then they became bewildering, and he felt as if he knew less than he had at the outset.

One day, grey and drizzling, he found a path he had not seen before, and followed it for a short way through some undergrowth to a stand of hazel trees, some five or six feet taller than the top of his head. Their branches were bare for winter, and the ground was thick with old nuts and pale yellow leaves. In the midst of the clearing, as if it were a god worshipped by the bowing trees, stood a moss-grown stone about Emrys' height. It did not look natural, and when Emrys approached it more closely, he saw that it was fashioned to resemble a woman. Grass was sprouting from its crevices, and ferns had grown around it, but Emrys set about clearing all of that away, until he was confronted by a face both ancient and youthful at the same time.

The figure held something in its hands, and when Emrys cleared away some more vegetation, he saw that it was a sword. But it was not drawn; rather, it was in a sheath, and the ancient sculptor had taken some pains to depict the finely-wrought fashion of the scabbard. Emrys knew what that meant.

"Excalibur," he breathed; then, looking at the face: "Argante, great mother!"

He looked upon that ancient face with wonder. Argante, consort of Arawn, who had woven the sheath into which Excalibur fitted. It was said that no harm could come to the man who bore that sheath. Its worth was greater than kingdoms.

But the day was cold, and Emrys left the hazel grove at last, wondering if he would ever find it again.

* * *

That evening, as he entered Caermyrddin, one of his mother's women hurried up to him, holding her shawl over her head to fend off the rain. "My lord Emrys," she said, "your lady mother wishes to speak with you." Emrys nodded, and as she hurried back to the women's quarters, he followed at a slow pace.

His mother was combing her long, dark hair; Emrys could hear it crackle, and see faint sparks now and then fly from it. He stood beside the brazier, a small pool gathering about his feet.

"Emrys," said Viviane, without preamble, "you are now old enough to choose your own path in life. But others expect things of you. Why have you neglected your lessons?"

"My tutors can teach me nothing I don't already know," replied Emrys flatly.

"This is not true," answered Viviane, turning and fixing him with her dark eyes. Emrys flinched. For a split second, she had seemed a person utterly alien to him, dark and unknowable. "I speak not of languages, nor of song or traditions—in these you were far advanced many years ago. But Grwhyr has spoken to me. He says that your swordsmanship needs much attention—you fall behind your peers in skill and dedication."

Emrys bowed before her. "I shall dedicate myself to the study of the sword," he said flatly. And then he left.

* * *

He was true to his word. He hated every moment of it, but his mother had spoken, and he obeyed as if she had placed a geis upon him. He learned to control his movements. The sword ceased to feel like dead weight in his hand, but became instead an extension of his arm. He learned to respond to his opponent's movements, to the slightest flicker of expression upon his face, so that he could parry with blade or shield almost before his foe knew what he was going to do.

And indeed, it did seem to the others that suddenly he had an uncanny knowledge of what they were going to do next. Nobody beat him at sword or spear, and nobody could land a blow on him, so tight was his defence. Indeed, he seldom defeated anyone in combat, but neither was he defeated. And so he passed the summer, growing in his skill with the various weapons Grwhyr offered him, but dead inside. After practice, he went away to a quiet corner, and he thought. And no one knew what his thoughts were, but they began to grow fearful of him.

* * *

The leaves were falling from the trees when, one grey morning with the keen-toothed air nipping at his flesh, Emrys trudged along the riverbank towards the sacred spring of Tylweth. He followed a path he knew well; but all at once, it seemed to him that he was no longer following the path, but watching himself follow it. Then he saw all the paths in the forest that he had come to learn in the springtime. And more—paths unseen by him, drove roads winding through mountain passes, wide roads connecting mighty fortresses, narrow streets threading through the close-packed houses of cities. He tried to follow the thread of his own movements, but he saw so many paths that he could not distinguish one from another. He could not see where he was going, nor where he had been, nor even where he was now.

And now, his mind was crowded with these paths, threading, intersecting, joining or running parallel for a while and then separating and going he knew not where; and he saw many travelers, and they moved along these paths in an infinite variety of courses, taking a left turn where others chose right, or passing through a tunnel where others crossed a bridge. And Emrys understood that the Sight was not enough, for he could see all this, but he could understand nothing. And when the vision went away, he was left alone in the cold forest, bent double with the burden of vision without light.

"Prince Emrys!" Cathbhad, who had been gathering firewood, cast aside his bundle and hurried over to where Emrys was standing, his hands on his knees, shaking like the leaves all around them. Cathbhad put an arm around Emrys' shoulders and steered him to his bothie. There, he parted the bull's hide, and deposited Emrys on the edge of his pallet. Then he went outside. Emrys fell over sideways. He did not sleep, for ever in his mind's eye, he saw a path extending from his feet towards infinity, joining others, crossing narrow streets and wide highways, always going, and he knew not where. Then Cathbhad returned with a mug of steaming broth and held it to his lips. He sipped, and felt its warmth suffuse his body, from the ends of his toes to the crown of his head.

"I wish," said Cathbhad, when Emrys' eyes were able to focus on him, "that the gods had chosen me as their emissary. I should gladly spare you the pain."

"It will be my burden always, won't it?" said Emrys miserably.

Cathbhad nodded. "It is something we all have," he said, "in greater or lesser measure. But you have it in greater measure than anyone I have ever seen. The gods must have singled you out for something special."

"Excalibur," said Emrys. "It must be Excalibur. Now is the time I must set out upon my journey!"

Cathbhad did not answer at once. "Perhaps," he said, as if someone unseen had forced him to speak. There was a stool on the other side of the bothie, and it was upon this he sat now, his feet planted wide, his hands upon his knees. "Emrys," he said, "it is often you've come to this little hut, and much have I taught you. I believe you remember everything you hear, and so I know you know the tales of the Morforwyn, the Lake Folk, and of

39

their war with the giants before the coming of Brutus. You know of the Seven Treasures of the Island of the Mighty, how they were given by the Morforwyn to Brutus and his captains, and how, one by one, they were lost. You know the history of the kings of Britain, from the days of Brutus even to this very day. But of Excalibur I have told you little."

"But I know much about Excalibur," Emrys contradicted him.

"What do you know?"

"It has been the sword of kings, it can only be wielded by the High King of Britain—in another man's hand, the blade would turn, and prove unfaithful. It was given to Brutus by Argante, Queen of the Morforwyn. The last High King to wield it was Cassivelaunos, who entrusted it to his friend, Belinos; where it is now, no man knows."

"And what of the other treasures?"

Emrys took in a deep breath, and blew it out again before replying. "The Bridle of Gwynn," he said, "which could tame any beast of burden on which it was placed, was kept by the kings of Albany until the time of Conla. He was enchanted by a dark-haired sorceress, and rode his stallion across the boundless ocean, and he and the Bridle were lost. The Veil of Gold was lost when, smitten by a woman he had seen in a boat, Gweir of Cameliard leaped from a cliff and into the boat, and was never seen again. The Cauldron of Garanhir was in the keeping of the kings of Cambria, until it was stolen by men of Eirin; Bran the Blessed sought to recover it, but it was seized by the Addanc, a winged serpent, and lost. The Harp of Teirtu was held by the kings of the Summer Country. Belgabarad, High King of Britain over a hundred years ago, demanded the Harp as a mark of King Cynar's loyalty, and fought a war with him over it. When the war was over, no man could find the Harp. The other two treasures were the dangerous throne—the Siege Perilous, it is called properly, and the Chariot of Manawydan, but no man knows what has become of them."

"It is good," said Cathbhad, with some satisfaction. "You have been attentive. But there is something more I would tell you." Emrys sat forward on the pallet. His weakness and vision were forgotten now, and his eyes shone with his eagerness for knowledge.

"The sword of kings," Cathbhad went on, "was forged by Arawn in the time before men ever came to these lands, when it was named Albion by its fortunate inhabitants."

"May I ask questions," wondered Emrys, "or should I hold my peace until you are finished?" Cathbhad nodded his consent. "Why should there be need of swords, when there is no enemy upon whom to use them?"

"A good question," Cathbhad said, "and worthy of a mind of your calibre, little hawk. But bring to mind the image of a sword." Emrys did so, and saw it there as if he could reach out and touch it: the sword of his mind was simple of design, curved along either edge like a woman's hips, with short quillions and a leather-bound hilt. The pommel was rather large, and set with no jewel. "Consider," said Cathbhad quietly, "that there are two sides to the sword, and two sharp edges that keep them continually apart from one another. One side of the blade may never see the other, unless the whole sword be consumed with a fire so fierce that it will melt all into one piece. Consider the sharpness of the edge. Consider how the quillions cross the blade, how the hilt is smooth so that a man may handle it. Consider the pommel, how heavy it is, and how its purpose is to balance the weight of the blade, and make it light in a warrior's hand—but how it should not be too heavy, lest the blade follow not the path its wielder chooses for it.

"The sword is a message, a word, for it is like justice. Justice knows two sides, good and evil; and to those who choose evil, it is indeed sharp, like the edge. Just as the quillions protect the hand, so those who support justice, and are therefore of a greater breadth than it, protect those who are weaker than they. And justice is balanced—it is meted out to the rich and poor alike, to men and women both. Yet, just as the pommel is lighter than the blade, so the mercy of justice is lighter than its retribution.

"Excalibur was not designed as a weapon; it was a work of art."

"Is it wrong, then, to use it as a weapon?" asked Emrys.

Cathbhad shook his head; but he looked troubled. "Yes and no," he answered. "A sword should be used for a just purpose—thus the work of art has become real in the world. Life is breathed into the artifice. But this is inevitable because men are at heart evil."

"Do you believe this?" said Emrys with wide eyes.

41

Cathbhad gave a wry smile. "Some less than others, perhaps," he admitted, "but the tendency of all men is towards evil. And that is why the blade of justice is heavier than the pommel of mercy. There is no balance in the world. That is why we need sacrifices at Beltane. Even human sacrifices." Emrys made a startled movement, and Cathbhad nodded slowly. "Yes, little hawk. So far you have been protected from the full truth, but you should know that it happens. The gods will be propitiated with sacrifice. Perhaps there was once balance, perhaps. But if the gods demand sacrifice, as we know they do, then perhaps the imbalance is part of the way the world is."

"Which gods demand sacrifice?" asked Emrys.

"Balor, for one," said Cathbhad. "Morgana we do not worship, for it is said that she has taken human form, and wishes to accomplish all her ends within the world of men. All the Morforwyn had human form when Brutus came here, but one by one, they vanished from our world. From time to time, they return; Morgana perhaps more than the rest. And it is of her I wished to warn you, for if you seek Excalibur, be certain that she will linger in your footsteps, lurking ever at your heels."

Emrys' eyes were wide with terror at this thought. "Will she do so?" he asked breathlessly.

"It is very certain," replied Cathbhad. "It is said that she had a son by Balor, a thing forbidden by the Morforwyn among themselves, for they may only bear or beget the children of mortals. They may not beget immortals. And when Arawn refused to breathe life into the deformed creature, she swore her revenge upon the Morforwyn. She withdrew into the north, and there she called upon her great magic to bring forth ice-giants out of the snow and the mountains. And for many years, she threw these giants against the Morforwyn and the other long-lived ones. And they strove mightily while ages passed. At last, the Morforwyn fled to the island of Avalon, and wound about it many spells and enchantments, by which Morgana's giants could not find them.

"And thus things stayed, until the coming of Brutus. And Argante, Queen of the Morforwyn, gave to Brutus and his generals the seven treasures that had been forged by the Morforwyn in the dawning of days. It was

Brutus and Excalibur who drove the giants back, and they fled to Morgana's realm of Annwn.

"But ever has Morgana sought to dominate this realm, and what she could not take by storm, she had procured by stealth, for all the treasures now have been lost, and no other than she has taken them."

"Then why has she not seized the Island of the Mighty from the hands of men?" asked Emrys.

"Because, although all the treasures have been lost, not all of them have been stolen. One treasure remains hidden to both us and her, and that is Excalibur. No man knows where Excalibur can be found, but neither does Morgana. And she has sought it long in her bitterness and her loneliness, but yet she cannot find it.

"If you seek it, she will follow you. If you find it, she will take it from you. If you resist, she will crush you. She is remorseless, and utterly powerful. There can be little real hope, if you strive against her. She is mighty."

"Surely she will not see me as a threat?"

"Not at this time; but if you come nigh Excalibur, doubt not but she will. Beware, little hawk. Always, she will be watching you. You may not perceive her—indeed, when you are hottest on the trail of the sword of kings, she will be least visible to you, for she will not wish to reveal herself too soon and mar the work you do for her."

"How can I avoid her?"

"Only by refusing to seek the sword."

"But I cannot do that," protested Emrys.

"Then you must learn the best ways to meet and overcome the wiles of Morgana. The way is fraught with danger, little hawk, but it is not impossible."

"This would be thought on," said Emrys. He got to his feet and walked blindly to the door. Without bidding Cathbhad farewell, he staggered from the bothie and wound his way home by paths he saw not.

V

Emrys did not begin his journey to Ynys Mon immediately. Indeed, Cathbhad's words had struck such fear into his heart that sometimes he doubted if he could ever take his courage in both hands and begin the expedition. And so he remained in Caermyrddin as the snows came and left Rhydderch's stronghold blanketed in virginal white. January was bitter, with a sharp wind sweeping from the Eirish Sea through the mountain passes of Cambria. The people of Caermyrddin huddled about their hearths and told grim stories about the kings of long ago.

Emrys' visions began to intensify at this time. Sometimes, he found himself pursuing a path across an undulating, treeless plain, and it seemed to him that he could see the road beyond the horizon. At others, he took wing, and saw all the paths of the world winding and crossing each other. Sometimes, the path was ankle-deep in blood, and sometimes he was accompanied by a she-wolf. Always, though, a great fear was upon him, as if he were pursued by some unseen but remorseless power, and fled into dangers whose peril he could only glimpse in his darkest hours.

Finally, in springtime, when the buds were beginning to swell upon the trees, and the melted snows were cascading down the mountainsides, the vision came that stirred Emrys to action. He was a hawk, wheeling through the mountain-tops of Cambria, the wind whistling through his feathers. He was weary, for he felt he had flown many leagues, and found no rest. At last, below him, he saw a wondrous sight: in the midst of a forest, surrounded by vertical precipices, he glimpsed the hilt of a sword. It was thrust into a great rock, as massy itself as a mountain. The quillions would afford him rest. He tipped his wing down, and in wide wheels swooped down and rested on the quillions of the sword. He knew there was danger all about him, but while he rested there, the sword would protect him.

The vision faded, and Emrys wept upon his pallet while the moonlight shone down upon him through the louvre above him. "I can do no other," he wept; and upon the rising of the sun, he ran to Cathbhad. He found the bard kneading dough for bread, and he raised a white hand in greeting as Emrys hastened up to his bothie.

"I have to go for Excalibur," he said bluntly.

"It is well," answered Cathbhad. "But it is well also that you go with your eyes opened to the perils."

"I cannot stay," said Emrys, as if Cathbhad had entreated him to remain. "All paths go that way. Whichever I choose, I shall finish in the same place." He looked with imploring eyes at the bard. "Cannot I choose my own way?"

"Yes, little hawk," answered Cathbhad, and there was pity in his eyes. "It is not a path the gods have chosen for you, but a destination. How you get there is your own business, but get there you must."

"Will the gods protect me until I reach it?"

"They might." Cathbhad frowned. "The gods are not all-powerful. Their purposes may be thwarted by other gods, or even by men. And their word is not the last, for there is that in the universe that rules even them."

"What is it?" asked Emrys, fascinated by Cathbhad's words in spite of his fears.

"Another god, perhaps," said Cathbhad, "greater and more powerful than those we know. Always, he is remote from men, but he controls all. He could crush this whole world in his fist, should he choose to, or resolve all its troubles with a single word."

"Who is he?"

"I do not know," replied Cathbhad. "It is the world's great mystery. The Saxons, a barbarous people who live in a cold, northern land beyond the Narrow Sea, call him Wyrd. But no man has ever seen him, and few are aware of his presence. Perhaps he does not exist at all." Cathbhad's voice trailed off, as if he would say more, but could not find the words. Then, all at once, he returned to the present and fixed his eyes upon Emrys. "Go, little hawk," he said, "go like the wind, and speed upon your way to Ynys Mon. There, seek out Gwelydd, the druid who taught me my trade. He will place your feet upon the proper road, and show you the marks by which you will know the right course. Yours is a great destiny: listen to the words of the gods. Tarry not upon your way, but go directly!"

"Farewell, old friend," said Emrys, and he embraced the bard.

"Farewell, little hawk; return when you can," answered Cathbhad; and they parted company.

* * *

Emrys set out during the middle of the night, without saying goodbye to anyone else, especially not his mother. He took an old sword no one would miss from the armoury and thrust it, without scabbard or any other wrapping, into his belt, and shouldered a pack that contained a few scraps of food liberated from the kitchens. Then he stole up onto the battlements. It was a cloudy night, and the wind bit keenly, but Emrys seemed to know, as if it were broad daylight, where the sentries were. He glanced over the palisade, and dropped his provisions and the sword. They landed, with a thud, below. With a glance in both directions, he snaked over the parapet and hung for a moment by his hands. Then he let go. Hitting the ground, he rolled twice, picked up his pack and sword, and disappeared into the forest.

It was a journey of many days to Ynys Mon, through appalling weather and terrain that seemed ever moving around him. There were times when Emrys felt that the sea must churn with less turbulence than the mountains that rose and fell about him. At length, he emerged from the mountains upon a coast, running due north, and this he followed for many miles, with Cereticiaun Bay on his left hand and the cries of seabirds around him. He had seen gulls before, of course, but now, he took particular pleasure in the soaring joy of their flight.

When the coast began to bend westwards, Emrys cut through the Enlli Peninsula to the northern coast, which he followed eastwards. There were many strange birds there, black and white with brightly-coloured beaks, all like small druids, but involved in obscure and trivial matters. Emrys watched them with delight for a while, but at length moved on with his head down and his collar up against the sting of the spray. At last, he saw a long, low body of land across the water, and knew he had reached Ynys Mon. He gave his last few pieces of silver to a ferryman and, stepping off the ferry, planted his feet at last upon the hallowed ground of Ynys Mon.

"How do I get to Afallach?" he asked the ferryman.

"Why would you want to go there?" asked the ferryman.

"The desire is upon me," replied Emrys, evasively.

The ferryman planted his staff in the mud and leaned upon it for a moment. "There's magic in that place, mark you," he said. "Those as live there"—he struggled for words—"well, they live in another place too, and it's not wholesome to be among them."

"Thank you for your warning," said Emrys. "I shall be careful, but my errand takes me close to that place, and I may do nothing else until I have seen it."

"Then follow this road north," said the ferryman, pointing. "There's a town of men nearby, look you, called Aber Alaw, and the sacred Apple Grove is not far distant from it."

Emrys thanked him and pointed his face to the north once more; turning, he was sure he saw the ferryman making the sign of the evil eye, to ward off misfortune.

* * *

In ancient days, according to the lore of the elders of Britain, there had been a mighty war among the Morforwyn. Morgana and Balor had rebelled against Argante and Arawn. Morgana, by her dark arts, had brought forth the race of ice giants out of the cold and barren mountains of the north, and for many centuries the long-lived ones had clashed until all the menfolk had been laid low, and the womenfolk of the Morforwyn had retreated to Avalon, where the magic of Argante had hidden them from the eyes of Morgana and her servants. There, among the sacred apple-trees, the Ladies of the Lake dwelt long, fearing to emerge lest Morgana's thralls beheld and crushed them. It was Brutus and Corineus, sailing from far away over the sea, who finally drove the army of Morgana from Albion, as the realm was then called, and they were the first men ever to tread upon the soil of the Island of the Mighty. For many years, the Ladies of the Lake and the men of Britain dwelt side by side, but as the centuries passed, the Morforwyn appeared ever more seldom among mortals, until none could say when last they were seen. But the druids with loving care raised up the sacred grove of Afallach on Ynys Mon as a reminder of the grove on Avalon, and there they stayed, deepening their lore as the long years slowly passed.

Those who served the druids built for themselves lodgings nearby, though not within sight of Afallach itself. And, in time, those lodgings became a cluster of houses and fields and a small market known as Aber Alaw. But seldom came any, other than those with the high calling, from the outside world to Afallach or Aber Alaw. Highly respected were the druids, whithersoever they went, but no man wished a long association with them, for it was well known that the gods of old, with whom the druids were as familiar as partners over a pint of ale, were of terrifying aspect and unpredictable nature.

This was the township to which Emrys came, footsore and weary, with a pack empty of provisions, two days after the ferryman had dropped him off on the shore of Ynys Mon.

Emrys looked with wonder left and right as he walked through the main street of Aber Alaw, for the buildings were far different from those he had become used to in Caermyrddin. They were mostly circular in plan, and built out of stone, with low thatched roofs. Fields that had not yet yielded a crop, for the year was young, ran right down to the back doors of the huts. It looked as if the town had been built around the trees of a small forest, and they had been given precedence of place over dwellings or roads. One oak, wrinkled and crouching, like a bent old man, stood in the midst of the main thoroughfare, untouched by hewer. The largest house of the collection, a hall of about the same size as Rhydderch's in Caermyrddin, actually had an elm growing through its midst—the budding branches could be seen emerging from the thatch of the roof.

In the midst of the town was a small square, where a number of merchants had set up their stalls. A small inn stood there, overshadowed by an oak and a beech, and several customers sat outside, nursing mugs of frothing ale and watching the merchants and customers going about their business. Emrys stood still for a moment, watching. They were odd clothes the people wore—long robes of wool, rather than the short tunics to which Emrys' eye was used. Their legs seemed to be bare, and all wore sandals rather than the boots and cross-gartering common among the folk from which Emrys came. The women's arms also tended to be bare, though they often wore shawls over them. Most of the women wore black, and the men also were clad in dark hues, mostly brown. The warriors, who moved casually among the ordinary citizens, wore a deep russet, with leather armour; they carried swords, but no spears, and their shields, slung mostly over their backs, were small, round and of beaten bronze. No one wore plaid, not even the warriors. Hair tended to be short, chins shaved, and women mostly wore their hair piled high with ringlets framing their faces.

Emrys strode with as much purpose as he could muster across the town square to the inn, and nodded to the old men sitting outside it. They regarded him with placid curiosity, bordering on hostility.

"The gods' blessings on you, friends," said Emrys. "I have traveled from afar, and seek the sacred grove of Afallach; can you direct me there?"

One of the old men replied, but for a second, Emrys could make nothing out of it. He stood dumbfounded for a while, regarding the old man who had spoken like a stunned rabbit. If Emrys had asked him to place his grandson's head in a noose, he could not have worn an expression of greater outrage.

"Can you direct me to the place I seek?"

The old man spoke slowly and carefully, but his voice was edged with anger. "Know you nothing of this place, boy? Afallach is forbidden to all men save the druids."

His speech was strange, like Emrys' Brythonic and yet unfamiliar, like the speech of a man from a distant land or ancient time. Emrys had not expected that.

"Why is it forbidden?" he asked, too surprised by the odd dialect to feel fully the disappointment that the man's words should have occasioned.

"Why is it forbidden? Ask not why, just know it is. Your errand has been in vain; return whence you came, or stay here a night, but go your ways ere long, for you have naught to do here."

Emrys put a hand to his head. The old man spoke again, but he heard no words. The world seemed very remote. He put out another hand to the table to steady himself, dropping his pack upon the ground. A mist seemed to be

49

rising all about him. He felt a cold dread clutch him. Why did the gods do this to him?

All at once, unbidden by his own will, Emrys opened his mouth. A song came out. But it was not the kind of song he would have expected—it was an indecent ditty, about a warrior and a maiden, with a lively tune and a catchy refrain. He had never heard it before in his life.

> A warrior and a maid
> Together one day played.
> The soldier was in jest,
> The maiden did protest
> And bade him do his best:
> Put in all! Put in all!
> She bade him do his best:
> Put in all!

Heads were turning towards them. The old men watched him with slack jaws. Under strong compulsion, Emrys sang on, though he had no harp or other instrument to accompany himself.

> And then her lovely eyes
> Rolled upwards to the skies.
> "My skin, so white, you see;
> My smock above my knee!
> What more would you of me?
> Put in all! Put in all!
> What more would you of me?
> Put in all!"

A crowd had gathered now, and several of the menfolk were tapping their feet. There were smiles on the faces of most of those listening; they could tell which way the wind was blowing.

> "My swan-like neck and breast
> Lie here for your request."
> The soldier he did fret
> And broke into a sweat,
> Much further for to get,
> Put in all! Put in all!

> Much further for to get,
> Put in all!

Even the old men were smiling now; a few others had emerged from the inn so that Emrys was surrounded by an admiring audience. But the fog still swirled about him. He felt that he could never reach out and touch any of them. They were in a different world.

> According to her will,
> The soldier tried his skill;
> But the story here does tell
> That, tried he ne'er so well,
> For an inch she'd take an ell!
> Put in all! Put in all!
> For an inch she'd take an ell!
> Put in all!

Emrys wondered if he could stop the mad career of the song. Was it possible the gods would inspire such things? This was no heroic lay, this was no song of piercing beauty about the gods of ancient times. And yet, what he could see of the faces through the fog was covered with pleasure. The song was suited to the audience. He sang on for one last stanza:

> When ended has their sport,
> She found him all too short;
> For when he'd done his best,
> The maiden did protest:
> 'Twas nothing but a jest!
> Put in all! Put in all!
> 'Twas nothing but a jest!
> Put in all!

The song ended in a guffaw of laughter. The mist dissolved into the sunlight of a spring morning, and Emrys found himself surrounded by laughter, with a mug of ale on the table before him. One of the old men he had spoken to earlier slapped him on the back.

"Oh, that were a good song!" he cried. "You must sing it again tonight, you must!"

Emrys smiled. The gods knew their business well. He had been accep-
ted.

VI

Emrys stayed in Aber Alaw while March died with a gusty sprinkling of rain, giving birth to April with fresh winds off the Eirish Sea. Young shoots sprouted from the fields that surrounded the town, and golden and violet flowers bloomed in the hedgerows. The great oak on the main thoroughfare flourished with bright green, and swallows dived out of the air and played between the houses. Emrys gained something of a reputation around Aber Alaw, partly for his singing. He was able, after a short time, to buy himself a harp; Cathbhad had taught him to play, but he had never thought of himself as much good at it until now. Curiously enough, though, he found he also had a talent for conjuring tricks. He could make an acorn disappear from under a cup, and then reappear wherever he wanted it. He could cut a rope in half and then restore it to its full length. And he could see into the minds of men, and see something of what they saw. He became a very popular figure around Aber Alaw, and rather than lodging at the inn, as he had done at first, he passed his nights in a small hut on the edge of town, which an appreciative villager had built for him for revealing the location of a small cache of silver coins in his field.

Emrys' visions did not go away completely during this time. But they seemed to come during quiet moments, mostly when he was alone. Once, he saw a woman from behind, her hair a flaming red, and she raised a bare arm, the blade of a dagger pointing downwards from her fist. It was already dripping with blood, but down it plunged, seeking death once more. On another occasion, he saw a dark-haired woman, beautiful and perilous, and he could not decide whether she was friend or foe. She was accompanied by a great cat, its fur as dark in hue as her hair. In some of the visions, he saw flames, leaping high and devouring all they touched, men, beasts, homes, fields. He put out a hand to quench them, but he could do nothing to stop their spreading. And he knew that something—he told himself Excalibur, though a doubt gnawed at his heart—was missing. Something there was that he lacked, and he knew not for what he needed this thing, nor what it was. And Emrys began to take long walks in the forest about Aber Alaw, learning its paths as he had done around Caermyrddin, and on his wanderings he pondered at great length the feelings and the visions he was experiencing.

From time to time, the druids visited Aber Alaw, usually to purchase goods from the market. They wore animal hides or coloured robes, but they did not have an otherworldly appearance. Their regalia was slightly strange, but not so strange that they would have occasioned more than one or two remarks upon the streets of Caermyrddin.

One day—a fine day with bright sunshine and a shower in the early morning that left the ground pleasantly spongy and the flowers brighter for their wash—there seemed to be an ill mood upon Aber Alaw. The merchants closed their stalls up early, and long before night fell, all doors were shut and bolted. Emrys wondered why this should be, and strolled along the main street towards the tavern, his eyes moving this way and that in wonder.

"Emrys!" came a hissing voice. Emrys turned, and saw Llywarch, one of the old men to whom he had spoken on his first day in Aber Alaw. Llywarch was peering out from the window of his darkened hut, and beckoning. Emrys moved closer. "Emrys," the old man went on, "know you not what day this is? Get you from the public streets, or you will be taken!"

"I do not know the day; what is it?"

"Beltane!" hissed the old man. "Beltane!"

"But I have celebrated Beltane many times at home in Caermyrddin," protested Emrys. "I see no reason to fear."

"Aye, boy," replied old Llywarch. "But this is Afallach, and the fifth year; 'tis unwise to be abroad on such a day."

"I shall heed your words," said Emrys, returning the way he had come.

But he did not enter his own hut, once he got there. Instead, he slipped behind it and into the deep forest that surrounded Aber Alaw. He got along fairly well at first, but night was drawing on, and before long, he found himself moving through deep gloaming, and the ways looked unfamiliar.

At home, Emrys reflected, ritual fires were built upon the hills on Beltane, and bulls were driven through the flames to purify them, before being sacrificed to Angharad, goddess of love, who would then bless the crops

54

for the coming year. Later on, the children of Caermyrddin would leap through the fires, and there would be feasting.

Emrys stopped. Ahead rose the dark silhouette of a hill, visible through the trees as a great black hole in the stars. And sure enough, there was a fire burning on top of the hill. Emrys could see a narrow thread of smoke winding its way among the stars. He plunged on through the forest.

The way was hard, for though the hill was not tall, it was steep, and he spent an hour dragging himself through brambles and clambering over them. But before he reached the crest, a curious noise came to him on the night air: a keening, like the mourning of relatives at a funeral. Emrys pushed on, and presently, the ground leveled off, and he found himself peering through the trees at a clearing. A ring of bonfires had been set up around the edge and, in the centre, stood a tall apple tree with a stone well at its foot. A drum was beating in a slow, heavy pulse, and unclothed men and women danced in and out of the fires, their skin shining in the light of the bonfires. On the edges, swaying slowly in time to the drums, were the druids in their finery. It did not look much like Beltane in Caermyrddin, but neither did it look particularly ominous.

But then the drums stopped, and the celebrants paused in their dance. They all looked towards the forest on the opposite edge of the clearing. Emrys had noticed a break in the trees earlier, but that was gone now. Trees seemed to have grown there in the short space of time he had been observing the dancers. In the silence, he could hear the eerie sound of keening once more.

The trees moved. The gap in the forest appeared once more, starry. And the light of the fires fell upon a thing that made Emrys start backwards in fright.

It was a man, thirty feet in height at least, his arms outstretched, his head erect. He moved with fluid steps towards the centre of the fire-ring. He was clad all in green.

No.

Emrys gasped. For from the ends of his toes to the crown of his head, the man was overall vegetable green. His clothes were green, his skin was green, and from the crown of his head flowed long green locks. Emrys watched in horrid fascination.

But then he noticed something else. Around the giant's feet moved dark shapes, and he saw that some of the women in black robes were hauling the giant to the space between the fires, using ropes. It was on wheels. And now that he observed a little closer, Emrys could see that what he had taken for green skin and clothes were really leaves and verdant twigs. The giant was in reality a huge effigy, woven from osier-work, and twisted through with vegetation. He was not a real giant at all, but a huge wicker man.

But it was from the wicker man that the mourning noise emanated, louder now, like the sound of many men weeping for grief. Emrys caught his breath. There were men tied to the wicker framework of the giant figure, and it was they who mourned.

The drums struck up again, and another dance began. The drums increased their pace, and the dance grew more frantic. Quicker and yet quicker went the drums, and the firelight flashed upon the naked dancers as they cavorted in and out of the bonfires. Then someone cried out. The dancers were still, but yet the drum went on, slowly now. Each druid moved to one of the fires. Moving in perfect unison, they took up bows, lit their arrows, and sent them flying into the green man.

Emrys whirled around and leaned against a tree, his stomach heaving. Behind him, the lamentation turned to a scream of terror and pain. And Emrys fled. He fled as if he had turned into a hawk, and could fly over the tree tops. He fled as if the Wild Hunt were upon his heels, and after his soul. And he did not stop until he had reached his hut, and flung himself on the pallet, where he could bury his face in the straw and scream silently.

The smell of roasting meat, he thought, would never leave him.

* * *

Emrys did not emerge from his hut the following day, nor the day after that. On the third day after Beltane, though, he at last came out, his cheeks hollow and dark circles about his eyes. The people of Aber Alaw, who generally liked him well, took one look at him and gave him a wide berth.

Emrys purchased some scraps of food, and drew a pail of water from the well, which he guzzled down fast, letting it stream down either side of his face. Then he went back to the darkness of his hut, and stayed there without appearing for another day.

He was much more presentable now, but in his heart he had struggled with his quest, and his need to consult the wise ones of Afallach, and he had decided that he wanted no part in their world at all. He made for the market-place, where he would purchase the provisions he would need for his return to Caermyrddin.

The day was bright, and when he reached the marketplace of Aber Alaw, he saw a druid buying some leather from a tanner. Emrys recoiled a moment, then watched him with a frown. Something about him was not quite right. He walked with a stoop, and Emrys thought that there was a shadow about him, over his face and hands, and that was strange, for the sun was bright overhead. And suddenly, Emrys was struck with a great sadness. All about him, men and women and children went about their business, such small matters, while overhead the sun shone, as it had always shone, and would always shine. Emrys felt as if he could see the ends of all things: the concerns of princes, the ambition of courtiers, the practices of lawmakers, all would come in the end to nothing, for all daily business ended with night. And suddenly, this druid's petty concern for leather to mend his shoe seemed ridiculous. Emrys gave a shout of laughter—not merry laughter, but a gust of breath that sought to relieve his soul. But all around heard him, and suddenly, all eyes were upon him. The druid bent his gaze upon the youth. His eyes were dark, his brows bushy, and he had a full beard.

"Do you laugh at me, boy?" he inquired.

"I do, my lord," replied Emrys, "I crave your pardon."

"Why do you laugh at me?" Emrys looked away, and did not answer. The druid moved a little closer. "Are you the conjuror and singer of ballads of whom noise has spread through the town of late?" Emrys nodded. There seemed to be contempt stamped upon the druid's features. But there was something more, and Emrys' eyes widened at what he saw in this man's future. "Tell me, boy," insisted the druid; "why have you laughed at me?"

"Because," Emrys blurted out, "you are buying that leather to patch a pair of shoes, but you will never wear them."

"Why not, boy?"

"Because you will die before you return to Afallach!"

There was a short pause. "Wretched boy," said the druid at last. "Afallach is but a mile hence, and though I am advanced in years, I am in good health. Go back to your conjuring tricks."

Emrys gaped at him, and wished wholeheartedly that the ground would open and swallow him up. He averted his eyes from the incensed druid, and hastened back to his hut.

There was virtually nothing in the hut: a pallet of straw, his harp, a small bundle containing food. He dropped himself onto the pallet and put his head between his knees.

What a fool he had been! What a fool! He had no purpose in life if not to find Excalibur. Nothing was as important as that—no scruple about human sacrifice. He did not have to like what they did, he just needed to get information from them. And now, he would never get into Afallach! He had spoken to one druid since arriving in Aber Alaw, and he had used the opportunity to display nothing but his own utter stupidity. This had set him back months in his quest.

Emrys reached out and picked up his harp. With a disconsolate hand, he began to pluck the strings.

The music kept him in a reverie for some minutes. He was shaken out of it by a shout from outside. Someone was calling his name. Slowly, he put down his harp and pushed aside the door.

A whole collection of villagers stood outside, regarding him with grim expressions. Their leader, the man who had built Emrys' hut, said, "You were best pack your things and be off. We have no need of your kind in Aber Alaw."

Emrys nodded, and returned to the gloom of his hut. He picked up his harp, shouldered his pack, and stood for a moment thinking of what had transpired over the last few months.

He had been a fool. To think that he could influence the course of history, that kings would be grateful to an urchin like him! It was past thought.

58

The villagers were right to expel him—he had offended one upon whom they depended, a valued customer at their market, one whose rituals interceded for them and made the gods look with a favourable eye on their crops. How could he have been so stupid?

Emrys emerged onto the village street and turned his back on Aber Alaw. He heard a few terms of abuse from behind him and, out of the corner of his eye, saw one make the sign of the evil eye as he passed. A few moments later, and Emrys was on the road south, making his slow way back to the ferry, and thence to Caermyrddin.

He had not been on the road an hour, when he heard hoof beats behind him. Turning, he saw a young man, no older than himself, approaching from the north. He seemed to be in haste, but reined in as he drew even with Emrys.

"Are you Emrys, the prophetic youth who foresaw the death of Rhufawn?" he asked. Emrys nodded. "Then come with me. My master, Gwelydd the Archdruid, bade me bring you to him, for he is much desirous to meet one who prophesied so accurately."

Emrys looked up with wide eyes. "Is it true then?" he asked. "Did the druid die?" The youth nodded. "I am sorry," said Emrys.

"I am not," replied the youth. "Rhufawn always ate more than his share, and he hoarded parchment." He held out a hand. "I am Aled," he said. "Climb up behind me, and I shall take you to the Archdruid. He begs you to return to him."

Emrys did not speak, but regarded the youth on the horse for a moment with an uncertain heart.

"He implores you to come," said Aled, sensing Emrys' indecision.

Emrys put his hand to the hilt of the old sword for comfort, then climbed up behind Aled. A moment later, they were cantering back northwards along the road. Emrys watched the hedgerows flash past, and a foreboding grew in his heart.

* * *

They passed through the village of Aber Alaw, where sullen faces followed them and several erstwhile friends of Emrys made the evil eye or whisked their children indoors as they passed. Emrys was grieved; in the short time of his residence in Aber Alaw, he had come to love its people and their strange dialect. The horse cantered on, and the ground began to rise.

Before they had gone very far, Emrys saw that they were surrounded by apple trees. They rose with the ground before them to the summit of a hill. They were divesting themselves of their delicate springtime garb. The ground was thick with discarded blossoms, and they drifted through the air thickly, like pink snow. Aled reined in the horse and bade Emrys dismount.

"Here, you must leave your sword, and I must blindfold you," he said, taking Emrys' sword and wrapping his eyes in a black cloth. "I'm afraid you may not see the secrets of the Gate of Afallach. Not yet, anyway."

Emrys went on in darkness, led by Aled, but his lungs filled with air laden with the aroma of apple blossom, and his ears filled with birdsong delightful to hear. The ground rose under his feet, so that it was soon laborious. For some time, he thought he could hear harp music and singing. Then, at last, Aled put a hand to his arm to stop him from going forward any further, and removed the blindfold.

Emrys blinked a few times, but then saw that he was at the crest of a tall hill. In the centre stood a single apple tree, fair to behold and laden with blossoms, with a well at its foot surrounded by neat and clean stones. Below him, the slopes were clad with apple trees in blossom.

There were charred patches in the grass.

Beyond the hill, he could see the Eirish Sea and, beyond it, Eirin, long enemy of the Island of the Mighty. Turning, he thought he could also see the Island of the Mighty itself, lying in splendour about the hilltop. There was the fastness of Dinas Eryri, amidst the mountains of Cambria; beyond them, he could see the rugged cliffs of Cornwall, where the frenzied sea spent its anger upon crumbling rocks. Turning more, he saw Logris of the many fortresses, and Lundein and, beyond that, the land of the Saxons and the world of the Romans; turning to the north, the mist and mountains and bare islands of Albany and Orkney. Beyond that, a wide expanse of cold, grey sea stretched even to the end of the earth. But there was something there, not quite at the edge: an island, shrouded in mists, hardly visible, and gone as soon as Emrys looked directly at it, like one of the fainter stars in the heavens.

"Welcome," said a voice, "to Afallach, the Isle of Apples, the Centre of the World."

VII

The man facing Emrys was incalculably old, but his age did not seem to have weakened him. He wore robes of white, but cast about his shoulders and obscuring them almost completely was a cloak made from the hide of a deer; the deer's head, including antlers, formed a head-dress. He held in his hand a tall staff, surmounted with the curved blade of a sickle, whose edge glinted with gold. His beard was long and white, but not unkempt, and his hair spilled almost geometrically over his cloaked shoulders. He wore a golden torc about his neck, the terminals fashioned into the heads of stags; but oddly, feathered wings spread backwards from the heads along the curved rod. A white girdle encircled his waist loosely, and a golden buckle hung below his navel.

"I am Gwelydd, Archdruid of the Island of the Mighty, and guardian of the sacred apple grove of Afallach. I speak to one who has the Sight, do I not?"

"Yes," replied Emrys, stepping forward. "The gods speak to me in visions."

Gwelydd closed in upon Emrys, reached out with his free hand, and placed his palm against the young man's forehead. The grip was firm, the hand dry and a little cold. Strong fingers curled over the crown of Emrys' head.

"I see the Mark upon you," murmured the old man, deep creases appearing between his bushy brows. "How is it you have eluded us so long? Ten summers have passed; ten times, the white bull has gone to the gods as our springtime offering, and now we cannot retrace our steps. We cannot take you back to your childhood, and train you as you should have been trained. Ah, what might have been!" He sighed deeply, and the crease between his brows vanished. "It is no matter. The gods have sent you here now." For a long while, the druid scrutinized Emrys' face in silence. His eyes were like deep wells of brown water. Then he withdrew his hand and stepped back. "Those of the village," he said, "they are a simple folk. Their thoughts are of small beer and distaffs. They do not understand. They think you cast a spell upon Rhufawn and killed him." He smiled, and there was affection in his eyes. "A simple folk, but good; and in time, you will regain their confidence. But I wanted to see you with my own eyes, for I felt I could divine whether you had the skill they guessed at or not. Now I see that you caused not his death, but foresaw it merely." He smiled at the irony of his choice of word, and repeated it softly: "Merely."

"Please," begged Emrys, "I don't understand."

"Not yet," Gwelydd replied. And now there was some sadness in his expression as he looked upon Emrys. "It is a lonely path that you must tread, I fear," he said distantly; Then he blinked and turned to survey the panorama that the hilltop afforded. "When you look from this hilltop, what do you see?" he asked.

Emrys looked west and then south. "I see the Eirish Sea," he said noncommittally. "And, to the south, I see the village, Aber Alaw, and the mountains of Dinas Eryri." Emrys gasped. He felt as if he had been pulled, as if his body had been thrust forward at enormous speed. Mountains and lakes flew past beneath him. He saw Caermyrddin, and his grandfather's castle, and a dark-haired woman, alone in her chamber. "Mother?" said Emrys.

Viviane was tying up her raven hair and preparing to face the business of the day. But her eyes were moist. She had been weeping. Emrys' heart reached out and touched hers, blended with it. He could feel her heaviness, and he knew that he had caused it. Gasping a little, Emrys staggered a few steps backwards.

"Mother," he pleaded, "forgive me. I shall return, and I shall explain myself."

"Every mother," said another voice, a man's voice, a little sternly, "must endure the departure of her son." Emrys turned and saw that Gwelydd was looking levelly at him; the miles had contracted beneath him to nothing in a second. "I do not say it is wrong to feel your mother's pain," continued Gwelydd; "but you must learn to control your response to the pain that others feel—and that you yourself feel. All boys become men, and that is little to be wondered at. But look again." He extended a hand into the east. "What do you see?"

The apple trees were becoming misty, and Emrys' vision hurtled out from Afallach. It was like having a rug pulled out from under his feet, and Emrys hit the ground, sprawling. Gwelydd reached out and helped him up, smiling faintly and dusting Emrys' shoulders off.

"What place is this?" asked Emrys.

"This," replied Gwelydd, "is the Great Centre. This is where the soul of the Island of the Mighty makes its home. The people of Britain are like a great oak, and their roots delve the earth here. All wisdom comes from this place. And from here," he added in confidential tones, "one who has the Sight may see many things. Look again."

Emrys had barely got his breath back, but he did look again. He cried out and staggered against Gwelydd, but kept his eyes fixed on the south.

"I see a great city," he stammered, "on a river. And I hear . . . oh, it is as if all the people in the city were suddenly crying out to me!" His knees gave way, but Gwelydd bore him up.

"What do they say?" demanded Gwelydd

Emrys twisted in Gwelydd's arms, but the old druid held him firm. "What!" cried Emrys, and his voice was shrill, like a woman's. "What— what will become of my child?"

"Good," urged Gwelydd. "Look further."

Emrys twitched again, and this time, Gwelydd could not hold him. Together, they sank to the turf, but the old man kept Emrys' head fixed facing the south. "Give me more ale," said Emrys, his words slurring almost incoherently. "Give me more ale, let my veins run with it, that I may not know who I am!"

"Further," said Gwelydd in his ear.

But Emrys spoke in his natural voice now. "Get them away! Get them away! I cannot hear them all! They are too many for my soul!" He shrieked, pulled himself away from Gwelydd and, as if impelled by some supernatural power, writhed upon the grass of Afallach, his limbs thrashing, his lips foaming. Gwelydd took two steps, bent at the knee, and breathed gently into his face. Instantly, Emrys' limbs relaxed and his eyes closed.

Gwelydd breathed deeply, contemplating Emrys' still form for a moment. Reaching out, he smoothed a few strands of hair away from the young man's brow. Then he called out, and Aled approached from the shadows of the apple trees, where he had waited all this time. He bent down and picked Emrys up, limp in his arms, and followed the old druid from the summit of the hill.

* * *

Emrys was following a path, through open country. The sky was bright above him, and the grass vivid on either hand. He strode forward with a light step, for he knew his goal was near at hand.

"Emrys!" cried a voice. "Heal me!"

Emrys turned and faced a leper, his face disfigured by his disease, holding out the rotting hands of a corpse towards him.

"Emrys!" called someone else. Emrys spun around. A young man was addressing him. "Help me to the love of my fair lady!"

"Emrys, I need bread!" cried the voice of a wretched woman crouching beside the roadway.

"Emrys," said one who bore a sceptre, "I need men. I need spears, and shields, and horses. What can you do?"

They were barring his way forward, and hemming him in on either side. Hands reached towards him, voices implored. He could no longer see the road for the crowd that pressed in upon him.

"Emrys!" they called. "Emrys! Emrys!"

Emrys turned his eyes upwards. Only the sky was free. If only he could fly like a bird, soar like a hawk! But the hands clawed at him, clutching, grabbing, fawning. He raised his own hands over his head, twisting, the corners of his mouth turned down.

"Leave me alone!" he cried. "Leave me, I say! I have important business along this road. My business is most urgent! *Leave me alone!*"

"Emrys!" they cried; and, above it all, he could hear one voice, the voice of an old man, gentle and soothing, calling his name in soft tones.

And suddenly, the vision was gone, and Emrys knew that he was in a dimly-lit chamber, flat on his back, covered with soft sheets, and a pillow under his head. He could smell hot tallow. And soup.

Gwelydd held the bowl out to him. The tangy aroma of parsley and basil wafted to his nostrils. He sat up in bed and took the proffered bowl eagerly. Lifting it to his lips, he sipped. It was good.

"You have slept the whole day," observed Gwelydd.

"What place is this?" asked Emrys.

"You are in Afallach still. These are the apprentices' quarters in the Cave of Knowledge."

Emrys looked about. There were four beds in the room. The walls were lined with shelves, and upon these were many books, bound in leather. There was a desk in the centre of the room, with a pair of benches. Scattered upon the table lay goose feathers, a few small knives, and a stack of parchments, the corners curling upwards just slightly.

Gwelydd smiled indulgently. "The Cave of Knowledge," he said, as if he were introducing a friend. "It is truly named, for it is the cave that contains the knowledge, not those who dwell in it. Oh, we can acquire its knowledge, of course, by reading the books. But it's not the same as having the knowledge ourselves, as a man who has learned something so that it is graven upon his heart. We always know we can consult our books again, and so we do not learn it quite so well. But the cave—yes, the Cave of Knowledge is well named. And there are some secrets, known to no man, that the cave alone possesses." Gwelydd drew a deep breath. "There are almost as many volumes here," he concluded, "as in the great library of the High Kings in Caer Lundein."

Emrys put aside the soup. "When you look from the top of Afallach," he said, "what do you see?"

"Only what mortal eyes can see," answered Gwelydd, a little sadly. "I have not the Sight. Many are the years since I first took the way of the oak and the stag and dwelt upon the sacred hill of Afallach, but the gift with which the gods have blessed your eyes is not mine."

"What do you want of me?" asked Emrys.

Gwelydd hesitated, turned his eyes down for a fraction of a second. "If I may speak plainly," he said, "I should very much like for you to join our order. As a druid, a Seeing One may achieve much in this world."

Emrys sat back, resting his head against the cold stone wall, and shut his eyes. An image was printed upon the backs of his eyelids: a ring of blackened spots in a forest glade and, in the midst, a pile of charred sticks, still smoking. He felt a tightening in his stomach, as he opened his eyes and turned them once more to Gwelydd. "That cannot be, at this time," he said.

The old druid paused a moment, frozen as if time had stopped. Then he nodded. "You will perhaps change your mind in time. The wind blows not every day from the same quarter. I hope, after thought, you will choose differently."

Emrys said nothing. He was still thinking of the Beltane fires.

"Rest," advised Gwelydd, placing a gentle hand upon Emrys' shoulder. "Older and wiser heads than yours have been turned by what they have seen from the crest of Afallach's sacred hill."

Emrys closed his eyes. The pillow beneath his head was soft and warm, and the blankets enfolded him in their cozy embrace. He was asleep again in a matter of seconds.

* * *

When he awoke—hours later, or minutes, he could not tell—the cave was empty. He felt refreshed, and rose from his bed, glancing round as he did so. The room was much the same as it had been before. He noticed now a pair of braziers, one of which was lit, filling the room with soft warmth. Tapestries hung from the walls, bearing scenes from old stories that Emrys could not understand. Taking a torch from its bracket, he held it up close to one of the tapestries. He saw a mighty throne of marble, and sitting upon it a man—no, a god—who bore a crown on his head. But there was no peace nor dignity in his face. Rather, his eyes started from his head, and his mouth was twisted into a shape that looked like death, or worse. At his shoulder stood a queen, with long, dark hair and, for a moment, Emrys was reminded of his mother.

A spark lit in his mind, and he suddenly knew what the tapestry depicted. "The Siege Perilous," he said quietly, touching the image of marble woven in the fabric. "Balor," he said, looking upon the mad king, "and Morgana," he concluded. He reached out to touch the image of the dark-haired queen, but flinched, and could not bring himself to do it. A raven, he saw, perched upon her shoulder, its wings beginning to spread, as if it would fly hence upon some errand of mischief or evil will.

Emrys looked away. There were several doors. Glancing around once, he opened one and left the room.

He found himself in another chamber. This one was wide, and many tapestries hung from the walls. All depicted stories from the remote past, and most had lettering running around the edges; some were bordered with abstract patterns, and in many cases, Emrys was hard pressed to discern which were letters, which were meaningless abstractions. He pulled one tapestry aside, and found that there were shelves behind it, and books resting upon the shelves. This, then, was a library. What had Gwelydd called it? The Cave of Knowledge.

Another desk stood in the middle of the room, but this one had only one bench, a selection of quills, and a small stack of neat sheets of parchment. The small figure of a bird, a hawk, fashioned crudely by some primitive workman, rested upon the parchments. There was a fire-pit in the middle of the room, smouldering even now, and sending its thin trail of smoke to a louvre in the ceiling. Other doors led off from this chamber, and Emrys saw that, beside each door, a niche was dug into the wall, and a small statue nestled in each niche. On closer inspection, he saw that the statues were of men, dressed in the robes of druids, like Gwelydd.

At last, he turned away from them and scanned the chamber with his eyes. Which door? There were many, and no way of telling which led where. Emrys, making a choice at random, opened a door and found himself in a dim chamber with no books. In the centre of the floor stood a pair of statues. A man and a woman, the man crowned like the king in the tapestry he had examined, the woman surrounded by black birds. Between them, they held a book. A small flame burned just in front of the book. The figures were life-size, hewn from oak, and painted in so lifelike a manner that Emrys watched them for long minutes, expecting one or the other of them to move or speak.

Emrys looked away from the statues, and saw that the walls were lined with recesses, wide but not high, about three in height. They were like the book shelves in the previous chamber, but the shapes were not books. He could see very little in the dim light, and the yellow pool of his torch did not reach far enough so, curiosity rising in him, he approached with infinite caution the nearest of the recesses and held his light over his head the better to see what was within.

A gaunt face stared at him from the darkness, its eyes empty sockets, its teeth grinning in a mockery of life. Emrys gasped and dropped the torch. It struck the uneven floor without going out, but the shadows danced, and the dead men were covered with darkness once more. Emrys clawed for the torch and, snatching it up, scrambled for the door. He slammed it closed behind him, leaning against the door frame and gulping air. His heart was pounding, and his knees were weak.

"Gwelydd?" he called, his voice quavering; he heard a sound from beyond one of the other doors, as if in acknowledgement of his call, and he staggered towards it, pulling on the handle and throwing it wide.

Daylight flooded past him into the Cave of Knowledge, and a great horned figure stood before him. The antlers seemed to divide the rays of the setting sun into a million shafts of gold, and for a moment, Emrys was blinded.

"Gwelydd," he breathed, "I am sorry—the cave, I explored the cave. I found the dead men. I am sorry—"

He paused, for the figure did not respond in words. It was not Gwelydd, but a tall stag, noble in mien, pawing the ground with a hoof. It looked down upon Emrys, and fixed him with its gaze. Its eyes were like deep wells of brown water, and Emrys caught his breath.

The stag lowered its head, and nodded, once, twice. Then it turned and, with measured paces, walked across an empty space of ground towards an oak forest; and Emrys trotted obediently after it.

VIII

The forest was full of oaks, ancient and, it seemed to Emrys, whispering to one another about him. The stag followed no path, but chose the easiest way through bracken and fern. The moist smell of humus filled Emrys' nostrils, the sound of birdsong his ears. A cuckoo gave throat, not far off, to its mournful notes. Every so often, when it seemed that Emrys would get left behind, the stag would stop, look over its shoulder, and wait for him to catch up. This seemed to go on for hours, perhaps days. The forest stretched on, the oaks like gnarled old men bending over him in every direction.

At length, the stag slowed. Emrys could see, ahead of him, a clear patch of sky showing through the oak and rowan. With one last glance over his shoulder, the stag plunged on, through some hawthorn brakes, into a glade. Emrys took three steps forward, and peered into the glade.

It was full of deer. It looked like a pool of soft chestnut backs, with here and there the great red island of a head. Mightiest of them all were the red deer, stern and muscular with branching horns that had just begun to sprout, or heavy bellies from the imminent delivery of fawns. There were fallow deer too, marked by their tawny colour and spotted backs. The young bucks leaped about on the edge of the clearing, clashing their heads together in a light-hearted way, like young boys practising with their fathers' swords. Interspersed with the red and fallow deer were the diminutive roes, invisible because of their shortness among the crowd, except at the very edges. But it was to these intelligent-looking creatures that Emrys' heart warmed most. Their ears, larger than the others', were pricked and alert, their soft muzzles bearded with short dark fur and white patches. The coats were a warm grey for the most part, but they were beginning to shed their winter livery, and a fiery reddish-brown showed through in most of them.

In the midst of this cervine throng, Gwelydd sat mounted upon the tallest of the red deer. Beside him, on a smaller deer about the size of Emrys' guide, sat a young boy in the robes of an acolyte.

The stag which had led Emrys to this place regarded him for a moment, then dropped its head and shoulders. Emrys stood for a moment, unsure; then he understood fully the beast's intention, and climbed, very gingerly, upon its back. The fur was a little coarse between his fingers, but he felt great power in the solid muscles beneath him. The stag trotted towards Gwelydd, the sea of brown fur parting at its approach.

"Have no fear, Emrys," assured Gwelydd. "Do not hold on—Cerngwyn will not cast you off."

"What is happening?" asked Emrys.

"What is happening?" repeated Gwelydd. "This is the third night of Beltane. Tonight is sacred to Gwynn. Tonight we ride! Tonight is the Wild Hunt!" Gwelydd leaned forward a little, and added, "It is most fortunate you should arrive at this time. There is something that you must do at the end of our ride." Emrys framed a question, but Gwelydd dismissed it with a wave of his hand and turned to the cervine host, uttering what sounded like a single word in a strange, inhuman language. All the deer immediately looked at him, some with bowed heads. He said nothing, but turned about with his arms outstretched, as if blessing them all. Some stepped in close to him, rubbing their heads against him before returning to the forest, where the shadows swallowed them. One by one, the deer departed, until there were only the three left upon which Gwelydd, Emrys, and the acolyte were mounted.

* * *

Gwelydd leaned close to his mount's ear, and whispered a few words. The great beast nodded its mighty, antlered head. Then, it leaped. Emrys had just a moment to admire the perfection of its motion, forelegs stretched out as it met the air, its head erect, its great antlers sweeping backwards. But then, Cerngwyn leaped too, his head reaching forward a little. Emrys felt his stomach churn for a moment; then they landed, with the lightest of footfalls. They were speeding through the night forest. Dark branches swept past on both sides. The hoofs beneath them drummed faintly on the turf, but the ride was smooth, as if the only barrier were the air. At first,

71

Emrys ducked as the branches hurtled past his head; but then he realized that Cerngwyn knew what he was doing, and would let no harm come to his rider.

It was a clear night, and the stars and a half-moon shone down upon the silvered forest. The three riders flickered as they passed through shafts of moonlight that reached the forest floor through breaks in the oaken canopy overhead. Emrys rode a little behind Gwelydd, and he could see the muscles moving easily beneath the flanks of his stag. The chill night wind blew in his face, the ground flew past beneath him, and Emrys felt his blood sing in his veins. This was living! This was life!

Then, all at once, they were slowing. The forest thinned, and they began to climb a hill. Their pace had slowed as the stags laboured up the slope towards the summit. It was a treeless hill for the most part, not like Afallach and, as they finally mounted the crest, Emrys beheld a circle of mounds, within which stood four great stones, silvered by the moonlight. There was something primeval about the place. It seemed to have been wrought by men who had passed away eons ago, who had raised them by arcane magical skills. Emrys shivered to think of the long ages of dirt that had gathered over these men's bones.

"Emrys," said Gwelydd quietly. He indicated the acolyte, who was unfastening the stopper on a large flask. "Iolo may not see all that you see. Remain still, and do not speak, and what you see will not harm you."

Gwelydd took the flask from Iolo and, holding it at arm's length, rode slowly into the middle of the standing stones.

"Come forth, creatures of coldness!" he cried. "Come forth, shades of the living! Come forth for Gwynn's ride!"

Gwelydd rotated his hand through a half-turn. A dark liquid fell from the flask's mouth. Emrys saw it spatter upon the unkempt turf beside Gwelydd's stag.

Emrys looked across at Iolo. His face in the moonlight was pale, and there was a faint crease between his eyebrows. His eyes shifted from right to left. He noticed Emrys observing him, and flashed a quick smile; but the smile seemed overconfident, rehearsed. Emrys returned his attention to Gwelydd. The druid still had his arm outstretched, though the flask was empty. A single drop of the liquid hung from the lip of the flask, as if refusing to leave.

A trail of dark smoke had emerged from the side of the hill.

Emrys could see no fire from which the smoke originated; and it did not behave like smoke, for it did not dissipate into the atmosphere, but clung together and hovered above the ground. Emrys felt a deep coldness creeping along his spine. The cloud resolved itself into the shape of a woman, the tatters of a winding sheet shrouding her wasted body, her dark hair flying, her eyes empty, like dried-up wells. Emrys could make no sound, and no movement.

Another phantom appeared, a man in battered armour. Through the open face of the helmet, his eyes gaped and his mouth grimaced. More were appearing all the time: old men and young, children, warriors, farmers, wives, the whole motley array of human endeavour, in this dark and hideous mockery of life. It was a dark host, dark against the moon-silvered mounds: hollow eyes, sunken cheeks, ribbons of flesh hanging from bony fingers, tatters of clothing streaming from ribcages. And black, black as the grave, black as the most terrible night, as the heart of the basest villain known to men. Jaws opened wide. Empty sockets stared. Emrys felt his skin crawl.

One of the dark host stepped forward. It had a look of ruined nobility about it, like the shell of an ancient fortress crowning a hill overgrown with weeds. It bore the shadow of a crown about its temples, a decrepit shield upon its back, and a long sword upon its hip. It opened its terrible mouth, and words, soft as the final breath of life, came out. "Why have you summoned us from our slumber?"

Emrys felt a tugging at his sleeve. It was Iolo. "Cover your ears," he said quietly, and did so himself. Emrys frowned. All was already so terrible; how could the terror be increased?

Gwelydd was steadfast, as shadows of the dead surrounded him in a dark cloud. He said, "Be it known that you who have answered my summons have done so because you have passed from this world. You are in the world, but not a part of it. Death has taken you!"

There was a murmuring of disbelief amongst the shades, and their spokesman said, "How do we know this is true?"

Gwelydd pointed to the liquid he had dropped upon the ground. "Behold," he said, "the blood of Gwynn's sacrifice!"

The spectre regarded him for a moment, then stooped, reaching greedily for the blood upon the ground. But when he touched it, he opened his mouth wide, and uttered a scream of unutterable anguish. Emrys' hands went unbidden to his ears.

Another ghost stooped towards the spilt blood; and another, and another. Each one screamed, the scream driving nails through Emrys' spine. A bitter lamentation rose from the host as they realized that Gwelydd had spoken the truth. At the sound, fishermen at their trade miles down the coast made the sign of the evil eye, or crofters turned their blankets up and huddled within their beds. Woodland creatures awoke and ran, as if from hunters, and birds were scared into the air.

Still, the howling went on. Emrys had stopped his ears, but it drove through his hands and worked into his heart, piercing it with the coldness of utter despair. Will it never end? thought Emrys; and a voice somewhere within him replied, No; death is never-ending.

But the noise, at last, subsided to a weeping, over which the wraith that had spoken before asked Gwelydd, "What does the living ask of the dead?"

"I have summoned you," said Gwelydd, "for your final journey. I offer peace, for those who wish it."

"Or else, what follows?" asked the ghost who spoke on the others' behalf.

"Longing without fulfillment; existence without life; hunger and thirst for all time."

The spirits conferred. Their talk sounded like the north wind through the dead branches of a winter forest. At last, the spirit spoke again: "There are those who still do not believe what you say," he said.

"Those are free to return," said Gwelydd. "You who are dead are free in that respect. But it will be as I have described to you, and you will come to regret your choice, a solitary and unheard lamentation until the end of days."

More whispering. One or two spirits floated away, drifting like gossamer on the wind towards the land.

"Make your choice," said Gwelydd. "The hour is upon you, and the door will not be for ever open to you."

"We come," said the phantom. "Lead, and we shall follow."

So began the most ghastly journey of Emrys' life, the Wild Hunt.

Before too long, the half-moon shimmered on the peaks of tall mountains, glimpsed between the trees of the forest they hurtled through. They rode on, the beats of the deers' hoofs making little or no noise, the dark host behind them sighing with grief. Every now and then, Emrys could see lights —homesteads, hamlets, lonely shepherds warming their hands over crackling fires. A fortress, glimmering from the top of its battlemented hill, showed as a golden constellation above them for a moment; then it too dropped behind.

And all the while, the dead were just behind, and Emrys rode as if they pursued him, feeling their clammy breath on the back of his neck, their cold fingers clutching at his warm flesh. He heard a fell whispering from behind him, more than the sighing of the wind past his ears. He felt his eyes drawn to the grim host behind, and there they were: dismal spirits all, darker than the night that surrounded them. One clutched his chest, as if the wound were still a source of pain. Long weeds trailed from the flowing hair of another. Another fingered the welts on his throat. Winding sheets flew behind them. The empty sockets gaped, holes in the universe, leading nowhere. Bony hands reached out. Emrys swallowed, and turned his face forward.

Now the half-moon shimmered on a dark sea. A lone island protruded from the pool of moonlight, like a discarded vertebra. It was bare, treeless.

The Wild Hunt slowed, until it paused on a narrow grey beach opposite the island. The sound of the surf mingled with the whispering of the dead. Gwelydd made a motion to Cerngwyn, and the stag carried Emrys aside, so that he stood beside the old druid and the acolyte. Gwelydd held up his staff.

The host of the dead was gathering upon the beach. Emrys felt a coldness growing from his stomach outwards.

Gwelydd spoke at last. "You," he said, "creatures of coldness, behold! This is the place of peace you have sought. You will not find rest in this world again; seek it in the next!"

One of the phantoms turned from the group and made his way across the water to the island. Another followed, and another. One by one, the spirits floated disconsolately towards the dark shoulder of rock, and the darkness swallowed each one. A few more drifted away from the group, towards their erstwhile homes, and were soon consumed by the dark air. At last, only the spectre that had spoken remained.

"As you are now," he said, "so once was I."

"As you are now," responded Gwelydd, "so I shall be."

The spectre nodded, and followed the others. He reached the margin of the beach and took one longing backwards glance at the world that was no longer his home. Then the darkness of the Otherworld engulfed him for ever.

Gwelydd turned to Emrys. "You too," he said, "must behold what awaits you upon that island."

"Me too?" stammered Emrys.

"On the island is a cave," explained Gwelydd. "Look, but do not enter. That is no place for the living. Look in, but do not cross the threshold."

Gwelydd pointed. On the beach, about fifty yards away from them, a small boat with oars had been pulled high up on the beach.

"This is the test," said Gwelydd, "that all must pass. Now is the moment. Go."

Emrys swung his feet down from the stag. He felt a prickling up and down his spine, and his knees, he was sure, wobbled visibly. Taking a deep breath, he pushed the boat out into the dark waters.

IX

The crossing was brief, for the distance was not great, and few minutes had passed ere Emrys drew the tiny boat up on the gravelly shore of the island. A thin fog hung about, as if the dead, passing this way so recently, had sighed out a contagious breath before departing the world for good. Emrys shivered. The air bit with shrewd teeth this night.

The western tip of the island, to which Emrys had rowed, was low and flat, but at its eastern end, it rose steeply to a rounded hill, like the back of some sea beast, bare of all but grass and rough gorse. The lower slopes of the hill, where the pale rock showed through the dark grass, plunged directly into the sea. It was a calm night, and the slap of the waves against the rock was a soft pulse, like his heartbeat, as Emrys walked towards the hill. He had not gone far before he saw his destination.

The cave yawned, dark like the eyes of the spectres it had recently consumed. The sea came right up to the cave's mouth, and rocks bulged on either side of it, so that approach to it by a mortal was awkward at best. Cold, clammy air unfurled from its obscene mouth, and Emrys shivered again. He looked across the narrow stretch of water to the mainland beach. There stood Gwelydd and Iolo, and the three deer.

There was a hint of pink on the rock, and Emrys looked over his shoulder. The sun was beginning to rise. He squared his shoulders, and clambered down among the rocks.

There was, in fact, a narrow ribbon of beach before the cave's mouth. Emrys slid down the rounded side of the rock onto it, his feet sinking a little as they hit the wet sand. He looked at the cave mouth. It seemed, if anything, darker now that he was close to it.

Cold breath issued from the cave and blew against Emrys' cheek. It carried with it a reek like rotten meat. And it seemed that, carried by this foul air, something spoke from the cave to Emrys. "Come," it said, in a leprous voice. "Come, for this is every man's fate. What is the use of striving? All effort ends in the grave."

Emrys stepped away from the boulder, almost hypnotized by the sick voice. The beach was not wide. One more step would take him to eternal rest. He felt drawn. One more step, and the end of cares.

He reached the mouth of the cave. He peered inside.

Dimly, he could perceive shapes—whether massive rocks or lurking creatures or the spirits of men, Emrys could not tell. He strove in his mind to resolve them into something he could recognize. And then, at once, he saw the shapes take a form, like a ship emerging from a fog bank.

He saw another cave, a cave full of ice. He saw a woman with long, dark hair, black as a raven's wing. She smiled, but the smile was not good-humoured. Emrys saw a mighty fortress, with many towers pointing to-wards the sky; but the darkness behind showed through it, as if the walls were made of crystal. And he saw a tree, cloven by ancient lightning, and the mound of a grave between its roots.

Fear clutched at Emrys' heart, and he shut his eyes tight.

Then a low rushing sound began, somewhere deep in the black heart of the cave. Emrys reached out and clutched the rocky entrance. *I must stand firm*, he thought. What was it? Some mighty beast, out of the depths of the ocean?

The rushing sound became a roar, and against his will, Emrys opened his eyes. A stinking cloud of foul air blasted from the cave and, screaming in spite of himself, Emrys was catapulted backwards against the cliff face.

The air was full of dark spirits, fell of face. They rushed, moaning, about Emrys, and he could feel their cold fingers plucking at his clothes, weakly, but persistently. Emrys obeyed their promptings, and they led him, inexorably as death itself, back to the cave mouth.

What was there to trust? Emrys thought of his mother, but her face seemed inappropriate. Cathbhad? Gwelydd?

"Come," said the spirits. "Rest with us." Their eyes stared, their jaws opened wide. Emrys felt as if he were being pulled into the cave, as if the cave were some deep pit into which he was falling. And why should he not? Why not give in to the cold and the dark? What really had he to live for?

All he had was the quest. Excalibur. The sword that would save a kingdom. And the girl—a woman now, and a ruler of people—who had set him upon the quest, so many years ago.

Emrys forced his eyes away from the terrible mouth of the cave.

And in the brief fraction of a second as Emrys yanked his eyes away from the terrible cave, he saw something else, another cave. Wide was this cavern, high as the roof of a hall. And in the midst of the cavern was a lake; and in the midst of the lake a rock thrust up from the bosom of the waters. On the rock stood a boy, and in his hand he held a sword.

Excalibur.

And then the vision was gone, and he was gasping upon the narrow beach. The sun rose, and warmth lay upon his skin.

In the blind dawn, Emrys clambered back up the rocks and staggered across the level beach to where he had drawn up the boat. He pushed it into the bobbing waters and stumbled into it, lying for a moment recumbent before taking up the oars and striking out for the opposite shore.

He did not speak upon his return, and neither Gwelydd nor Iolo pried. They rode in silence through the forest back to Afallach, and then released the deer. Gwelydd sent Iolo on ahead of them, and he and Emrys walked alone back through the forest.

"I know what I saw," said Emrys at last, "but not why."

Gwelydd did not answer at once. "That," he said at last, "you must determine yourself, for no man sees the same as his neighbour. Each man must face his fate alone."

"I don't understand."

"Perhaps not now. But what you have seen this night, all men must see who are to become men. You must understand that. Knowledge is barren, without that which you beheld in the cave, for wisdom begins on the threshold of death." Gwelydd stopped. They had emerged from the forest, and stood now before another cave, a cave Emrys felt he had not seen in long years of his life, though it was a bare few hours ago. Afallach was stirring. Acolytes were moving to and fro on their masters' business. Gwelydd turned to Emrys. "Rest," he said. "You will begin to learn our ways tomorrow."

Emrys nodded and entered the Cave of Knowledge, where he found his bed welcoming him into its soothing warmth. He lay awake for some time, thinking of what he had seen that night. He felt somehow different, as if his childhood had passed beyond recall in a moment. He had faced what was to most men their greatest fear: he had looked upon his own death. And now, wrapped up in the warmth of his blankets, it did not seem so fearsome. The phantoms had called up fears from deep in the pit of his stomach while they had flown around him; but now they were gone, and he could see them for what they were: wraiths, insubstantial as the image of a flame imprinted on the back of one's eyelids. He had faced death, and the spirits of the dead could lay no claim upon him now. And there were, he reflected, worse things than death. How would he respond, he wondered, to the death of a loved one? There weren't many people he loved, he realized, and he did a quick inventory of people he knew.

The image of a woman's face flashed upon his inner eye for a moment: Boudicea, her red hair fanning about her, wisps of smoke crossing her face, a spot of blood, no bigger than a fingernail, in the corner of her mouth.

Emrys writhed in his bed, thrust his knuckles into the sockets of his eyes. Yes. Yes, there was something worse than his own death.

In a nearby bed, Iolo heard Emrys' thrashing, and felt sorry for the boy. But he felt sorry for the wrong reason. Soon, he was asleep; but Emrys lay long awake, until the sun stood high in the afternoon sky.

* * *

Emrys began his education promptly when the sun rose on the morrow. Gwelydd did not teach him at first. That was left to Aled, Gwelydd's senior acolyte. He took a tablet of slate, covered with honey, and drew in the honey shape after shape, which Emrys copied meticulously, stroke after stroke, curve after curve, until the figures danced through his mind in his sleep. And each symbol was accompanied by a sound, which Aled insisted Emrys make as he formed it with his finger. When he thought Aled was not looking, Emrys surreptitiously sucked the honey from his finger. Aled noticed him, but instead of reprimanding him, said, "Learning is sweet, is it not?"

But reading and writing were not the extent of his education. There was a rather plump druid called Dergen, who taught memory. "Child," said Dergen, upon his first meeting with Emrys, "knowledge is like a chest in which you keep great treasure. As you study knowledge, you store up for yourself treasures good, incorruptible, immortal, which never tarnish or decay. But your strongbox cannot become disordered. Just as you organize your chest so that jewels go here, coins of this value there, coins of a greater value there, so you must dispose of your various memories into different places in your mind, so that you can retrieve them later, when it is necessary to do so."

Under Dergen's guidance, Emrys learned first how to commit a thing to memory. It was like following signposts, or landmarks. Emrys learned to associate one thing with another, to make connections between things and ideas. The thing did not have to be closely associated with what Emrys was trying to remember. On one occasion, Emrys was trying to memorize the names of the High Kings of Britain. Dergen said to him, "Imagine for yourself a tree, and see the trunk itself as the Island of the Mighty. Now the first, the highest branch, that is Brutus. Look at the branch until it is firmly fixed in your mind. Do you see it? Good. Now, proceed to the next limb down. That is Locrin, the second High King of Britain. And so on, down the one side of the tree, until you reach the bottom, the twenty-fourth branch. That branch will be Guithelin. Now begin at the top again, on the other side of the tree. This new branch is Marcia, who was but regent to her son, Silicios. And proceed to do the same thing on the right-hand side, until you reach the bottom branch, which will be Cymbeline and Coroticos. Now begin again, and proceed slowly, committing every detail of each branch to your memory, until you have done. Then you can divide each branch into the families of each High King."

To Emrys' amazement, he found that history opened up before him, that he could tell story upon story, and the tree was a reminder not only of the names of the High Kings, but also of the events of their lives. Emrys felt he walked with those kings of ancient days, fought beside them in battle, strove with them against the realm's enemies.

And Dergen showed him also how to find his way around in his own mind, until Emrys walked like a traveler in the pathways of his mind, and he found things there long forgotten. He remembered the warm comfort of his mother, a little blurred. He remembered the tender words she spoke to him, and how he had stretched wide his lips to tell her how he loved her. Dergen took him back further, and he found a place of darkness and repose, of comfort and safety: the beginning of things.

Another druid called Iorwerth—tall with white hair and black bushy eyebrows—taught rhetoric, a subject that delighted Emrys. "Composition," said Iorwerth, "is the proper joining together of words in such a way that the ear shall observe no mismatch, no impediment, no jarring note. No man shall be dulled with overlong sentences, nor confounded with the mingling of clauses, needlessly heaped together without reason or number. By such means, hearers will forget what they heard. But you shall speak fluently, all shall hear your words, and all shall believe what they hear from you. Language, above all, governs men, manages, guides, and reins them in their affections, more than do their swords!"

By Iorwerth's tuition, Emrys gradually became the master of speech. Language ceased to be a haphazard mess. Now it marched for Emrys or crept with a slow and stealthy pace. Sometimes, it danced, or shuffled. But for the first time, it obeyed Emrys, and he understood what was the power of poetry.

Law, history, the gods, the ways of trees, prophecy—Emrys learned all with enthusiasm. And slowly, from the strokes and curves in the honey, words emerged like the shapes of familiar trees and hills out of a mist as one rode towards home.

Emrys' visions did not go away while he studied in Afallach. Once, one came to him during one of Dergen's lessons. The other acolytes regarded him thereafter with dread, reminding him of Gwelydd's contention that the Sight was both a blessing and a curse.

Emrys described all his visions carefully to Gwelydd, who recorded them in a book he had sewn together himself for the purpose. Gwelydd would listen carefully, writing down everything Emrys said, and then pause a while afterwards, brushing the feather of the quill lightly against his lip as he pondered.

"What does it all mean?" asked Emrys, on one occasion. Usually, Gwelydd would dismiss him soon, but today he had pondered longer than usual. The way his eyes blinked and refocused on Emrys implied that he had forgotten about his presence. He laid down his quill and closed the book, tying the cover together with leather thongs.

"Ill news, I fear," he said. "I believe the eagles you see in these visions represent the Romans. And I believe they are poised to attack."

"Attack? The Romans? What can we do?" cried Emrys, leaping to his feet.

Gwelydd took Emrys by the arms and stilled him. "We can stop panicking, for one thing. I must send a message to the High King. For the moment, we can do no more."

That night, Emrys lay sleepless upon his pallet in the Cave of Knowledge. He thought about the threat, paused to strike across the Narrow Sea. Now was the time to find Excalibur, and place it in the High King's hands. But the vast library Gwelydd and his predecessors had collected and which, he felt sure, held a clue to his quest, was dark to him. A whole summer had passed, and still he could do little more than sound words out very painfully. Frustrated, he tossed and turned this way and that in his bed.

Eventually, he slept. And in his sleep, another vision came to him.

It seemed to him that he stood upon the crest of the Hill of Afallach, the scent of apple blossom in his nostrils once more. He was not alone. There was a woman with him. Dark of hair she was, and slate-grey of eye, and at her side a large black cat stood, rubbing its head against her leg. She wore a long dress of crimson with flowing skirts and sleeves. A simple belt of pale leather, secured by a golden buckle, hung low from her waist.

Emrys felt drawn by this woman. He wanted nothing more than to lose himself in those eyes, to die upon her command. He took a few steps closer.

She continued to regard him levelly. The dress clung to the contours of her body, the deep, rounded breasts, the smooth, curved thighs. Her lips were parted, and slightly moist, as if she had tasted but late of some fruit.

83

Her hair stirred, as in some breeze. Emrys longed to seize her and ravish her with a primitive passion. She held her hands loosely at her sides, her long fingers touching her thighs lightly. Now she raised one hand and, extending a slender index finger, pointed into the north.

There, hovering over the waters of the sea to the north of the Island of the Mighty, its hilt towards the heavens and its tip towards the bosom of the ocean, was Excalibur.

Emrys reached out, but the sword was beyond his grasp. He turned to the woman. Her eyes were on him, inviting but laced with menace. The eyes slid sideways, an invitation to look once more.

The whole of the Island of the Mighty stretched out before him, in all its splendour and diversity, from the craggy islands of Orkney to the shining palaces of Lundein, from the open flatlands of Eicenniawn in the east, to the mighty mountains, muscles of the realm, in the west. All of Britain lay open before him. Wherever he cast his eye, there he could plumb the depths of men's hearts. Understanding and knowledge were his.

He looked beyond the Island of the Mighty, to where Excalibur hung like a great silver and gold sunset. But now he saw something different. A ship, not large, but venerable, its sail full, plying into the mists of the northern waters. In the forecastle stood a warrior, his bearded face grim, his woolen cloak drawn close about him. In his hands he held a bundle, and a corner of the wrappings had slipped away sufficiently to reveal the hilt of a sword. Emrys knew that the warrior was Belinos, and he was carrying Excalibur to its final resting place. He trembled, feeling a strange power surge through his body.

Then, once again, Emrys was on the hilltop with the woman. And he saw, as he never had before, history unfolding around him. He watched as Brutus and his ships landed off the southern coast of the Island. He watched the battle against the giants. He watched Corineus cast the Chief Giant Gogmagog from the cliffs of Cornwall, to dash his brains out on the jagged rocks below. He saw Gwendolyn, and Leir, and Cordelia. He saw Bran the Blessed, hanging from the terrible talons of the Addanc, and Excalibur swishing at the beast's underbelly. He saw Cassivelaunos, and his last farewell to his friend and comrade, Belinos.

And now Emrys saw the future. He saw himself enthroned beside the raven-haired woman, a goblet of wine in his hand, his subjects cowering before him. He turned his head towards his consort. There she was, beautiful and deadly, the sum of all his fears and all his longings.

When the vision left Emrys, twitching in his bed in the Cave of Knowledge, her face yet lingered in his mind, and he wondered who she could be.

X

mrys did not tell Gwelydd about this new vision; there seemed to him something private about it. Telling someone about it would be like confessing to some great guilt, he knew not how. But, seeking Gwelydd out in the forest on the following day, he asked, "Can I see the past and the future from the crest of Afallach too?"

They had been striding through the oaks, Gwelydd two paces ahead of the scurrying Emrys, but now Gwelydd halted. He spun around and peered with intensity at Emrys. "Do you think that the gods would give such a gift lightly?" he demanded. "You are but young in our ways. There are many things you should have learned by now, had you come to Afallach when the time was right. One of them perhaps is how to manage this gift of yours. Learn and study, Master Emrys. Then you can master this gift, or this curse, and you shall see what you need to see."

Gwelydd strode on. Emrys hug back a moment, his nails digging into the palms of his hands. Then he hurried after the Archdruid. "But that doesn't answer my question," he said. "I know I can see all places from the top of the Sacred Hill, but what about all times? Can I see things that happened in the past, or that will happen in the future?"

Gwelydd stopped beside an ancient oak, bent over almost double, like a man of ancient years. He seemed to be thinking of other things, though. His expression, when he turned, was no longer penetrating. His brow was furrowed, and there was curiosity and fondness behind his dark eyes. "What is it you would see, my young student," he asked, "that is hidden by the darkness of passing time, or would be revealed by it?"

Emrys took a deep breath. He had not mentioned his quest before. He said, "I think I should like to see Belinos, who hid the High King's sword. I'd like to know where he put it."

Gwelydd did not speak at once. He examined Emrys carefully, wonder growing upon the features of his face. "Is this why you came to us?" he asked in hushed tones. "Indeed, the gods sent you. This is a great thing you seek to do and, if you achieve it, Britons will thank you down the long centuries." He stood still and quiet for another long moment, and then said, "Yes, the Sight can show you the past and the future. I have read of its powers in the books of Llygat, the last of our order who possessed your power."

Gwelydd reached up into the branches of the tree and pulled loose a few small objects, chestnut brown in colour and spherical in shape. "I think," said Gwelydd, putting them safely into his pouch, "that I have collected enough gallnuts for today. Aled will be pleased that he can begin making ink again. Perhaps he will show you how it is done; one's learning should be complete, beginning with the roots, and proceeding thence along the trunk to the branches and the outermost twigs."

They walked silently through the whispering woods for a while, and Emrys said nothing because Gwelydd seemed to be pondering something deeply. At last, the old druid stopped and looked at Emrys again. But this time his eyes held no searching expression. He was not evaluating Emrys. Indeed, he looked upon him with affection. He said, "No one here can see what you see from the crest of Afallach, and so I know nothing of its secrets. Perhaps you can peer into the past and future from there. But first you must be very strong. All I say is this: beware."

"Beware what?"

"Not what: who. Beware of the Dark Lady."

"Morgana?"

"She. She will not rest until she has Excalibur."

"Why?"

"Because it is the last of the Seven Treasures. Each of the others she has already stolen. One by one, they disappeared from the world of men, and she took them to herself. Excalibur is the last. It is the prize, the king of the Seven Treasures and, although it has vanished from our sight, she took it not, for she knows not where it is. The other treasures are powerless without Excalibur. At least, their power is limited and local. But when she has Excalibur, she will use it to rule the Island of the Mighty, and nothing will avert her plans." He paused. "Better it should stay hidden than that should happen."

"But she doesn't know where it is?"

"No; or she would have used it. And that galls her, deep in her heart. If she knows you have the Sight, and that you seek Excalibur, she will not rest until she has you within her power."

Emrys gaped at his mentor, but said nothing. Gwelydd looked about him, and then at Emrys. He reached out and placed his hand on Emrys' shoulder, and Emrys could see some discord behind his eyes. There was something he found himself unable to say, Emrys could see that, and he was struggling. Emrys remained silent, to allow him to say it. Then, all at once, the struggle seemed to cease. But it was as if a wall had been built between them.

"I think," said Gwelydd, "if a man arose who could wield Excalibur, he might be able to hold Morgana at bay. There could be a truce."

"Otherwise?" Emrys prompted.

Gwelydd sighed deeply, and came near to shrugging his shoulders. "She is powerful," he said at length. "There may in any case be nothing we can do. Who can stand against her might? Many are the men she has bent to her will, and broken as she has done it."

Emrys' eyes were wide. "How can I avoid her?" he asked.

Gwelydd shook his head. "You cannot," he said. "If it is Excalibur you seek, you must seize your courage with both hands. Think not of the cost." Gwelydd's eyes narrowed as he looked on Emrys more. Then his brow relaxed. His lips formed a sympathetic smile before he spoke. "These are hard sayings," he said, placing one of his large hands upon Emrys' shoulder. "Seek Excalibur when you have grown strong in our ways. And remember, this may not be your path. There are other ways of serving the gods."

"What is your way?" asked Emrys, more as a way of stalling for time than for information.

Gwelydd sat down upon a massive tree root, and motioned Emrys to sit beside him. He did not speak for a long while, but his eyes had a distant look, as if they gazed upon worlds and lands many thousands of miles from Afallach.

"At first," he said, "I thought I could serve the gods best by serving kings. The gods are stern masters, and I thought that the best way to evade their wrath was to govern the realm according to their wishes. So I have spent my life advising kings."

He fell silent. When several minutes had passed without elaboration, Emrys said hesitantly: "That was a good plan."

"Was it?" Gwelydd turned to contemplate his face, and Emrys saw that he had not lost his thread, but was trying to unravel it from a complicated skein. "The gods are stern masters," he repeated, "but they are also secretive. They do not often make their wills plain to mortal men. There, you exceed me, Emrys, for the gods do speak to you directly. You must learn to understand their tongue, and perhaps to speak a little of their speech yourself. But they have seldom made their wishes known to me." There was something of a lament in Gwelydd's voice, and Emrys' heart sighed plaintively on his behalf.

"And then there are the kings," said Gwelydd, with almost a snort. "What do they really care about the gods? They seek not wisdom, but expediency; their hearts are full not of those they serve, but of crowns, and sceptres, and thrones. They would rather be served than serve. I think, in the end, you cannot change the lives of a nation of individuals. You must touch each man and woman and child, one at a time. And so, after many hard labours, I finally came back to Afallach."

"And have you found peace here?" asked Emrys.

"There is no peace beneath the moon," answered Gwelydd. With a brusque gesture, he got to his feet and picked up his staff. "Come," he said. "I have enough gallnuts now, and Aled will be wanting to crush them for his precious ink. He is so impatient."

But Aled had other things on his mind as they approached the Cave of Knowledge. A chariot, faced with bronze, its team champing at the bit and stamping their hoofs with impatient nobility, stood at the entrance. Another cart rested behind it, and servants and warriors wrapped in plaid stood beside them, conversing with each other and with the druids. Spears and shields were propped against the wall. Seeing Emrys and Gwelydd, Aled detached himself from a small group and hurried over.

"An emissary," he said, "from the lord of the Eicenni, Lord Gwelydd."

"Where is he?" asked Gwelydd.

Aled hesitated a moment, confused. Then his face cleared, and he said, "In the Cave of Knowledge." But by that time, they had arrived at the door, and Gwelydd entered, Emrys and Aled upon his heels.

It was Boudicea.

She stood by the brazier, resplendent in the regalia of a powerful lady among the Britons. But more splendid still was the regalia of her beauty, too great for one person, that rolled from her like perfume and filled every cranny of the cave.

For a moment, Emrys could not move, but only stare at her with wide eyes, his jaw slack. An uncomfortable pressure growing in his chest told him that he had forgotten to breathe.

Gwelydd and Emrys bowed before the Lady of Eicenniawn. "May the gods give your ladyship health and happy days," said Gwelydd.

"May they rain blessings upon you and all in Afallach," replied Boudicea. The Lady of the Eicenni inclined her head to Gwelydd, her hand upon her heart. "My Lord Archdruid," she said, "my husband Prasutagos, lord of Eicenniawn, stands in great need of your wisdom."

"Certainly, my lady. Emrys, perhaps you would continue with your studies . . . ?"

"That will not be necessary, my lord Gwelydd," interjected Boudicea. She fixed Emrys with her eyes, and Emrys thought there was a smile in them. "My business concerns perhaps Emrys as well." Gwelydd must have looked puzzled at this, for Boudicea hastened to explain: "Emrys and I were friends in childhood. We grew up together, you could say, and were very close friends. Very close." The last two words she almost whispered; they were barely perceptible. But Emrys heard them, and he thought of their last meeting.

"How can I help your ladyship?" asked Gwelydd, as all three of them took seats.

Boudicea unclasped her cloak, and laid it on the writing desk. Her shoulders and arms were bare, torcs circling her long throat and each of her upper arms. Her dress was tight-fitting, with narrow skirts. The green showed off her red hair, long and loose, and there seemed to be gold thread woven into it, for every now and then it caught the light and shimmered, like sunlight on the sea.

"You sent a message of late, my lord, to the High Kings in Lundein, concerning your fears that an invasion by Rome was imminent."

"I did."

"My husband believes your fears are correct, and he wonders how you knew." She paused, but not for an answer. Instead, she continued with her message. "My husband has concluded that you must have a Seeing One with you here in Afallach." She smiled, but it was barely a whisper upon her lips. "Now I see Emrys is here, and remember his gifts, I must conclude that my husband was right." Her tone became serious again. "My Lord Gwelydd, my husband urges you to send him your Seeing One to serve as his druid."

Gwelydd took a deep breath. "Alas, your ladyship," he said, "regretfully, this cannot be done. Emrys is at the beginning of his studies, and many more years must pass before he is ready to serve as a druid."

Boudicea looked down at her fingernails. Her arms were graceful and flawless, and Emrys remembered them around his neck, pulling his body down onto hers. She said, "I was afraid that might be the case. Can Emrys not return with me to Eicenniawn as our prophet? Surely he possesses the gift of the Sight, whether he has had any training in the ways of the druids or not?"

"He does indeed possess the Sight, my lady," answered Gwelydd, "but, without the special training he can get only here, that gift is useless. Emrys must learn to control the Sight. Otherwise, the gift is more a danger than a benefit."

"And Emrys has no words of his own to speak on this matter?" Boudicea turned her green eyes upon him, and her gaze was like a caress.

Emrys swallowed deeply and said, "I incline my agreement with Gwelydd, madam. The Sight possesses me at the moment, I do not possess it. Let me finish my training here, and then I can serve the Lord of the Eicenni as he deserves to be served."

Boudicea smiled; she understood his full meaning. She said, "Then let it be so. I shall regretfully return to my husband empty-handed."

"But let it not be with an empty stomach," said Gwelydd. "Please accept our hospitality this evening, before you begin your return."

"I should like that very much," replied Boudicea; and she was looking at Emrys, not his master.

* * *

Afallach possessed a refectory, and on most evenings, most of the druids would eat there. It was customary for Gwelydd and, increasingly now that he was becoming advanced in years, for Aled to read from a book after the meal, and they would spend perhaps an hour in discussion of the matters raised by the reading afterwards. But on this evening, all the druids turned out, as did Boudicea's retinue, and the kitchen became a busy place indeed. Emrys spent the evening in a trance. Everything in the refectory seemed dark and colourless, all save Boudicea herself, a jewel of iridescent vermilion and jade and flashing sapphire. He did not sit near her, but he saw that her eyes were turned frequently upon him and, when the meal was finished and Aled had begun his reading, she rose from her place and sank onto the bench beside Emrys.

Boudicea had also brought her two daughters along with her. Red-haired like their mother, the twins dashed about the feet of the druids with an energy none could duplicate save their tireless nurse. Emrys caught Boudicea looking upon them with pride shining in her eyes.

"They are fine girls," observed Emrys. "Prasutagos must also be very proud of them."

"He is," replied Boudicea distractedly. For a time, they listened to Aled. He was reading the story of Bran the Blessed and the victorious wars in his youth. At length, Boudicea sighed. "History is so sad," she said, her moist lips forming the words precisely.

"Yes," agreed Emrys. "There were moments of glory, like lonely stars shining from a dark sky. But most of it is sad, with a sadness that pierces the heart." There was a question that Emrys longed to ask, but he did not know how to begin. "How does it suit you," he said, "being Lady of the Eicenni?"

Boudicea's eyes shone. "It suits me well," she said. "I steer the destinies of many men, I am adored and obeyed by all."

"The gods have smiled upon Prasutagos in his choice of wife," observed Emrys.

Boudicea looked directly at him, and there was some hurt there, deep down. "In his choice of consort, he could have done no better," she said, with emphasis on the verbal change. She added, "As one to share his power, he has found a matchless sovereign."

Emrys was surprised. "He loves you, surely," he said. How could he not? he thought to himself.

"He loves me, yes," replied Boudicea. She turned suddenly and with passion to Emrys. "Oh, Emrys," she said, "we have known and loved each other too long to have secrets. Prasutagos loves me, after his fashion; but he is thrice my age! His love is what you might expect of one so old. I love being sovereign," she added, her voice dropping to a whisper as she leaned close to Emrys and her breath caressed his skin, "but I do not much love being his wife. That is why I came here. I thought that, if you were at Afallach, as the prophecies Gwelydd sent to Lundein implied, then you might be persuaded to return with me to my people, to be our druid. And then I should have a man to love, as well as a man to be my husband."

"To love the wife of a great man is no small risk," observed Emrys.

"To love without risk is not to love," countered Boudicea.

Emrys cast his eyes down towards the floor, and said nothing for a long while. Boudicea observed him keenly the while. At length, Emrys raised his eyes. "But as you know, my own love," he answered, "it cannot be. I am no druid yet, nor like to be for another twenty years." He finally raised his eyes and met hers. "But I shall always be your true lover."

The magic of the moment was broken as one of the servants poured Emrys another cup of wine and, for a while, he and the Lady of Eicenniawn watched the twin girls playing between the tables. One of the Eicenni warriors was chasing them and tickling them when he caught them. Sometimes, he would catch them both, parcel them up under his arms and tickle them both so that they kicked their bare feet and squealed with delight.

"Prasutagos has given you fine daughters," Emrys observed at last.

But Boudicea shook her head. "You provided them," she said.

XI

Soon after Boudicea had left, winter exhaled its cold breath over the world. It was a particularly cold winter that year. Snow settled seldom, for they were close to the sea, but bitter winds drove in from the west, flattening the withered grass and rattling the dry branches at the tops of the apple trees like dead men's teeth. Hardship was extreme in Aber Alaw, where the death of livestock became a common incident.

But spring returned eventually, and with it came hope. And when the trees were just beginning to bud, and the villagers in Aber Alaw were breaking up the soil and sowing seed for the year's harvest, Emrys was at last given permission to use the books in the Cave of Knowledge.

It was slow going at first, for he had to pick out the words carefully, sounding them out as he had been taught. But it came easier with time. Some of the scrolls contained history, some speculations upon the gods. Some were books of spells, some of science, and some a curious blend of both. Emrys spent a week contemplating a small book upon the movements of the heavenly bodies, a month upon a cumbersome volume containing the histories of King Brutus and his son, Locrin.

Before Emrys knew it, the villagers were harvesting the crops, and the nights were beginning to draw in, and he had found no clue regarding the whereabouts of Excalibur. He decided to ask Gwelydd about it.

The old druid twisted his lips into a wry smile and looked thoughtfully about the cave at the shelves of books. "I have read but the tenth part of these volumes," he said, "for they were collected by those who rest yonder." He indicated the door to the Chamber of the Sleeping. "But I know of nothing here that would help you, except one brief rhyme."

Gwelydd spent a few moments pottering about looking at one shelf after another. Finally, he drew a small tome from a shelf at the very back of the room, opened it, turned a few brittle pages and, at last, lighted upon the verses he was seeking. He read the words, imparting to them a solemnity

and melancholy that made Emrys think of eons of yearning, centuries of un-
fulfilled longing.

> Bright was the blade   of Brutus the brave
> Loyallest of lords,   beloved of men,
> Forged by fäerie   in the freshness   of the first day
> Sundered from men   the sword of kings
> Through stone,   over sea,   under sod,
> Unseen by eyes,   Excalibur of old,
> Fear-maker in foes,   ancient heirloom.
> The brand abides   the best of all Britain
> To raise from the rock   and reign over all.

Emrys said nothing at first. Gwelydd handed him the tome in silence.
Emrys read the lines over two or three times, mouthing the words as was his
custom, but hardly making a sound. At last, Emrys looked up. "I have
heard these verses before, from Cathbhad, my grandfather's bard."

"He heard them here, from me," observed Gwelydd.

"Who wrote them?"

"The last of our order to be possessed of the Sight," answered Gwelydd.
"His name was Llygat, and he lived three centuries ago."

Emrys frowned. "Excalibur was not lost then."

"No," agreed Gwelydd. "But he had the Sight. These verses are a
prophecy. They are, I am very much afraid, the only clue we possess as to
the whereabouts of the Sword of Kings."

Emrys read the verses one more time. Then he noticed, below the last
lines, more words, written in an ink that had faded with time. He could see
some loops, some horizontal slashes, some vertical lines; here and there, he
could even make out whole letters.

"What words are these?" he asked, pointing them out to Gwelydd.

Gwelydd peered closely at the manuscript, and held it up to a taper, tilt-
ing the page this way and that to get a better look. "It is another prophecy of
Llygat's," he said. "The Three Great Sea-Maids of the Island of the
Mighty."

"What do the words say?" asked Emrys. "I can make nothing of them."

"No more can I," replied Gwelydd; "they are too faint for my old eyes."

Emrys tapped his teeth with his knuckles. "Perhaps this is important," he mused. "Llygat seems to have thought that these words were connected with the rhyme about Excalibur, or he would not have written them down here. I can copy these words onto another piece of vellum. They might be important."

Emrys spent the morning at his studies, returning to the Cave of Knowledge in the late afternoon. He sharpened a quill, filled an ink bottle, weighed down the errant corner of a fresh piece of vellum, and bent low over Llygat's old book. The first character was clear, and he copied it painstakingly onto the fresh leaf. He could make nothing of the next few letters, though. He moved the taper closer, lit another one, and still there was not enough light.

With much labour, Emrys dragged the bench outside and set up the parchment again under the late sun of afternoon. Afallach stood behind him, and the sun was sinking towards it, so Emrys knew he had not much time to complete his transcription before the light failed, even out here. He peered closely at the ancient page. Sure enough, in the better light, he could make out the characters better. He dipped his quill in the ink and scratched a few letters. Before long, they formed a word. "*Mordraig*," he read. "Sea-dragon?" He reflected for a moment. "The Three Great Sea-Maids of the Island of the Mighty," he mused. "This is the name of a ship." He bent back over his task, working quickly now, as he grew used to the labour. He went a little faster with the next line, for by now he had a system, and it was not long before a few words stood out black against the light tan of the parchment. Some characters were missing, but he could infer what they were easily enough: "*Annwyl* reached a safe haven."

"*Annwyl*," said Emrys aloud. "Beloved. Another ship. A sea-maid *must* be a ship." He smiled to himself. "What else?" He dipped his quill again and resumed his work.

The last line proved harder than the rest. The original scribe's ink had blotted at one point and obscured two characters; at another point, some water had spilled on the parchment, and a whole word was nearly lost.

And then the sun sank below the brow of the hill, and shadows gathered all around him. Emrys lit a candle, but the wind snuffed it instantly. Grunting and sweating, he shuffled back indoors, the bench in his arms, and set up many candles, all around the parchment. So far, he saw, he had "The world's wonder;" and from the mess beginning with *P* at the end of the line, he could tell that the line related to the *Prydwen*. But it was the very next word that was so intractable, having suffered so much water damage.

The slow, dark hours of night passed while he struggled with that one word. One by one, the candles burned low, until only one retained its flame. Emrys sat up, rubbing his knuckles into his eyes. He needed more light. Stumbling with weariness, he pushed open the portal to the Cave of Knowledge and went outside. The night was cold, the sky pricked with the blazing light of many stars, and Emrys paused a moment to consider their beauty.

He was close, he knew it. What was the world's wonder, and how was it related to the *Prydwen*? "World's wonder," he knew, was a bardic formula, and it meant "mystery." Something related to the *Prydwen* was a mystery. But what? Its location? Silently, Emrys cursed the person, long ages ago, who had spilled water on the manuscript. Had it not been for that accident, he would have solved the riddle by now.

Emrys hurried on along the path around the Hill of Afallach. It rose above him, a silent silhouette. The community of druids slept; no man was stirring, and Emrys had to tiptoe into the storehouse. He took as many candles as he could carry, and returned to the Cave of Knowledge.

"Arawn," he muttered, "it was you who forged Excalibur, when the world was young, and bird and beast and flower were one with man, and death was but a dream. Show me the words, I beg you!"

One by one, Emrys lit the candles. One by one, a flame rose from the wick of each of them and stood, trembling, above the wax. Each one shed more light over the manuscript, and when all eight had been lit, Emrys turned his eyes upon the antique book, still open upon the desk.

As if he was seeing the whole thing afresh, the word stood out from the leaf as it had never done before. The water damage was a mere background irritation, blurring the characters but by no means obscuring the meaning.

"Celliwig," said Emrys. With a few more strokes from his quill, he had the whole rhyme:

Mordraig rests beneath the waves,

Annwyl reached a safe haven.

The world's wonder Celliwig, where *Prydwen* rests.

"Now," said a voice at his shoulder, "you have only to find out where Celliwig is."

Emrys jumped, startled in spite of himself. Gwelydd had moved up behind him silently, or else he had been so intent upon his work that he had not noticed the Archdruid's footsteps. He turned back to the page in front of him.

"Celliwig," he mused. "It almost sounds like a word in our speech, but not quite."

"Words change," Gwelydd said, "and these verses were written many long lives of men ago. The tongues of men are never still."

Emrys got to his feet. His mind was racing. "The tongues men speak," he repeated, "are always changing."

"Yes," responded Gwelydd. "That much you may even see today. Listen to a man who was raised in Albany, and another who was raised in Cornwall. Neither can speak to the other in words they can hear aright. Over time, it is the same. Our forefathers spoke our language, but the fashion has changed since then."

Emrys closed his eyes and reached out with one hand to steady himself against the table. "The second part of the word," he said, "*llewig*. It sounds like a word. How could it have changed? Perhaps to *llewych*, 'shining.'"

"Perhaps," said Gwelydd slowly. "And there is Caer Lloyw in the south of this land, in the Summer Country. Perhaps that is the place."

Emrys frowned. "Is it near the sea?" he wondered. "Still, there might be a clue there. I must go at once to Caer Lloyw!" he declared, seizing the parchment and tucking it away about his person once more.

"Perhaps," said Gwelydd again. And when Emrys looked at him, he saw a deep sadness in the old man's eyes. "But you have not completed your training here." Emrys paused a moment, the corners of his mouth turning downwards. "Our ways," urged Gwelydd, "could help you control the Sight. Such has been the way in the past."

"How? How was it done? How can a man give commands to the gods?"

"Llygat was able to do it," Gwelydd answered.

"But how?" persisted Emrys.

Gwelydd did not speak at once. His thoughts were in his face—many and contradictory, it seemed. Emrys waited patiently. At last, the old druid said, "I do not believe the time is ripe for you to know these things. You have been in Afallach only a year. Most young men have been here twice seven years ere they reach the age you are now."

"My Lord Archdruid," said Emrys, "you heard Boudicea's message."

"I saw a young woman," said Gwelydd penetratingly, "who was not in love with her husband, who had manufactured a means of seeing the man she truly loved once more and more often."

Emrys ran his fingers through his hair. "Yet it is true that Britain stands in need. The Eagles watch from just across the Narrow Sea, awaiting but the command of this stammering new emperor of theirs. The High King of the Island of the Mighty needs Excalibur now. Even a short delay may be too long."

"I do not believe you could find it without the Sight as your servant," said Gwelydd, whispering now, casting a glance over his shoulder at the sleeping quarters of the acolytes. "But this can wait until morning. Get you to bed now. We can speak further of these things in the light of day."

Weariness descended suddenly upon Emrys, and he yawned widely. Quite suddenly, he wished for nothing more than his bed, and he shuffled into the sleeping quarters, where the other acolytes snored peacefully, and lowered himself into the gentle arms of his bed. He was asleep in seconds.

But it was not a dreamless sleep. He dreamed that he was sitting in the Cave of Knowledge, a quill in his hand and a piece of parchment before him. He instantly knew that this was not real, that it was a dream. His mind even went over recent lessons from the druid Ibar, who taught prophecy. There were, he remembered, five types of dreams. Some of them would come true, and some were prophecies that the gods made obscure. Some dreams, which came to dreamers betwixt waking and asleep, were strange fantasies. Others, like this one, were just a continuation of one's waking concerns. What was the term Ibar had used for it? Nightmare. That was it. This was a nightmare. He was dreaming of doing the thing he had been doing just before he had gone to sleep.

At least, he thought, it wasn't one of his visions.

It was curiously silent, though. Normally, one could hear the muted sounds of Afallach, even at night: snoring from the dormitory, sometimes Gwelydd moving about in his own chamber, perhaps even the muffled sounds of men conversing outside. But at this moment, Emrys was sharply aware of his own breathing, his own heartbeat.

A spot of light appeared on the wall opposite. Carefully, Emrys set down his quill and moved towards the light. It illuminated a shelf at the back of the cave, a dark recess that remained dark in spite of the light that shone around it. Emrys stared into the recess and, suddenly, he felt fear begin to worry him, like a dog at a bone.

Somehow, he knew that the other great secret of Afallach was here. Somehow, he knew that the secret to controlling the Sight was within his grasp.

But the recess seemed to be growing larger. The edges vanished. There was nothing but darkness now, and he was falling, falling through the pitchy darkness. His arms spread wide. His mouth opened to yell, but no sound issued from his lips.

He came to the bottom with a jolt, and now he could see. He was in the open country, and paths extended from his feet in all directions. But there were corpses, twisted and mangled from battle and sacrifice, scattered and heaped around him. And among the bodies lay the still form of a wolf, its side gouged out and its wound still steaming. Emrys felt his shoulders begin to shake with great sobs, and he sank to the ground.

A moment later, he was back among the sleeping acolytes in the Cave of Knowledge. His eyes were wide, and all sleep had drained from him as water from a bottle.

Instantly, Emrys leaped out of bed. The air was cool, as it always was in the cave, and it raised goose bumps on his arms as he shrugged off the blanket and crept past the still forms of the acolytes into the next chamber.

All was still. The moon shone through the louvre in the ceiling, and a patch of silver light fell on the wall opposite. Carefully, Emrys tiptoed towards the light. It illuminated a shelf at the back of the cave, a dark recess that Emrys had not yet consulted. Slowly, Emrys reached out and wrapped his fingers about the spine of an old book. There was no need to wonder if it was the right book. *He knew*. He drew it from the shelf, and opened it.

It was written by Llygat, the Seer of the Druids, and it began, "This book was begun in the sixth year of the reign of High King Eliud, when I am advanced in age, and have struggled with this gift of the gods for many years. I write for those who come after me, who also possess this gift—or this curse."

XII

When the sun rose, sending its youthful shafts into the Cave of Knowledge through the louvre, Emrys was still reading. He felt sick, as if something had reached inside his body and turned his stomach upside-down. He looked up a moment from his studies, and saw a soft, rosy patch of light on the wall, where the patch of moonlight last night had directed him to this book. He looked down at his hands, and turned them over, examining minutely the lines across his palms, the whorls on the ends of his fingers, made more prominent now by the ink that had settled deep in them.

Could these hands, he wondered, do what this book suggested they must?

He felt, for a moment, giddy and, closing his eyes, pressed his forehead against the table-top. For a second, a vision came to him, clear, crystal clear, as if he was seeing it before his eyes: himself in druids' robes, standing in terrible majesty upon the height of Afallach. And before him, to please the gods that they might send him the visions he needed, its feet and hands tied behind its back and the obscene garrote already around its neck, lay . . .

Emrys shuddered. No. He could not look that way, not even think of it. He must shut his eyes, and stop up his ears against the dreadful sound that rose up from the World Centre to the gods.

Was that what they wanted?

"Emrys?" Emrys leaped up and whirled around, the stool rattling beneath him as he turned. It was Gwelydd. "Still at study?" asked Gwelydd, a faint smile pressing his lips as he moved closer. The smile turned briefly to a frown. "What is it you read?" he asked.

Emrys closed his eyes. The future stood before him, a path drenched in blood. That was the secret. That was how the Sight could be tamed. By the blood of those dearest to the community. He opened his eyes.

"I must leave this place," he said. "Too long have I neglected the quest that the gods have placed upon me."

"There is so much more to learn," said Gwelydd.

"I cannot learn it." Closing the book, Emrys turned to face his mentor. "I cannot do what you do," he said. "I cannot become the slayer of unarmed men, and of women, and of children."

Gwelydd was silent for a moment. His eyes traveled from Emrys to the book upon the table. His lips grew thin, his eyes narrowed a little, and he looked up at Emrys. "So," he said, "you have read Llygat's book. And now you know how you can control the Sight."

"I know that I will not do it," said Emrys, his voice trembling.

Gwelydd dropped his eyes from Emrys'. "I once believed that too," he said in a trembling voice. "And every Beltane, I hope beyond hope that it is nothing but a horrid dream, and that I may awaken." A tear ran shining down his cheek as he spoke. "And the worst is that the way I feel can hold no comfort for the mother whose arms are empty, the man whose daughter will not come home again. It is a terror from which I cannot awaken, for it is the real world." He looked up once more. "How did you find the book?" he asked. "How did you know what to look for?"

"Does it matter?" asked Emrys.

"I suppose not," said Gwelydd sadly. He sighed deeply. "This is bad," he said. "You were not ready for this information."

"Not ready!" cried Emrys in disbelief. "Not ready! The Sight is *my* gift —I have a right to know this!"

"Yes," agreed Gwelydd, "but not at this time. Not all truth can be known at once, and this I would have spared you until much, much later. It is a hard lesson, and you are not yet ready to learn it. I do not mean this to dispraise your abilities, but I mean merely that you have spent but a little time learning our ways."

"How could I ever be ready for such foulness?" demanded Emrys. "I am sorry I ever came here. This is no place for me. I don't want . . . I don't want blood on my hands. And I don't want to . . . to hear . . . that *noise!*"

Emrys was weeping, his face contorted and scarlet. He looked up at Gwelydd, and instantly ice froze in his spine. The old druid's eyes were glassy, as if he would weep. He said, "In time, all noises are one. A man can endure anything, even that. In time, you will understand."

"No," said Emrys. "No, I will not. This is a thing I cannot do!"

"It is what you must do," answered Gwelydd. "None of us likes it, but it must be done." His eyes had lost the glazed look, and he was once again the Gwelydd that Emrys had known and loved for two years. "If your visions are to be useful to anybody," he went on, "and bearable to yourself, give the gods the blood they demand."

Emrys shook his head. "You can do it," he said, "but not me."

Gwelydd's features hardened. "We do not have the luxury, as you do, to choose our own paths," he said, and there was almost a sneer in his voice. "The gods do not send us visions. We must propitiate them. The gods demand sacrifice. That is life. Life is a long scream, terminated by oblivion. What we do alleviates that."

"I meant no offence," stammered Emrys.

"Learn your masters well," answered Gwelydd, closing in upon the younger man. He was so close that Emrys could feel the warmth of his breath on his face. "We are their sport. For their entertainment, they will grind us, break us, utterly digest us. If we do some of the breaking, that will satisfy them, and they will leave the rest of us alone. We do what we do so that no one else has to do it. That is *our* sacrifice."

"I did not understand; forgive me."

"All over this island, men and women sleep peacefully in their beds at night, and murder is not a part of their lives because it *is* a part of *our* lives. We are but one step up from the beasts. They live in hunger and fear, and so do we. A few lives offered in sacrifice is a small price to pay to take that step."

Emrys felt small and overwhelmed. He said nothing. Silence, like a great boulder, weighed upon them long. At last, he said, "Not because I am better than you, but because I am weaker, I cannot do this thing. I am like a ship, buffeted this way and that by the prevailing winds, but I can steer myself nowhere."

"Which is why you need a helmsman," observed Gwelydd.

"No," said Emrys firmly. "This I cannot do, even if the whole of the Island of the Mighty were swallowed up, and all I love with it. There must be something else. I cannot see what it is, but I cannot believe that this is the only way. And now I must go to Caer Lloyw." He returned the book to its shelf in silence, and strode past Gwelydd into the dormitory.

Half an hour later, he was ready to leave. He had brought few possessions with him, and had collected fewer in the two years he had dwelt in Afallach. He had intended to leave without ceremony, but Gwelydd was waiting for him. He was holding Llygat's book.

"How did you know where to find this?" he asked.

"I had a vision."

"Then . . . " The Archdruid's voice trailed off. His bushy brows dropped a fraction of an inch in the centre of his forehead. "Then it was the gods . . . "

"Yes," replied Emrys tersely. "It was the gods who directed me to Llygat's book. *They* thought I was ready."

Gwelydd looked away from Emrys, and then back again. He seemed, for the first time since Emrys had known him, to be truly carrying all the years he had lived through. "It occurs to me," said the Archdruid awkwardly, "that we may have misinterpreted *Celliwig*. *Shining fortress* it seems to mean, indeed, but I wonder. In ancient tradition, we hear of Caer Fedwit, the Fortress of Mead-Dreams, and Caer Rigor, the Fortress of Hardness. Then there is Caer Goludd, the Fortress of Hindrance, and Caer Ochren, the Fortress of Imprisonment. They all mean the same place: Annwn, Morgana's abode, raised from the northern seas in her flight from Britain in the elder days. It is in my thoughts that Caer Llewych might be the same, another name for Morgana's stronghold of Annwn, Caer Siddi, Faërie Fortress. Mayhap you will travel to Caer Lloyw, endure great hardship, and still be no closer to your goal than you are now."

"I have to begin looking some time," replied Emrys, avoiding the older man's eyes. "I seek not to blame you for what you do. I thank you, rather, for I would not do it myself. And because I cannot do it myself, I cannot continue to learn the way that leads there."

106

"Perhaps . . . " began Gwelydd; but he did not finish his sentence. Instead, he said, lamely, "One with the Sight could be a powerful ally to the High Kings of the Island of the Mighty."

"So I hope I shall be," said Emrys. "I shall find Excalibur, and deliver it into the hands of the High Kings. And perhaps," he added, completing the thought Gwelydd had left unfinished, "at some later time, I can return here, and finish what I have begun."

Gwelydd nodded, a smile gradually turning the corners of his mouth upwards. He held out a hand, and passed a small object on to his erstwhile acolyte. Emrys unfurled his fingers and looked at the small, hard object Gwelydd had given him. It was fashioned like a bird, with a hooked beak, and Emrys recognized it as the little figure he had seen often upon Gwelydd's desk in the Cave of Knowledge. The ancient sculptor had been a crude workman, but somehow the fierceness of the eye glared from the time-polished face. Emrys looked up.

"When I was young, and in the service of Cynfarch, Lord of Caer Luel, I found this. It is a merlin, beloved of the Picts, who live in the far north of the Island of the Mighty." He looked up, and for the first time, Emrys met his eyes. "Merlin Emrys I name you: as a merlin sees its prey from afar, so by your gift you too see further than other men. You are the Seeing One of our age."

Emrys lowered his head in reverence to the old one. Then, without another word, he turned and strode away from Afallach without looking back. Soon, he had turned a corner, and the old man was hidden from sight. Not long after, he had left Aber Alaw behind too, and before him was the road to his destiny.

* * *

Emrys took the same route south as he had taken north, two years earlier, but in reverse. It was in his mind that he would like to see his mother again, before going on to Caer Lloyw. Caermyrddin was, in any case, on the route to Caer Lloyw. His grandfather's stronghold was almost due south of Ynys Mon, and then a sharp turn eastwards would take him, along the southern coast of Cambria, across the wide stream of the River Wysg, and then along the banks of the Sabrina to Caer Lloyw.

He made better time on the southward journey, for it was now high summer. The wide beaches of Cereticiaun Bay shone like a strand of gold between the azure promise of the sea and the grassy cliffs along which Emrys tramped, sweating slightly under his light burden and the unblinking sun. Above him, the gulls wheeled and mewed, and below him, cormorants dove into the sea or sat and bobbed there, like black, ungainly ducks. There were sea pinks flowering in the cliffs below him, and on his inland side, the broom was glowing with golden life in the grasslands that reached as far as the mountains, denuded now of their snows. Emrys walked in a trance, his soul rejoicing in the life and vivacity of the Cambrian summer.

He paused frequently in his journey to enjoy this world, so full of life. It seemed like a new world to him, freshly created by a benevolent god. The grass shone in its greenness, as if it had just been washed, the sea roared against the beach or the base of the cliffs with an energetic fervour, and the gulls cried one to another about how good it was to be alive. The world seemed more full of life than he could ever remember it before.

But he did not stay long on such occasions, for as he traveled south, a feeling of foreboding grew upon him and, especially when evening was drawing on and the shadows were gathering about him, Emrys cast his eyes nervously over his shoulder. It seemed to him that he was being followed.

When he had been traveling for about a week, and knew that he must soon leave the road he was taking, for it went to Gorsedd Arberth and Caermyrddin lay almost due east of there, he met another traveler.

The man appeared first as a black dot against the voluptuous green of a hillside, rising from the cliffs towards the mountains. The wind was blowing stiffly in from the sea, and Emrys bent his will against it in order to remain upright, wondering who this person could be. He had seen no other traveler on his journey, and such people as he had encountered were lonely drovers or herders. This was no such person, as there were no beasts anywhere else in sight, except an untamable kestrel, hovering nearby, its eyes keen for prey.

The man was dressed wholly in black, Emrys saw as he drew near, and was reclining against the hollow of a hill, a beech spreading above him to provide shade. He seemed to have a wide-brimmed hat, replete with flowing feather, with which he covered his face. Emrys thought he must be asleep, though he had never had such a keen feeling of being observed.

His clothes were fine, Emrys noted, when he was close enough to be able to make such judgements. His boots, supple and shiny, reached up close to his knees, and had ample turnovers at the tops. His tunic was close-fitting, and seemed to be woven with a satin brocade that shone in the sun, contrasting with the absorbent black of the garment. A white lace collar was laid over the outside of the tunic. The sleeves were wide, and slit so that a red fabric showed through the black. There was red piping on his sleeves and hems, and around the brim of the hat. His belt had a wide silver buckle, and a thin-bladed sword hung from it. Right now, the sword was held vertically, the man's hand resting on the hilt. It was an ornate hilt, of a type Emrys had never seen before. A hand-guard arced from the pommel to the juncture of the quillions, all etched with floral designs of intricate complexity. The sheath was black, with red tracing in bizarre and energetic lines down the whole length.

As Emrys stopped to gaze at the spectacle, the free hand reached up and removed the hat from the face. Emrys saw dark ringlets framing the face, almost like a woman's hair, and a pointed beard and small moustache. But the eyes were hard and bleak, as if they had seen much suffering, and enjoyed it. Above the lace collar, there were old welts on his throat.

"Greetings to thee, Emrys the Seeing One," said the man. "Whither wanderest thou?"

"How do you know my name?" asked Emrys.

"It was told me by another."

"Who?"

"She whom I serve."

A sudden chill froze Emrys' blood and, though it was high summer and a warm day, he shivered. "Morgana?" he said.

"Even she," answered the man. He got lightly to his feet. His motions were slightly effeminate, but nothing Emrys could put his finger on. "She wishes to speak with thee."

"Then why did she not come herself?" demanded Emrys. "Why did she send her lackey?"

The man's countenance froze. With two smooth paces, he closed the distance between himself and Emrys. His hand rested upon the pommel of his slender sword, and the faint aroma of civet wafted from him. He said, "Thou dost mistake thy place, if thy thought is that the Great Lady shall serve thee! I am sufficient for thee. Wilt thou come willingly, or shall I use other means at my disposal?" His features softened a little, though the eyes were still those of one who is cruel to a puppy. "Come, she will not harm thee. It is to consult with thee on a matter of great moment that she hath sent me to thee. Long hath she watched thy progress, and well pleased is she with what she hath seen. Come."

"And who are you?" asked Emrys.

"I am Herit," answered the other, "though that can mean little enough to thee. Come. Too long has the Lady awaited thee. Must we delay her any longer? Rich are the rewards of her service."

Emrys stood irresolute, the sea whispering at his back, and the bright June sun beating down upon him.

"At the least, hear thou what she hath to say," urged Herit. "She can perhaps help thee in the achieving of what thou most desirest."

"No!" cried Emrys, turning sharply away from Herit and beginning to run. But even as he did so, a mist rose about him, and darkness descended upon him, and he pitched forward into the soft turf, his senses dead to the world.

XIII

When Emrys awoke, he thought he must be dead. He was surrounded by light, light of all different hues. Under him was a fur; he seemed to be reclining upon a bed of some sort. He felt no pain—his unconsciousness had not been the result of a blow to the head, then. But his throat was dry. He felt as if he could drink oceans of water.

He looked around him at the lights. As he moved his head to and fro, they flashed and scintillated, sometimes shifting hue as they did so. Emrys reached out with his hand: his fingers touched something cold, flat, and hard. He sat up and peered at it.

He was in a fortress, or large building of some sort, but it was constructed entirely from transparent crystal. The crystal took the light from the outside world, refracted it into a thousand shivering pieces, and then threw it with cold contempt upon those within it. Emrys held his eye close to the surface of the crystal. He could make out the green shapes of hills, and above them, blue and white swirls that indicated the sky. He could recognize the real world, but it looked alien, as if it had been created by a slightly perverse child.

He sat back and looked around him at the fantastic kaleidoscope that surrounded him on all sides. It made his head spin a little. He was not sure whether he was looking up or down, for there was no frame of reference in anything familiar. He scrambled to his feet, just so he would know where "down" was.

He decided that he did not like the fortress of glass. Besides, it smelled faintly musky, as if many cats lived there.

Some of the lights jumped aside as something black moved beyond the deceitful walls and, suddenly, Herit stood before him, his hat doffed, his hand upon the hilt of his sword.

"Where am I?" asked Emrys.

"Caer Siddi," explained Herit, "stronghold of Morgana, Queen of Annwn and the Island of the Mighty. She bids thee join her. Follow me, for she would speak with thee."

Emrys followed Herit through the flashing corridors of the castle. Shapes outside grew huge in a second, then squeezed to fingernail-size, then expanded again or else disappeared completely. And there *were* cats, cats everywhere. Some slept, some prowled, some regarded Emrys with sullen green eyes as he passed by. Some were small mousers or barn-cats, but Emrys saw also a wild cat with tufted ears, and once they passed a spotted cat whose head came up to Emrys' waist. A deep, throaty growl came from it as it watched Emrys pass along.

There was no knowing whither they went through this most confusing of all mazes; but, at length, Herit stopped and pushed what appeared to be a door.

Emrys found himself in a wide hall. Trestles of a dark wood, ebony perhaps, were laid perpendicular to the passage from which he had just emerged. The place was warmed by fires lit in small crystal cups mounted upon the walls: fires hanging in space, surrounded by crazy, otherworldly patterns of light. And the walls reflected these little fires a thousand times, so that the place seemed to be consumed by fire.

Morgana awaited him, standing upon the dais at the far end of the hall.

She was taller than most women, and her hair was the colour of a raven's feathers. Her skin was pale, but not unhealthy. It was a complexion that scorned to be out of doors except under dire emergency; it preferred to be under a roof, sheltered from even the kinder elements. She wore a tight dress of red samite, the neckline cut to expose a generous cleavage. It clung to her swelling breasts and rounded hips, hinting at pleasures it did not reveal. A wide gold necklace circled her perfectly sculpted throat. Her arms were bare and, though slender, seemed to possess a superhuman strength. More gold sparkled from her ears and on her wrists. Her stone-grey eyes neither left him nor blinked as he approached the dais. Her lips, thin and pale, curled slightly downwards. She was exactly as she had appeared to Emrys in his visions.

And yet, for all that her form was appealing, her figure pleasing to the eye, her features alluring, Emrys felt at the root of his soul a mortal fear.

Emrys had not taken a step into the hall and Herit, noticing that he had not moved, turned and urged him on roughly. Emrys took a few stumbling steps. What did she want? Would she kill him quickly, or would she torture him? She was a goddess—surely she knew already that he neither possessed Excalibur, nor knew where it was hidden.

Reaching the foot of the dais, he threw himself face-down upon the floor. Herit took his arm, yanked him upright, and propelled him up the three steps to the top of the dais.

A great golden lion stood beside Morgana, and it growled deep in its throat at Emrys.

"Welcome to Caer Siddi, Merlin Emrys, Seeing One of Afallach," Morgana said.

Emrys narrowed his eyes at her use of the name, and looked sharply at her; then he looked away.

She seemed to know instinctively what he was thinking, and said, "The name is your destiny; you will not truly be yourself until you accept it. And only he who is truly himself can find Excalibur."

Merlin took a deep breath, but tried to be noncommittal. "Thank you, madam," he replied, his eyes sliding away from hers. He fixed them upon the ground.

He heard the rustle of her dress, felt her long fingers on his chin. They sent a thrill, like lightning, through his body. She turned his chin up so that she could look long into his face.

"Yes," she said quietly, "you have the Mark. Not that I ever doubted. I have sent you visions, and you have responded to them."

Emrys forgot his fear in an instant, and stared at the Lady of Annwn. "You sent me the vision of Llygat's book!" he said. Morgana nodded. "Why?"

"For many reasons," she answered. "Come."

Morgana turned and pushed open a door behind the high table. Beyond was a spiral stair, leading up through the dazzling colours into the sapphire above. The sun, Emrys observed, was low on the horizon, and it sent spears of golden light flying through the crystalline walls of the tower they were climbing.

At length, they reached the top, and Emrys found himself standing upon a battlement, overlooking a wide panoramic view.

Caer Siddi was situated upon a rocky plain between two rivers, each of which emptied into the sea in a wide bay to the north. Beyond the rivers, and extending up each arm of the bay, mountains marched into the distance, their snows pink in the rays of the late afternoon sun. To the south, Emrys could see a thick forest and, beyond that, a vast expanse of white, a desert of snow and ice.

But he could see more, scenes beyond the horizon of mortal sight. He saw an island shaped like a great hand, its fingers clawing into the north. Its heart was ice, but fire too lurked beneath its surface, erupting forth in livid columns of steam or molten rock. In the forests lurked fell beasts; in the towns and castles, slaves crouched under the whips of cruel taskmasters. Morgana's realm lay before the eyes of the Sight, beautiful but terrible.

"This is a land," said Morgana, "of contradictions. Great sheets of ice are neighbours to boiling kettles of mud, or mountains of fire. When first I came here, an exile from Albion, cold and alone, this place was a surging mass of forces, all striving to overcome one another. Fire and ice clashed, the great tumult of the sea rose under the lashings of the mighty wind to overcome the land, which gnashed its teeth and overthrew all who set foot upon it. And I used those forces. I threw the earth into the fire, and it arose new-made, as mighty mountains that gave resistance to the winds. I built a wall against the seething ocean all around. Annwn is my land. I created it. I formed it from the primeval matter of chaos. I brought life to it. It exists because of me."

Emrys said nothing, but gazed blankly out across the landscape.

Morgana went on, "This I can do for your land, the Island of the Mighty. Too long have contradictory forces striven to tear it apart. Now there are two kings. Use the Sight, Emrys. What do you see?"

Emrys' hand lashed out and he seized the wall for support. Out of the mist arose a scene: two men, bearded, struggling for a crown, while others, clothed in scarlet, looked on. One of the red-clad men stepped forward. On his breast was an armour plate, bearing the device of an eagle with wings outspread over the world. He reached out for the crown, but the men did not notice him.

"What I offer Britain," said Morgana "is an end to the chaos. Those who have spoken ill of me have spoken amiss. I wish to bring order to chaos. My way is hard, I admit. It is the way of discipline, the way of self-control."

Emrys was back in the real world, if it was real. The ice was sharp on top of the Tower of Annwn. He looked at Morgana. She did not seem to notice the cold.

"What do you want of me?" he asked.

Morgana looked down, like a little girl accused of stealing apples from an orchard. "I want to end the strife," she said. "The men of the Island of the Mighty have spoken evil things of me. They are not true! I have endeavoured always to protect Britain from her enemies. I have struggled to bring order to the Island of the Mighty, in spite of the best efforts of her kings to destroy her with civil war and other contention."

"Is that why you stole the Treasures of Britain?" demanded Emrys sharply.

"Stole, you say?" Morgana seemed offended. "Stole! Yes, that is what *they* would say, the Druids. Ever have they opposed me! But it is not so. The Treasures were placed in the hands of fools who could not protect them. I took them to me, so that they would be safe. Here, they are in the keeping of the wise, and still they protect Britain from afar. But they are talismans of mighty power. When I return them to Britain, as I shall, they must be under the strictest supervision. Such power should not be in the hands of fools."

"When you return to Britain?"

"Yes, bringing all the Treasures—Excalibur too."

"You know where Excalibur is?" Emrys' tone was excited.

"I do not," replied Morgana. "But you can help me find it. Will you do this, Emrys, and bring order and peace to Britain, and with them the greatness that belonged to it of old?"

Emrys looked at his hostess. She was inestimably beautiful, and she regarded him with imploring eyes, a supplicant. He tried to remember all the warnings he had heard about her—from Gwelydd, from Cathbhad, from the stories he had heard in his childhood. But they all seemed unreal, gossamer blown away by a breeze. Could all the storytellers have been wrong?

"We both want the same thing, Merlin Emrys," said Morgana. "And we want it for the same reason. Britain can be great, a power to be feared in the world. The Dragon can challenge the Eagle. Together, we can find Excalibur far more quickly than we can separately. And time is pressing—the Eagles are poised to stoop upon the Dragons, when the Dragons have no claws."

"I—I don't know, my lady," stammered Emrys. Why didn't it seem simple any more?

"You do not trust me." Morgana recoiled from him, like a hurt kitten. "You have heard the lies that men have breathed about me, and you believe them." She sighed. "Well, it must be so, then. I must continue my labours alone. I must—"

"No, lady!" cried Emrys, stepping closer to her. "No," he said again, more quietly now. "I *want* to help. I think you are right: we can find the sword together."

Morgana smiled. "Then I have a friend among the Britons," she said. "At the end of all these years, once more, I have a friend." She moved away from the transparent parapet and started her descent once more. Emrys followed. Once inside the castle, the green hills and distant mountains turned again to bizarre, distorted shapes. What had been natural became fantastic. Emrys gazed with wonder at the shapes as he and the Queen of Annwn returned to the hall.

Once they had reached the foot of the stairs, Morgana turned to face Emrys. "We shall talk again, you and I. There is much I would say to you —much that you should know about me that I think your bards have not told you." She smiled with a kind of fondness for these poor, misguided wretches. "They do not mean to tell such lies, of course," she explained, "but it has been my sad lot to hear my name dragged through the mire and made the petty antagonist of every story they can devise. But what cannot be changed must be endured with patience. And I have been so very, very patient." Her eyes snapped onto Emrys, and there was an almost hungry gleam in them. "But now is the moment. Now is the moment because you have appeared. Here you are, with the Sight—the first in three centuries. Now I can do what I have planned to do all along, and bring order and harmony to the Island of the Mighty. I am glad that you will help me in this, Merlin Emrys."

"I will do what I can, my lady," Emrys replied.

"Good. We shall speak again, on another occasion. For now, you must return to Britain, and carry on the work, with what guidance I and my people can render you."

Morgana, Queen of Annwn, stepped forward and took Emrys' face between her hands. He could feel warmth emanating from her. Her head cocked a little, her lips reached out, and she kissed him, long and slow, upon the lips.

"There is no limit to what you and I can achieve together," she said. And then she left him alone and wondering in the hall of fantastic colours.

* * *

Not long after this, Emrys was back in Cambria again. Herit had taken him closer to Caermyrddin than he had been when they had first met, saving him several days' journey. Before the sun set that evening, he was looking down from the crest of a hill onto the quiet calm of Caermyrddin. Threads of smoke drifted up from hearth-fires, and the muted sounds of commerce rose to him on the breezy air. Emrys drank in the air of home deeply, and galloped down the hillside towards the home of his childhood.

Surprised faces greeted him as he entered the courtyard through the thick wooden gates. Everything was exactly as he remembered it, down to the minutest detail. Everyone was doing the same jobs they had been doing when he left. The same cows stood in the same byres. The same weeds sprouted in the dark corners at the foot of the walls. And yet it looked to him like the landscape of some alien and enigmatic land, peopled by inscrutable folk whose customs were familiar to him only from dreams. A few of them stopped in their work to watch him, open-mouthed, as he strode with a purpose across the open space to the women's quarters where he expected to find his mother.

The women's quarters seemed dark to him after the brightness outside. Slowly, details resolved themselves out of the darkness: the vivid colours of the tapestries, the plethora of chairs, the chests covered with thick rugs.

Viviane stood at the far end, rising slowly out of her seat, wordless in her surprise and joy at seeing Emrys. She was magnificent in her beauty, and wore it as a mighty queen does a crown. But, Emrys noticed for the first time, there were the tiniest creases at the corners of her eyes and mouth; and unless the light were striking her oddly at the temples, there seemed to be a few strands of grey hair there.

"So," she said, "you have returned."

"I have, mother," said Emrys, dropping to his knees before her. "I crave your pardon, for I left without your permission."

Emrys felt her breath on the crown of his head, and she kissed him lightly before raising him up and folding him in her arms.

"That is in the past now, my sweeting," she said.

XIV

An hour later, Viviane and Emrys emerged from the women's quarters into a courtyard of lengthening shadows. Emrys noticed for the first time that three great wagons were ranged beside the Great Hall. One contained food: servants were still loading it up with smoked hams and baskets of bread. The other contained neatly-folded canvases and bundles of sticks and ropes, clearly the equipment needed for tents. The third was piled with a wide assortment of other things: weapons, a few items of treasure, clothing for men and women wrapped in oilskins to keep the elements out.

"Emrys!" came a voice. Emrys noticed one of the servants, loading the wagons with food, had paused in his work and waved. "Welcome home! How are things in the world?"

"It looks as if you'll soon find out, Alun," answered Emrys. "Do you journey with these wains?"

"No, it's here I'll stay. The world's too big a place for me! The gods give you joy, Emrys!"

"And you, Alun." To his mother, Emrys said, "What is all this busyness?"

"We set out for Lundein tomorrow," Viviane explained. "There is to be a great council, and the seven kings are summoned."

"It is for a choosing," Emrys said. "When the council is over, there will be but one High King."

Viviane's eyes darted across at him for a moment. "So, politics has been your study in Afallach," she observed.

"Nay, I—" Emrys hesitated. He had been about to tell her that his words had been but a guess, a lucky guess. But there seemed little point in telling her that. And now they had reached the doors of the Great Hall. The warriors who guarded the entrance nodded respectfully to Viviane, and looked with wonder upon Emrys. Then they pushed open the doors, and Emrys and his mother entered the hall of Rhydderch's fortress.

Nothing had changed; and yet, as Emrys had observed when he had first entered the fortress earlier in the day, everything was different. When he looked up at the oaken beams that supported the roof, Emrys fancied he could almost see a small figure scurrying along after a hawk. A merlin. A strange turn of events, he reflected, that had given him that name. And Morgana had used it. And there was the stone figure in the wallet hanging from his belt, the one Gwelydd had given him upon his departure from Afallach.

Rhydderch sat upon the dais, two or three councilors ranged about him. A small table stood to his right, upon which sat a flagon and a cup, and various pieces of curling parchment, which Emrys guessed were maps. Cathbhad was one of the councilors, and his eyes danced to see Emrys, though he said nothing nor moved.

"It is settled, then," said Rhydderch. "We choose Coroticos. He is the rightful inheritor, according to our law; we cannot choose Cymbeline, and choose the law of our enemies. Coroticos is to be High King of Britain. Are we agreed?"

"Coroticos," urged Clytwyn, one of the councilors, "will be strong in opposing Rome. Cymbeline seeks to negotiate. The table, and not the sword, is his way."

"So, if we choose Coroticos, we choose war. But I am assured by you that we are prepared for it, and so I believe."

"And yet, my lords, your majesty," said another of the councilors, a man named Digon, "Rome is mighty. No spear has yet prevailed against her. Cymbeline could buy us a little time to further strengthen our armies."

Rhydderch smiled grimly. "No spear has prevailed against the Eagles because no spear they have flown against has yet been a Britonnic one. I do not fear these upstart eyases." Then he noticed Viviane and Emrys.

Viviane bowed before Rhydderch, and Emrys did likewise. Viviane said, "Your grandson has returned to us, my lord and father."

The king of Cambria regarded Emrys for a long while. The other councilors looked on with indifference. Rising from his throne, Rhydderch descended from the dais and confronted Emrys directly. His eyes were appraising. Two years it had been since Emrys had last beheld that face, and many more than that since he had seen it so closely. It was a harsh face, beaten to toughness by the elements, but also toughened by hard choices. Emrys wondered if a sword-cut would make any impression on the iron of that cheek.

Slowly, Rhydderch paced around Emrys, inspecting him as if he had petitioned to join the household guard.

"My grandson the dreamer," he said. "They told me you had run away to Afallach, but you have not stayed away long enough to become a druid. What have you been doing? Not learning the ways of the spear, I reckon. That is much to be regretted—we shall have need of men who can carry spears soon." Rhydderch completed his circle around Emrys, and looked him in the face. He opened his mouth to speak, but saw something that made him hesitate a moment. There was a flicker of doubt in those stern eyes. Then it was gone, and the harshness returned. "You are welcome back to Caermyrddin," he said. "You may return to your former privileges, but if you have anything else to say, please wait until I return from Lundein. As you can perhaps see, at this moment I am very busy. The gods give you a good evening."

And, in a swirl of cloak, he returned to the business of planning the journey to Lundein. Emrys looked across at his mother. She wore an expression of pain, as if she had caught the lash of a whip across her face. Her hands, he saw, were balled into fists. Her lips parted for an angry word, but Emrys leaped before her, putting both his hands on her arms, and saying, "Peace, mother. This is as it has always been. Not now." Gently, he turned her about and steered her towards the doors. But a voice from behind them stopped him, and he turned to see his old friend, Cathbhad, descending from the dais.

"Welcome home, little hawk," he said, enfolding the younger man in a tight embrace. More quietly, he said, "The gods have trodden the path with you, I see: a light shines in your face that shone not ere now." He paused, and the trace of a cloud passed over his brow. "Much is there that was not before," he said. "We must find a time to talk."

"Thank you, old friend," said Emrys. "There is much to tell you."

"That must wait until this evening, at the earliest," replied Cathbhad, "and I must still make preparations for our journey. But perhaps you will

121

come with us to Lundein? There will be time enough on our journey, and you can tell me all that has befallen Afallach since I left, more years ago than I care to count."

"I am bound for . . . " began Emrys; but then he stopped, and his lip twisted at one side. Something was in his mind, a few words from Gwelydd two years ago. "Lundein has a library, does it not?" he asked. Cathbhad nodded. "Then I shall come to Lundein with you. But see: my grandfather grows impatient that you expend words on his simple-minded grandson. Have you not greater matters to attend to?"

Cathbhad's face splintered into a thousand wrinkles as he grinned back at the younger man. He put a hand on Emrys' shoulder. "You are welcome to Caermyrddin. Think not upon your grandfather. He has many cares, many burdens. He loves you well enough, after his own fashion," he assured Emrys and, turning, rejoined Rhydderch on the dais.

Emrys followed his mother slowly out of the hall, wondering why he should have agreed to go to Lundein instead of Caer Lloyw; but even as he emerged into the courtyard of the late afternoon, his thoughts were interrupted by the distant howl of a wolf. A mournful note it was, ululating upon the stiff breeze that blew in chilly from the south. Men paused in their work to make the sign of the evil eye, and mothers held their children tighter to their bosoms. Seldom did such creatures give tongue in daylight, and Emrys too stopped in his tracks. He blinked a few times. The wolf let out another pitiful cry. Perhaps, thought Emrys, hunters have killed its cubs.

He shuddered, as he crossed the courtyard with his mother, to think on the vengeance the wolf would take upon such hunters.

* * *

The journey to Lundein took many days, for bright June passed into a rainy July, with heavy clouds louring so low it seemed that anyone could reach up and touch them. The road they took through southern Cambria became slimy with mud, and the wagons bogged down frequently. The River Trybrwyt was swollen when they reached it, the ford under deep and swift water, and this slowed them down greatly, while scouts rode upstream to

122

find another place to cross. In the end, they trudged north along the western bank in any case, for most of them knew that, a few short miles away on the far side of the river lay the realm of Morgannawg, a place inhabited by sorcerer kings and priests with dark rites. Soon, they were able to make a brief march east, picking up the youthful River Wysg and following it along the eastern bank for a few miles before picking up the Ridgeway that would take them directly to Lundein.

As they emerged from Cambria into the Summer Country, the mountains dropped away behind them, to be replaced by rolling hills. It was like seeing a great man's fiery temper subside into grumblings. The road they took generally followed a ridge with a steep drop on either side to wooded valleys. Some days, mist rose up from the hollows in the nights, and when they awoke, it seemed that they were alone in the ghostly world, plying along the ridge that thrust forward through a sea of oblivion. The very hands of the gods seemed turned against them, their dark faces frowning through heavy clouds at the string of damp humanity labouring along the spine of the world.

Soon after leaving Cambria, they passed Caer Lloyw. They arrived when the sun had not an hour's life left, and what with pitching the tents for the evening, Emrys had no chance to enter the city at all. He heard the gate-horns braying to citizens outside the walls, and knew that the gates would be closing at any moment. He paused for a moment, and contemplated the city. A fitful rain was falling from the grey skies, and the city did not seem to shine. Nor was summer particularly evident in the country. Emrys pulled his cloak up over his neck and returned to his work, shoving his thoughts about his quest deep down inside of him where he would not have to reflect upon them.

It was a depressed body of warriors who huddled into the tent that night, heads on shields but eyes open and staring. Emrys sat among them, his fingers running over the strings of his harp. He felt that something was missing. He felt that he was ready to begin his quest, but he did not know how. And then there was Morgana. How did she fit in with the pattern? The dotting of rain on the canvas over his head, and the ripple of the harp-notes combined for a moment in a brief symphony, and Caled, one of the warriors, looked up at the sound.

"Come, Emrys," he barked, "stop caressing that woman there, and make her sing: give us a song to lighten our hearts in this gloomy place!"

"Our bard lies at my right hand," observed Emrys, indicating Cathbhad, who was curled up under a blanket next to him.

"But I am asleep," said Cathbhad. "Sing!"

Emrys muttered a few words of imprecation to Tylweth, dashed his fingers over the strings and, without thinking of his words at all, sang,

> Sweet apple-tree with branches sweet,
> Rich your shade and rich your fruit,
> Branches spreading over untilled land,
> Sweet apple-tree, with deep-digging root.
>
> Sweet apple-tree, a maiden I found,
> Shield on my shoulder, sword in my hand,
> But she spoke nothing when near I stood,
> Sweet apple-tree, with blossoms kind.
>
> Sweet apple-tree, with blossoms red,
> The ground beneath you stained with blood,
> And in the forest I slept alone,
> Sweet apple-tree, that grows in a glade.
>
> Sweet apple-tree with branches fine,
> The lords of Rhydderch make their moan,
> But in your branches, hid from sight,
> Sweet apple-tree, I recline.

"Humph," said Caled. "I wish I'd woken Cathbhad up. What did that mean?"

Emrys blinked, as if he had been woken from a dream. "What did it mean?" he repeated. "What did I say?"

"A lot of nonsense about an apple-tree," replied Caled.

Emrys thought for a moment. "I do not know," he said. "I do not ask the gods the meaning of the words they send me. There were apple-trees in Afallach."

Caled said, "Humph!" again, and settled his head upon his shield. The other warriors followed his example, and soon the tent was quiet but for their snoring. Emrys lay awake. Outside, the wind howled through the heavens, a wild dog harrying game. Heavy raindrops drummed against the canvas over his head.

What was it about? Apple trees, women in crystal castles, burning effigies on Beltane night? If he arose now, one short walk through the rain would bring him to Caer Lloyw, where, he believed, there was a clue to Excalibur's whereabouts. As silent as death, he rose from where he reclined and wrapped his cloak about him. Quickly, he pushed his feet into his boots and pulled the cords tight. Concealing his harp beneath the cloak, he picked his way through the sleeping bodies to the tent entrance. For a moment, he hesitated. Would not opening the tent-flap wake some of them up? And were there not guards posted?

And then again, why should he not go to Caer Lloyw? Was he not a free man, the grandson of a king? He was no peasant, bound to a certain plot of land for life. He could go whither he wished.

Emrys parted the tent flap and let it drop behind him. There were no guards in sight. The damp, rich smell of the wet earth was all around him, and the creaking of the trees and sighing of the wind were living sounds. He knew, roughly, the direction of Caer Lloyw, and pushed through some trees to begin his journey.

The going was rough—slippery, and in the darkness, pathless too. But for all that, it was not long before he emerged onto a hillside and beheld the town below him.

It was not quite dark, for the moon was full, its light diffused by the clouds but not swallowed up completely. It cast a faint silver radiance over the wooden houses below, where a few fires twinkled and from which spirals of smoke rose like offerings to the gods.

The rain had lessened, for the wind was blowing away the clouds, bit by wet bit. The city lay below, but Emrys stood irresolute. What, he wondered, as he hesitated on the brink, was he waiting for?

Long he stood, his mind leaning first this way, then that. Before his feet, there was no path, and no path led to the place to which he had come. He had got here not by following a road, but by leaving it. Gwelydd and Morgana. Between the two of them, they had erased his direction. He did not know which way to go.

It was in the pathless wood that Cathbhad found him, hours later, when sunrise had bathed the hillside in its grey light.

XV

Cathbhad stood for a moment and said nothing, for Emrys presented him with a strange sight indeed. He stood on the brink of a deep fall, a tangled forest below him. His hair was matted with last night's rain, his garments soaked. But he seemed unaware of the physical world around him. He stared out over the awakening routine of the township of Caer Lloyw but, to Cathbhad, he looked like a traveler from another world. He called his name, and slowly, the boy turned his head to face him. Cathbhad took an involuntary step backwards. Emrys' cheeks were sunk, his eyes haunted. Slowly, the eyes came back from far, far away, and focused on the bard.

"I have . . . lost my path, Cathbhad," said Emrys slowly, and with great effort.

Cathbhad stumbled forward through the brambles. "There is no path here, little hawk," he said. "Return with me to the wain-rout, for the king calls upon his wain-drivers to be on the road ere long!"

"I do not know the way."

"You do not need to." Cathbhad held out his hand. "Let me lead you. Come away from the brink!"

Emrys turned and looked towards his feet. For the first time, it seemed, he saw the precipitous drop before them. He turned his eyes again towards Cathbhad and, slowly, moved away from the edge and towards his friend. Cathbhad caught him by the arm and looked him up and down. He did not seem disturbed by the weather; it seemed that he was wind and ice itself.

"What is it," asked Cathbhad, "that afflicts your mind and soul thus?"

Emrys turned his eyes this way and that, as if he were searching for something, though he hardly even knew what. "Cathbhad," he whispered, "how can I tell right from wrong?"

"Emrys!" Cathbhad took Emrys' face between his hands and forced him to look into his own. "Emrys, listen to me. If the gods are guiding you, heed them! They will not let you lose your path."

"But which of the gods?" asked Emrys.

"Argante," urged Cathbhad. "Offer her sacrifices, pray to her, beg her to lead you. All the ancient tales call her the Queen of the Morforwyn. She it is you must follow. All wisdom proceeds from her. Come now, for we must return to the wain-rout. Your mother seeks you—you have been missed."

But Emrys pulled away from Cathbhad. "What of Morgana?" asked Emrys. Cathbhad did not speak. All around them, the wind chattered through the damp leaves while, down below, the sound of a dog barking came up clearly from the awakening city. Emrys said again, "Cathbhad, what of Morgana? What if she could help me find a path? What if she could show me the way to find Excalibur?"

"I don't know," stammered Cathbhad. "Morgana is . . . in all the stories, she—"

"I don't want stories, Cathbhad," replied Emrys. "I want the truth! If Morgana can help me, why not? Why not choose evil?"

"Good and evil," said Cathbhad. "There never is one without the other. After the summer comes the winter; after life, death." From back on the road, horns brayed, summoning the wain-drivers to their toil. "The horns call us, Emrys," said Cathbhad. "The wain-rout is leaving."

"We can catch up with it," answered Emrys. "Cathbhad, death is more powerful than life," he added. "No man can escape death; death always conquers life. Evil will always conquer good. We do best to be on the side of the conqueror, not the vanquished."

"Do you believe this?"

"I do not know." Emrys looked Cathbhad directly in the eye. "Why do I not know, Cathbhad?" he demanded. "I have the Sight. Why does it not reveal to me a way to go? Why must I still struggle?"

"This gift of the gods," said Cathbhad, "it is a burden most of us could not bear. Did you not learn anything of its ways in Afallach?"

"I learned many things," replied Emrys, "but I cannot put them to use. I have lost my way."

Cathbhad was silent a short time, while Emrys' mind turned over and over, thinking without any real direction about his experiences since he had

128

left home two years ago. Suddenly, Cathbhad seemed to reach a decision. Putting a hand on Emrys' shoulder, he waved a hand at the heavens and said, "Listen to that wind! How it howls! How the trees sigh as the breath of winter rattles their branches! That's what I mean, little hawk. Here we are in the middle of summer, when all around us should be flower and leaf, and along comes this cold blast of death. But, between now and Samhain, there will be more warm days than there will be between Samhain and Beltane. That is how it should be. The year must die, and be reborn. As with the year, so with all other things. You speak of Morgana. Perhaps it is she who sends you these visions. She is necessary, as the winter is necessary. What is old must die, making way for the new. What is good and evil, and how may a man know the difference? I do not think this world is a place where such distinctions matter. Evil will triumph for a time, and then good will rise and vanquish it. That is the way of things."

"Such words bring little comfort," observed Emrys.

Cathbhad shrugged. "You and I, Emrys," he said, "we seek not comfort. And he who seeks comfort beneath the moon is little more than a fool. Life is not comforting, but it is unavoidable."

"Life is a long scream, terminated by oblivion," said Emrys.

Cathbhad gave a short, indulgent laugh. "Those are Gwelydd's words, if ever I heard them," he said.

Emrys flushed. "But they are true, even if I said them not first. Come. We must rejoin the wain-rout."

"Little hawk," urged Cathbhad, staying him with a hand to his elbow, "the way is not so dark as Gwelydd would have us believe, you know. Good dwells in the same house as evil, pleasure with misery, wealth with poverty. Morgana and Argante are the two most powerful of the Morforwyn. Have you ever spoken with architects about their craft?" Emrys shook his head. "What keeps a building upright," Cathbhad explained, "is the fact that the walls constantly want to collapse. If you lean two collapsing things against each other, then the very force that is trying so hard to pull them down will keep them up. Now listen, Emrys." Cathbhad stopped the young man and spoke directly to him. Out of the corner of his eye, Emrys could see the wagons of the wain-rout moving slowly along the road.

"Good and evil are like these opposite walls. Take away one, and the other will collapse. The whole structure will topple down."

"Do you believe this?"

Cathbhad gave a snorting laugh. "It is two years of Guidgen's lessons in wisdom," he said. "Had you stayed a little longer at Afallach, you would perhaps believe it as well as do I."

Emrys moved off towards the lumbering wain-rout. "I did not stay," he said, "so I thank you for your lessons, Cathbhad my teacher. But I must think about these things."

"Wait!" called Cathbhad. Emrys turned back to him. Through the trees, the wagons were beginning to lumber along, and they caught the sound of Viviane's groom, calling Emrys' name. The undergrowth rustled as Cathbhad moved forward to join him. "Emrys," he said, "do you understand? Good and evil dwell together, so from that perspective, it makes no difference which one you serve. You could serve Morgana, or you could serve Argante; you could serve Mercury or Jupiter or Ashtaroth, and it would make very little difference. All are potent. All are terrifying. And all are equally indifferent to what happens to us."

"How do you know this to be true?"

"The gods are concerned only for themselves," Cathbhad went on. "They are too great to concern themselves with us. But some are more harmful to us than others. Whom do you serve?"

"That is what I do not know, and I cannot see a way ahead anywhere!" cried Emrys. He tried to move off again towards the wain-rout, but once more Cathbhad stopped him.

"Whom do you serve?" he insisted.

"Morgana!" cried Emrys. "Argante! Myself! What does it matter?"

"Emrys!" came Viviane's voice, from the Ridgeway.

The wild look in Emrys' eyes cooled suddenly, and he cast a glance over his shoulder. "Mother," he said.

"Whom do you serve, little hawk?" asked Cathbhad again.

Emrys turned his eyes upon Cathbhad, who felt a tingling along his spine at what he saw in them. For a moment, he looked very unlike Emrys.

There was suffering in the lines of his face, and blood trickling down from his temples. But no: that was a trick of the light. It was just rain.

"You," said Emrys. "It is you I serve, Cathbhad. You, and my mother, who loves me, and my grandfather, who does not. And Alun, and Caled, and Coroticos and Cymbeline, and even the Emperor Claudius in Rome."

"Anyone whose suffering you can lessen," said Cathbhad, with gratification.

"No!" Emrys had turned to join the wain-rout, but now he wheeled about again; and it seemed to Cathbhad that he was as tall as one of the trees, his great gaze searching over the canopy, surveying the world around. "No," he repeated. "It is to give meaning to the suffering," he said. And he turned from Cathbhad and stalked off through the forest to the wain-rout.

Viviane was indeed waiting for him, and her personal groom with her, his hand upon the bridle of Emrys' horse. Emrys swung himself up and rode out ahead of the column. Behind him was the king, his mother, and Cathbhad. They all watched the solitary figure plodding along at an even pace with the wain-rout; but each pair of eyes regarded him with a differing expression.

* * *

At last, after many days' arduous travel, at midmorning on a bright July day, they beheld for the first time Lundein, a great city that sprawled along the northern bank of the River Thames. Emrys paused in his journey to wonder at it, while the wain-rout lumbered past him down the gentle slope of the Thames Valley. Grander it was than his imagining had told him. In the centre was a small mound, the White Hill, and upon this was builded the many-towered White Palace. Winding out from it were many streets, along which thatched roofs huddled like bales of hay in an autumn field. Even at this distance, the streets seemed to seethe, and the market-places too, with brightly-coloured humanity. Bounding it all were the walls built by Lludd, a hundred years ago, stout and mighty, thick and impenetrable. The towers stood like great sentinels, watching with stern eyes the approach of enemies from afar. Emrys felt his hair prickle on his scalp. It was a sight that would inspire anyone with awe.

"Dun Lludd," said Cathbhad, giving the city its old name. He sniffed the air. "I can smell the bronze foundries!" he said, and rode on. Emrys shook his reins and followed. The hedgerows rose on either side, and the city was lost to view for a while, and Emrys pondered what he knew of the city's tale.

Most ancient of the twenty-eight cities of the Island of the Mighty, Lundein had been founded by Brutus, more than a thousand years ago, and called by him New Troy. There were caves beneath the city, vast and labyrinthine, which the second High King, Locrin, had furnished in a fantastic manner for his mistress, Sabrina. Another legend claimed that the head of Bran the Blessed, mightiest of all the High Kings of Britain, had been buried beneath the White Hill by his retainers after the final, weird battle that he had fought against his brother Efnissyen. And yet the city had been but a village until the time of Lludd, son of Beli the Great. Lludd ruled the Island of the Mighty prosperously, and built walls around the city of New Troy, and girt it about with innumerable towers; and when he had done so, he bade the citizens build fine houses within the walls so that there might not be in the world a city of such splendour. And there Lludd dwelt, and dealt out meat and drink to those who served him out of love; and though he had many castles in his kingdom, this one he loved most, and for that reason, his people soon came to call it Dun Lludd, and then Lundein.

Throughout the morning, Emrys caught glimpses of the city, but it seemed little closer. Indeed, it was not until mid-afternoon, when the sun was beginning to decline from its zenith, that they pitched their tents beneath the stockades. Then Rhydderch and his meinie passed through the great western gate of the city. Emrys swung himself up onto his horse and followed, for he wanted to see the city. Immediately, they found themselves on a narrow street between timber-frame houses that seemed to lean over them. The tops of their heads almost scraped the walls of the buildings; with a sharp crack and an anguished groan, Caled set the sign-board of a tavern flapping.

Cathbhad was again riding beside Emrys. "Ah, Lundein!" he declared. "When a man wearies of Lundein, he wearies of life! There is in Lundein all that life can afford, Emrys."

Emrys looked from left to right. The citizens of Lundein pressed themselves against the walls of their fine buildings to let the wain-rout pass. They were a happy people, a prosperous people; and yet, among the gaily-clad and brightly-coloured throng, Emrys caught sight of signs of weakness, signs of woe. Beggars leaned their backs against alley walls, and on the street-corners, youthful harlots stood cursing their infants.

"Everything," agreed Emrys, with tight lips.

Cathbhad caught his mood, and correctly divined the cause of it. "The poor there will always be," he said. "They cannot be avoided. Think not on them."

"They are suffering," observed Emrys.

"We all suffer, in one way or another. Why would you encourage them to neglect their duties by throwing them food or money they have not earned? It is no favour to give food to a man too lazy to get his own." They rode for a few minutes in silence. "This is a fine city," Cathbhad said at last. "What splendours must have been in the days of Belin and Brennios! They bent Rome to their wills—as we shall."

But Emrys was silent. A shadow had passed over the sun, and he shivered.

At last, the Cambrians rode into the wide, straight street that took them to the gates of Lludd's Palace. The walls were tall and mighty, and white-washed so that they reflected the sun with a dazzling splendour. A pair of towers, pierced with narrow slits, stood on either side of the road, and between them were the great gates that gave admittance into the palace of the High Kings of Britain. They were shut and barred from within, and out-side stood two thick-armed sentries, each bearing spear and shield and bronze sword. The Cambrians came to a halt, and Rhydderch drew rein before the gates.

XVI

The guards looked up at Rhydderch and the collection of Cambrians. Each of the guards wore a small helmet, nothing more than a cap of bronze, surmounted by the figure of a dragon, rearing with wings outspread. Their cloaks were held in place by bronze brooches in the form of a serpent, curling in about itself. The buckles on their belts were fashioned into the shapes of dragons' heads, so that the leather of the belt seemed to be the long tail, wrapped as if about the world.

Chief Dragon of the Island of the Mighty. That was the ancient title of the High King.

One of the sentries stepped forward and addressed Rhydderch. "Who are you," he asked, "that ride hither to the court of the High Kings of Britain? Tell me your names and your lineage!"

"I am Rhydderch, son of Gwenddolau, of the house of Bran the Blessed, king of Cambria and servant of the High Kings of the Island of the Mighty. These are men of my household, valiant in the defence of Cambria and of Britain. Why are these gates locked against us?"

The door-ward spoke again. "My lord," he said, "you come in the darkest hour of the Island of the Mighty. The gate is barred against all, until they have declared their lineage and purpose."

"We are no enemies of the realm," said Rhydderch, "but come at an urgent summons, for the High Kings would have all kings of Britain at their council. Let us into the palace; you would do well to obey us in this regard!"

The door-ward nodded. "We have not the keys, my lord. But abide a while. There is he within who can open the gates." He signaled to his comrade, who turned and rapped upon the door. A small hatch opened up in the face of the door, and a hurried conversation ensued, in hushed tones so that none in the Cambrian household could understand the words. Then the hatch snapped shut, and silence descended upon them. The noise of the city

—distant conversations, the rattle of cartwheels, someone singing a song about ale—seemed for the moment to swell and fill all their consciousness.

Then came a rattle of keys from behind the door, and the ancient hinges groaned as the great door swung open. The man who emerged was tall, close to his sixtieth year, his face seamed and tanned by the weather, his hair limed and his long moustaches white. He wore the splendid plaids of the north, and a gold-hilted sword hung at his waist. He held himself erect, placing his feet firmly apart and holding his grizzled chin aloft. One hand hung loosely at his side; the other rested on the pommel of his sword.

There was an air of command about him. He gave Emrys the impression that he was unused to disobedience. Emrys leaned over to Cathbhad and, in an awed whisper, asked, "Is it the High King?"

"Nay," replied Cathbhad, "it is—"

But he was interrupted when the man himself spoke; and now Emrys could see that he was smiling up at his grandfather, who was smiling in return. They looked as if they had been friends long ago, whom circumstances had parted, though now the winds of the world blew them once again together.

"Rhydderch, king of Cambria!" declared this old friend of Emrys' grandfather. "So it is indeed! A long way from Dun Guinnion, and the expulsion of the Eirish invaders; then, I recall, I could count the white hairs in your beard. Now that endeavour is past hope!"

Rhydderch leaped down from his saddle and folded the other man in his embrace. "Gwilym!" he cried. "The wealth and prosperity of the gods to you!" His eyes bent downwards a fraction, and he punched his friend lightly on the stomach. "And I can see where all that wealth and prosperity is going!" he said slyly. "How have the years treated you?"

"Well, as you can see," replied Gwilym. "These have been years of wine and food. We've had trouble with the Eirish, as usual. They cannot forget the deeds of your illustrious ancestor!"

"Bran the Blessed? Aye, now there was a man." At a motion from Gwilym, stable-hands hurried forward to assist the Cambrians, who dismounted and followed Rhydderch and Gwilym through the gates and into the courtyard of Lludd's Palace. Rhydderch paused inside the gate and turned his head slowly to take in the sight. The courtyard was wide, and in many places the grass had been worn away. A wide paved path led through it and up the shallow hill to Penfran, the Great Hall, whose walls were whitewashed, and rose in mighty splendour over their heads. "And this is where they buried him," mused Rhydderch. "All those years ago, after the Assembly of Bran, this is where they brought him for burial."

"The precise place has not been found, even now," observed Gwilym, "however hard Cassivelaunos tried."

"I did not know that Cassivelaunos sought the grave of Bran," said Grwhyr, stepping up beside his father.

"He did," answered Rhydderch. "It became something of an obsession for him, after he had repelled the Romans and lost the Sword. Gwilym, this is my son, Grwhyr."

"May the gods shine a light upon your path," said Gwilym, bowing from the waist.

"And upon yours," responded Grwhyr.

"I see you beget men as mighty as yourself, Rhydderch," observed Gwilym, as they moved on towards the guest-hall. "Would that we could meet under pleasanter circumstances!"

"What news, old friend?" asked Rhydderch.

Gwilym shook his head. "The factions grow more and more estranged." Gwilym hesitated. "Be wary of the queen of Cameliard," he said.

"Cartimandua," said Rhydderch, savouring each syllable with relish. His lip was curled back from his teeth as he spoke. "She is a witch, a dealer in death. Can the council have forgotten the fate of her husband? There is no kindness in the woman—she is all bitter, all gall. She lurks like a great bat, and her eye is upon all. What foul brew is she concocting?"

But Gwilym shook his head. "Not now," he said. "Later, my friend."

They had reached the guests' quarters. It was one of seven timber-framed buildings erected against the palisade, one for each of the seven kingdoms. Emrys saw that there was already smoke snaking out of the louvre and up into the bright July sky.

136

"Well," concluded Gwilym as they reached the foot of the steps leading into the Cambrian quarters, "all will be as it must be. The gods will have their way. Enter your lodgings. Who will you see first?"

No one but one who knew him well would have discerned the discomfort that this question caused in Rhydderch. A cloud flitted across his face for a moment, and then he spoke. "Well," he said, "let us first wash the dirt of the road from our limbs and hair; then we shall see!"

"Very well." Gwilym smiled. "My heart is glad to see you again, old soldier!"

"And mine to see you; will you call upon us?"

"I shall. In one hour."

They said farewell and, as the Cambrians ascended the steps to enter their lodgings, Gwilym strode back towards Penfran.

* * *

An hour later, when Gwilym had conducted Rhydderch, Grwhyr, and a few of the Cambrian nobles to the audience chambers, Emrys left the Cambrian Lodge with the aim of finding the library.

Lludd's Palace was a grander place than any he had ever been in.

The walls, thick and strong, enclosed a grassy area about two hundred yards across. In the midst of all stood the mighty hall Penfran, the Head of Bran, with its steep-sloping gables and the watch-tower in the north-west corner. Emrys' eyes went up, past the whitewashed ground floor, past the triple-windowed upper storey, past the oaken planking of the roof to the sentry who stood at the very uppermost peak of the fortress, black against the brilliant sky. Above his head, the wind tugged at a standard bearing the emblem of a crimson serpent, its tail coiled about itself, its jaws open wide to consume its enemies.

Emrys walked a little further around the inner circumference of the walls. Above him, he could hear the warriors on the wall-walks exchanging commands in voices like aggressive guard-dogs. In the courtyard, servants and nobles crossed and re-crossed the greensward, bearing food or weapons or other burdens. Some stood in knots, conversing with earnestness, their eyes flicking away from time to time to see who was near at hand. The guest-quarters were evidently not enough to accommodate all those who had been summoned to this great council, for tents had been raised between the outer defences and the whitewashed walls of Penfran.

Emrys stood still for a moment, and gazed again at the south wall of Penfran. The lower storey was featureless, except that wide steps ran from the cobbled path up to a platform and pair of oaken doors. The door stood open, and within, Emrys could dimly see more movement, like a brightly-coloured ocean. The doors were flanked by a pair of sentinels, dressed in a similar livery to those who had met them at the main gate. They stood perfectly still; it was almost possible to believe that they were the lower third of the door-posts.

Emrys mounted the steps towards the doors of Penfran. The guards at the top looked him over assessingly and, evidently thinking him not much of a threat, declined to move as he passed through the doors and into the hall.

To Emrys, entering the hall was something like entering a holy place. The floor was wooden, and strewn with rushes and sweet-smelling herbs. It was almost entirely taken up with trestle tables, and food was spread upon them that people idly sampled as they conversed. Emrys found a table of sweetmeats and picked up one glorious-smelling confection. There was honey and cinnamon in it, and Emrys felt as if his mouth were dissolving with pleasure.

All around the walls were wooden stalls that rose half the height of the walls; wrought from dark wood, cherry perhaps, these seemed to be the apartments of the High Kings and their immediate households. Steps ran up at regular intervals to a balcony over these apartments and, from the balcony, the light from seven tall windows shone down upon the hall.

Opposite the doors was the dais, and four thrones had been set upon it, with a table and other stools for honoured guests of the High Kings and their Queens. Behind the thrones was a series of great tapestries, each one depicting the founder of one of the seven kingdoms of Britain. Emrys crossed the hall and gazed up at these tapestries.

The central tapestry depicted Brutus, Excalibur in his hands, its sheath, bright with jewels and gold thread, upon his hip. Beside him stood his queen, Imogen and, to his right, his eldest son, Locrin, after whom the kingdom of Logris had been named. There were six other tapestries flanking this one, each of them depicting one of the other kingdoms, its founder, and its Chief Treasure. There was Corineus, slayer of the giant Gogmagog and founder of Cornwall, with his daughter Gwendolyn and the Siege Perilous, the dangerous seat that gave wisdom or madness to whoever sat upon it; there also was Camber, remotely the forefather of Rhydderch and therefore of Emrys too, with the Cauldron of Garanhir; Brutus' youngest son Albanact, whose tapestry was on the edge of the group, sat astride a mighty charger, whose teeth champed fiercely upon the Bridle of Gwynn. On the other side of Brutus were the other three founding kings: Camelus held the Veil of Gold in his northern kingdom of Cameliard; Badisomagos sat listening to the Harp of Teirtu among the fens of the Summer Country; and Orkinnes, king of the northern land of Orkney, drove the Chariot of Manawydan over the waves near his island fortress.

Emrys did not move for a while, so struck with awe was he at the sight of these tapestries, for it seemed to him that all the history of the Island of the Mighty was woven into these fabrics: the glory of victory, the pain of loss, the bitterness of betrayal.

Emrys took a few steps up the dais, examining the central tapestry of them all. Brutus, grandson of Aeneas the Trojan, stood in royal splendour between the first High Queen of Britain and his eldest son. His eyes were stern, uncompromising. They bored into Emrys.

Emrys blinked. Blood. Was there blood in the tapestry, or had he imagined it? He peered at it more closely. Gouts of blood were upon the blade of Excalibur, and Brutus waded knee-deep through a vermilion tide. The sky behind him was pricked with strange stars, and all around him writhed men who were his victims, slain in their sleep, without armour, without defence. Emrys clutched at his heart, took a step backwards.

Some hands caught him, and prevented him from tumbling backwards off the dais. He balanced himself, and looked back at the tapestry. It was very different now: as it had been before, it showed Brutus in his glory, the wind tugging at the scarlet cloak, the golden circlet binding his brow, Excalibur, the sword of justice, gripped in his mighty fists. Behind him, the

139

blue skies of Britain smiled down upon strength and integrity. Then what had been the vision?

Emrys turned his head to see who had caught him as he had reeled away from his vision, and caught his breath. The circlet and the rich robes were unfamiliar to him, but the burning hair and the parted lips could belong only to the Lady of the Eicenni, Boudicea.

mrys nearly cried out loud for joy, until he remembered where he was and to whom she was married. Even so, he caught her by the hands and gave her a long, admiring look. Under the plaid cloak, she wore a long green dress—she almost always did, as the colour complemented her eyes and contrasted with her hair. The plunging neckline exposed a little of the valley between her swelling breasts, and the fabric clung tightly to her waist and thighs, accentuating the former's narrowness and the latter's curves. She held one knee slightly forward, and her toes were revealed beneath the hem. Her arms were bare, except that, just above her elbow, she wore a torc, shaped like the slender body of a serpent. At her throat, she wore another torc; it was loose, and seemed to rest upon her collar-bones.

Emrys released one of her hands and raised his own to touch her cheek. Its softness and warmth almost overmastered him. Ever so quickly, she turned her face to one side, and her lips pressed against his fingers. Then he lowered his hands to his side.

"Boudicea!" he exclaimed. "My love," he added in a whisper, "what do you here?"

"It is with my husband that I have come to this place," answered Boudicea quietly, stepping in closer to him. "Yonder stand his men."

Her head moved a fraction, and Emrys looked in the direction the movement indicated. There stood two thick-bodied men in plaid. Their shields were laid aside, but their hands were on the pommels of short swords.

"They will report to Prasutagos in full that I have been greeted by you."

"He is a jealous husband, then?"

"He is many things."

Emrys swallowed. "Are the girls here?" he asked. "I would fain see them."

"They are; you shall see them during our stay. But what do you here? I had thought to see you only at Afallach these next years."

141

"I could not stay," answered Emrys. "It's not as a druid that I shall best serve the gods, my love."

"Gwelydd is here, you know."

"I did not; where is he?" asked Emrys, looking round.

Boudicea shrugged. "Probably with one or another of the brothers."

"Boudicea," gasped Emrys, stepping closer to her. The whole substance of his body yearned to be nearer to her; his skin was tingling with anticipation. "Boudicea, will we get time—"

"Perhaps," answered Boudicea briefly. She stepped away from him, her eye flitting quickly towards her bodyguard. "But we must take care." She frowned. "If you are not here with Gwelydd, then why are you here?"

Emrys grinned apologetically. "I heard there was a library in Lundein," he said.

"There is," replied Boudicea, "but why would you want to see it?"

Emrys shrugged. "There is a matter I would settle there," he said evasively. "Do you know where it is?"

Boudicea nodded. Emrys wanted to reach up and touch her cheek, caress her slender throat; it was all he could do to restrain himself. Her full lips parted. "I can show you," she said. "But first I must cast off the eyes of my husband." Emrys glanced over at the two warriors, who were watching them with mild interest. Now Boudicea spoke quickly. "In the south-east corner of this hall is a door beneath a statue of Tylweth. Meet me there presently. And if I am delayed, be patient. A great lady is not always mistress of her own movements."

She turned, and sailed away, a mighty ship subduing the element through which she clove, her bodyguard closing in behind her. For a moment, her faint scent lingered on the air like a temptation. Then it was gone, and Emrys was alone in the crowd.

Emrys scanned the interior of Penfran. He could not see the statue of Tylweth, but he made for the corner of the hall that Boudicea had indicated and, sure enough, there it was, in an alcove above a small door. Emrys looked up at the statue, and tried to think piously about Tylweth's beauty, and the inspiration she gave to poets; but all thoughts except those of Boudicea and the lightning that had seemed to fly from her body into his had been driven from his mind.

He felt her hand upon his arm and, in a flash, they were through the door and hastening away from her husband's servants.

The passageway beyond was dark. A single window, about a dozen yards away, threw grey light into it, but there was no other illumination. Just inside the door was a torch in a bracket. Boudicea took it down, and Emrys brought out his flint and tinder. Moments later, Boudicea was stooping close to the floor. Finding a metal ring set into the ancient flagstones, she pulled, revealing a flight of steps. Descending these, they found themselves in another passage. It turned hard to the left, and in moments was descending sharply by means of a series of steps. The orange light of the torch reached out ahead of them, but they went on, and still they could not see the bottom of the steps. And yet the air was not musty, or clammy, or anything but sweet as daylight.

Then the ground leveled off, and they stood before another door.

"How do you know of this place?" asked Emrys.

"I told you," said Boudicea. "I know where the library is. But I also know my history." She pushed open the door, and together they ventured within.

They entered a cavernous space, the further wall beyond the reach of the torch's light. Boudicea held the torch a little higher, and Emrys glanced at the wall behind them. He gasped.

It looked like a great frothing waterfall, frozen as it cascaded from an irregular ceiling to the leveled floor. Spouts erupted at different levels and poured, most lifelike, down the wall. It glistened like rushing water, but there was no sound. It was shot through with vivid pinks and blues, broad striped and running the whole height of the room. Emrys took the torch away from Boudicea and held it up to get a better view of the frozen waterfall. He reached out to touch it. It was cold and hard. Rock.

"Was this carved by man's hand," Emrys asked in awe, "or did the gods fashion it so?"

"No man wrought the walls of the Caverns of Sabrina," said Boudicea. "Look further."

143

Emrys moved along the wall, holding the torch so that it revealed more and then more of the wonders of the place. Thick columns held up the fretted ceiling like pillars in a hall of men; great bubbles of stone frothed out of fissures as if it were boiling strange, multihued soup; towers of rock reached like aspiring hands towards the roof of the cavern.

And everywhere, men had adapted the natural rock formations to their own comfort. Stalactites and stalagmites in one corner formed the frame of a picture, and Emrys stood long before it in study, for it showed a man of kingly aspect, and in his hands Excalibur. At his feet was a woman of great beauty.

"That is Locrin and his mistress, Sabrina," observed Boudicea. "Gwendolyn, his queen, would never have squatted like a wretched toad at his feet."

"Toad!" said Emrys. "I think she is very beautiful."

Boudicea made a noise that sounded contemptuous.

At the further end of the hall was a natural platform of rock. The ancient architect had used this natural feature, making it into the high dais. A tapestry, showing the splendour of Troy in its prime, hung behind a throne that had been carved from a thick stalagmite.

"Do the High Kings still use this place?" asked Emrys in wonder, trailing his finger along the smooth arm of the throne.

"Not for public matters," replied Boudicea. Emrys felt her hand on his shoulder. He turned and pulled her to him. Their lips met and embraced. Emrys' free arm circled her waist and he gathered her to him, like the fruit of the field during harvest, while with the other he still held the flame aloft. The aroma of sage and rosemary emanating from her hair enveloped him in a mesmerizing cloud. His lips moved from her mouth to her neck and throat. She gasped.

Then they parted. "Not here," Boudicea advised him. "We shall find a time, later. Haven't we always?" She took his hand, and led him to the back of the dais. Parting the tapestry, she revealed an opening, and disappeared into it.

"Where does this lead to?" asked Emrys, following her into another passageway.

"The library, of course," she answered. "Didn't you want to see the library?"

She led him along another passageway. At regular intervals, just above head-height, whoever had delved these tunnels had hollowed out a small opening, from which candles at one time had illuminated the way. They were cold now, though, and Emrys and Boudicea flitted on in a pool of golden light from the torch. Once, they passed through another grotto, this one smaller than the other, and with furnishings built into the natural rock formations that revealed it to be the bedchamber of a lady. Emrys paused to look upon the chamber. A pair of maple dragons' heads writhed about the foot of the bed, and a tapestry at its head showed a dragon entwined about a sword. It was the same sword that Locrin had borne in the tapestry upstairs. Boudicea hurried him on.

"I cannot long evade my husband's guards," she urged him.

Emrys knew the story, of course. Locrin was the youngest son of Brutus, never intended to reign as High King; but his older brothers were both killed by war or treachery. When Brutus died, Locrin had attempted to cement a political alliance with Cornwall by marrying the Cornish princess, Gwendolyn. But he had never loved her. When Sabrina, the daughter of an enemy king, was captured in battle, Locrin had fallen in love with her. Gwendolyn was popular with the people and with the nobles, and Locrin could not openly flaunt his mistress, so he gave orders, and tunnels were delved deep in the earth below the White Mound. There, in a splendid subterranean palace, Sabrina dwelt in luxury and was visited frequently by her lover.

Locrin, in the meanwhile, had neglected Gwendolyn; and at length, she discovered the underground palace. Taking Excalibur one night when Locrin was away with his mistress, Gwendolyn had fled to her father's kingdom, where an army flocked to her. She and Locrin met in open battle in the Summer Country, and Locrin was overthrown and killed. Sabrina was in the host, and Gwendolyn now gave her own orders. Nearby was the swift-flowing deep-banked river that bore even to Emrys' days the name of the king's mistress who was drowned in it; and some who lived near its willow-crowded banks said that, when that season approached in which the battle had been fought, her voice could be heard sighing through the tree-tops for her royal lover, for it was said that their love, though illicit, had been true.

Boudicea had paused outside a door. It was a new one, furnished with a shiny lock and hinges. Emrys reached out to push it open, but Boudicea held up a hand, and instantly Emrys knew why she had paused. Someone was in the library.

Emrys put the torch in a bracket beside the door and knelt down to listen at the keyhole. It was a strange language he heard, and from the measured way in which the words were spoken, Emrys guessed that the speaker was reading from a book. The words had a lilting quality to them, like small waves on a seashore sheltered from the wind, and yet there was a precision to them too that was almost mathematical.

"Enough!" snapped a voice speaking Brythonic. Emrys pressed his eyes shut. In his mind's eye, he saw a face framed with long, light brown hair, a beard and moustache. A golden crown circled the temples. It did not occur to Emrys to doubt that High King Cymbeline was the speaker. "Enough," he said. "Now tell me what it means."

The man who had been reading answered in Brythonic. In Emrys' vision, he wore a flowing white garment that wrapped him from the shoulders to the ankles. He held his left hand near his chest in an odd but regal posture. His chin was clean-shaven, and the wide curls of his grey hair were flattened against his head. "This is the passion of Queen Dido," he explained. He spoke Brythonic with a thick accent, overly precise in his vowels, clipped in his consonants. "She ached with longing, says the author, a longing that her heart's blood feeds, a wound of fire that burns inward, eating her away. Hapless woman, says the author, she is like a doe hit by an arrow fired from far away, by a shepherd hunting in a Cretan forest, who does not see the mark his arrow hits, but the steel barb is fixed in her, and she may not shake it free; it clings to her side."

Emrys felt Boudicea's hand on his shoulder and, turning, he kissed her on the lips. They were warm and soft, and he kissed her again. She held a hand up to his cheek. It was like being touched by lightning.

In the library, Cymbeline said, "Enough of Dido. It is of Aeneas, the man, that I wish to hear. What does he do? Have you heard this story before, Lucius?"

"I have, dread sovereign. This is the great national story of my people. It explains who we are. And it also explains who you are—Aeneas was the grandfather of Brutus, your ancestor."

"But what did he do? Did he father many sons on Dido?"

"Your majesty must read the story yourself," replied Lucius. "But rest assured, Aeneas cannot stay with Dido. Jupiter, the king of our gods, had planned a higher destiny for him. And so Aeneas leaves her."

Emrys and Boudicea parted. Their eyes were locked, but there was a sadness in them.

"What happens to the queen?" asked Cymbeline.

"She kills herself for grief when she learns that Aeneas has deserted her. Shall I go on?"

Cymbeline did not answer at once. He was evidently thinking of something. Boudicea reached out with her hand. Emrys took it and kissed each finger in succession.

"That Aeneas," said Cymbeline, "his blood runs in my veins, as well as yours. You and I are cousins, Lucius."

"That is great Caesar's opinion also, majesty," replied Lucius.

Cymbeline gave a small sigh. "We thank you, Lucius, for the handsome gift of this book, and we shall hear it at greater length at another time. We will not, however, hear your petition here, but in council. We are only half the kingdom, and our brother too must hear what words you have to speak. Come."

A look of fear flashed into Boudicea's eyes. The two of them leaped instantly to their feet. Emrys seized the torch, and they flew away down the passageway. Finding Sabrina's bedchamber, they crouched behind the bed, extinguishing the torch as they did so.

A few moments later, they heard voices approaching. Light filled the chamber as a dozen or more men filed through, conversing as they went.

"Yes," Cymbeline was saying, "this is the old palace of Sabrina, one of the wonders of my kingdom. Your Caesar should bring his Messalina here. I am sure she would find the place interesting."

"Yes," answered Lucius, drawing his word out with what Emrys thought was some irony. "The empress finds such places interesting indeed."

Then they were gone, and Emrys and Boudicea were left in darkness.

After a moment, Emrys said, "Should we not speak of this matter to someone?"

Out of the darkness nearby came Boudicea's voice: "I don't want to wait for another moment, Emrys," she said. "I want everything. Now."

Emrys reached out and pulled her to him. His fingers felt for the clasp on her shoulder, and the dress sloughed away from her trembling shoulders.

All around them, the splendour of Sabrina's palace was hidden by the darkness. But that did not matter to them. They came together in their own palace, and it was full of light and colour.

XVIII

That night, Emrys slept not, but lay awake through all the dark watches of the night, his eyes wide, his mind on the moments he had snatched with Boudicea. Three men of Rhydderch's household sat awake until past midnight, talking politics, but Emrys had paid them no heed. Then, just before dawn, the door opened and Rhydderch and Grwhyr stepped in. They were talking in hushed tones, but Emrys could hear every word.

"Then what are we to make of it, father?" asked Grwhyr. "If the gods—"

"If the gods would not accept the sacrifice, then we must stand alone against the Eagles," said Rhydderch.

"What can we do without the aid of the gods?" There was a trace of fear in Grwhyr's voice. "If the gods do not look upon us with favour, we can do nothing. Our swords will not avail against the Romans, unless the gods stand behind us."

"Perhaps." Rhydderch paused a moment, reflecting. Then he went on: "But perhaps too this is a time for men. Perhaps this is a time to show what men can do *without* the gods."

"*Without* the gods?"

"Aye, that was my word. I said *without the gods*. What do they care for us? Sometimes they kill us for amusement, sometimes they are pleased to take what we offer, but they never seem to me to think of themselves as being under any obligation because we have made a sacrifice. Listen, my son. Listen to history. Corineus, they say, was a friend of Brutus, and the first king of Cornwall. He married Argante, one of the goddesses who dwelt in this land before the coming of men. But as time passed, the Morforwyn mingled less often with men. The divine blood is thin indeed in Cymbeline and Coroticos. We are not the children of the gods. We are not even their grandchildren. Why should they trouble themselves over us? At best, our sufferings offer them some sport."

"Do you believe this, father?" Rhydderch did not answer for a long time. At length, Grwhyr prompted him again: "Father? Is this truly your belief? You have said nothing like this before."

"This is my belief," answered Rhydderch, "and the belief of many, though they do not speak it openly. It is a journey of many years from the landing of Brutus to our stand against the Eagles of Rome. And I do not believe the gods will stand with us."

"Then is darkness and death all that is left for us?"

"Yes," replied Rhydderch curtly. "Our way of life is passing away, Grwhyr. Would you wish to live and see such a dawn?"

As if on cue, a cock crowed, and the two of them broke up their conference, leaving Emrys wondering in the darkness.

* * *

The Great Council was to be held the next day, and all the nobles of the Island of the Mighty woke early to break their fast. It was a cool day for July, white clouds forming a solid barrier overhead between the world and its lord, the sun. A damp wind had blown in from the east, along the Thames, and now whirled around between Penfran and the outer wall. A light smattering of rain promised more to come.

As he was climbing the steps into the hall, Emrys heard his name called and, turning, found himself confronted by Boudicea, ascending the steps behind him on the arm of a man who was evidently her husband. His hair was white, and bound behind his ears; his cheeks were hollow, his eyes dark. Boudicea introduced him to Emrys as Prasutagos, Lord of Eicenniawn. For a moment, Emrys was frozen, embarrassed and a little afraid; then he held out his hand; Prasutagos took it, smiling warmly as they shook.

"I had heard that you were studying in Afallach, my lord Emrys. My wife," he said, giving the words a subtle emphasis, as if underscoring the ownership of a prize possession that all men sought to own, "entertained some thought that you might dwell among the Eicenni and be our Chief Druid. But I see you wear not the robes of the acolyte. Have you abandoned your studies?"

"For the moment, I have, my lord," answered Emrys.

"For the moment?" said Prasutagos. "Good. Yes, that is good. A man should be circumspect about his life. I don't trust a man who doesn't think very carefully about what he does. But what do you propose to do in the meantime?"

Emrys' eyes flashed over to Boudicea. She was regarding him as if he were the only thing in the world. He thought of her body yesterday, united with his own in the darkness. He hoped that Prasutagos would not notice his flush, but the Lord of the Eicenni had turned aside a moment to nod a greeting to one he knew. Now he returned his attention to the young upstart before him with inquiring eyebrows and tight lips. "At the moment," Emrys told him, "I am conducting some research. Perhaps, at a future date, I shall be able to return to Afallach and complete my studies."

Prasutagos nodded and patted him on the shoulder, leading him as he did so up towards the double-doors into Penfran. "I hope so, Emrys," he said. "Britain has need of good druids. They are not so many as once they were. I remember a time, when I was a lad, when every noble family from Cornwall to the tip of Orkney sent at least one boy, occasionally a girl into the Order. Now, it is the exception, not the rule. Families are praised for sending *one* boy to Afallach! Warriors, warriors, warriors! That's what modern houses seem to want—just warriors. Who's going to make sacrifices for their victory, eh? That's what I'd like to know!" Behind his back, Emrys and Boudicea exchanged glances.

Another gust of damp wind blew rain across their heads, and Prasutagos moved them all into the narrow passageway between the gathering gloom outside and the promised warmth of the hall. A pair of sentinels were stopping people before they entered the hall and collecting weapons, which a servant in the royal livery carried through an open door in the wall to the left of the entrance. Prasutagos slid his sword out of its sheath and handed it to the guard without looking at him. Boudicea took a long knife out of her belt. Its edges curved slightly, like a woman's hips. She handed it over to the guard, who turned to Emrys as if he would bar his entrance.

"This is Emrys, grandson of Rhydderch, king of Cambria," said Boudicea; "me you know, and Emrys of Caermyrddin enters Penfran with me. Is that well?"

The guard nodded, but asked for Emrys' weapon. Emrys looked down, but found that he had left his sword behind in his lodgings. He shook his head at the guard and shrugged. They entered Penfran.

Prasutagos glanced around at the interior of Penfran, and Emrys studied him minutely. This was the man who slept beside his own love every night, who believed he had fathered the two fine girls Emrys knew were his daughters. He tried to imagine what it might be like for those rough-skinned hands to touch the soft flesh of Boudicea. Did she shrink away from his touch in the middle of the night, or did she close her eyes and think of Emrys? Emrys felt faint, and closed his eyes. When he opened them, Prasutagos was still there, prattling on to some noble from Lothian. Boudicea stood beside him, her eyes on Emrys. Emrys tried to smile, but he could not make the muscles of his face obey his command. It was as if his body rebelled against him.

Emrys looked away from Boudicea and her husband, and saw that in the midst of the hall, a round space had been cleared away. At the precise centre of this was the hearth, raised by bricks about a foot off the floor, where bright coals glowed with a steady crimson. The trestles had been pushed back to form a kind of amphitheatre, the focal point of which was the dais, surmounted by a brace of empty thrones. Even as Emrys looked, he saw a pair of figures emerge and seat themselves upon the thrones. Boudicea leaned close. "The one on the left—" she began.

"Is Cymbeline, I know," interrupted Emrys. "Do not you recall? We saw him yesterday." He cast his eyes about quickly, but Prasutagos was elsewhere.

"No," answered Boudicea, puzzled. "It was dark, they were in the library and we outside, or we were hidden. I could neither see nor hear anything but muffled sounds. How—?"

Emrys' eyebrows sprang upwards in surprise. "Boudicea," he whispered, "it was the Sight! I stood outside the door yesterday, but I could

152

see them. I could see who was speaking! My love, I used it, I used the Sight! It did not take me—I took it, and I used it!"

Boudicea looked as if she wanted to embrace him. Her hand fluttered out and brushed his, and she smiled.

"Boudicea!" She turned, hearing the voice of her husband. He was approaching them, accompanied by Gwilym, who bowed courteously to Boudicea, excused himself, and departed. Emrys followed him with his eyes.

"Come, my wife," said Prasutagos. "We must take our places."

The Eicenni, who were vassals of the High Kings directly, with no lesser king intervening, were taking their seats close to the dais. Emrys, who had lost sight of Gwilym, now watched the lord and lady of Eicenniawn from afar, as they approached their meinie. The warriors bowed before them, and Emrys watched in wonderment how erect was Boudicea's neck, how regally she inclined her head to those who paid her homage. The lord and lady of Eicenniawn sat in high-backed seats among their retinue.

It suddenly occurred to Emrys how easily power sat upon the shoulders of Boudicea's husband. The men of his retinue were like greyhounds, ready to leap at his command. And what a fool was he, Emrys of Caermyrddin, nobody in particular, to cuckold this man? What would protect him from the wrath and vengeance of the lord of the Eicenni, should he discover Emrys giving him the horns? No one would blame him, of course—queens and ladies of the lesser nobility took lovers all the time. It was a privilege of rank. But nobody expected the wronged husbands to respond indifferently upon discovery. Emrys found himself unexpectedly standing upon soft ground.

But she is mine by right, he thought. She chose me. We were raised together from our earliest days.

And now he looked at her anew, and saw not Boudi, the little girl he had run and played with years ago in the courtyard of Caermyrddin, but Boudicea, the stern Lady of Eicenniawn, riding a towering chariot, with serried ranks of warriors at her back. Making love to her was a perilous privilege.

Boudicea was looking directly at him. As he watched, she leaned towards her husband and whispered something to him. Prasutagos nodded, lifted a hand, and crooked a finger at Emrys. Emrys followed the prompt, and went to stand among the Eicenni.

"My wife has reminded me," said Prasutagos, "that you stand in Penfran by our invitation; it is meet, therefore, that you sit among my retinue. Unless you would rather join the delegation from Afallach, or from Cambria?"

Across the hall, Emrys could see his grandfather and Grwhyr taking their seats on the front row. They were talking earnestly to Gwilym. He wondered what his grandfather would say if he knew he were in the hall.

"It is my honour to sit among the Eicenni," returned Emrys, and a warrior shuffled along the trestle behind the thrones to make room for him.

Emrys ran his eyes around the crowd gathering on the edges of the council circle. Here indeed were all the nobles of Britain! It occurred to Emrys, suddenly, that if the Romans were of a mind to do such a thing, they could set fire to Penfran and destroy the entire ruling estate of the realm in one fell action. Then he wondered who had been left behind in the seven kingdoms? Who was ruling in their stead, while the seven kings of the Island of the Mighty contended in Lundein?

He noticed Gwilym, who had moved away from Rhydderch, and was talking to one who sat upon a throne, dressed in the plaids of Cameliard. It was a woman, who had once been beautiful, though now her face was leathery, harsh, with a strong jaw and a hooked nose. With a chill he could not readily explain, Emrys realized that this was Cartimandua, Queen of Cameliard, Cartimandua whose name was spoken in whispers after nightfall.

What was Gwilym saying to her? Emrys was possessed suddenly with an insatiable curiosity. All at once, he saw not the nobles gathered around the council circle, but a great coiled dragon. Emrys gasped, for the vision was a powerful one, and it took all his effort not to cry out and tell others what he was seeing. The scales shone in the torchlight, massive muscles slid one over another beneath the brazen hide, and there, not on the dais, was the head: Gwilym was the eyes, the tongue, the teeth, the fiery breath of the dragon. Emrys blinked, and the vision was gone. As he watched, Gwilym left Cartimandua and went on to consult with another of the nobles of the Island of the Mighty.

Emrys looked away from Gwilym at the High Kings, seated upon the dais. Neither spoke. Cymbeline was eating from a silver platter on a small table beside his throne. Coroticos was smoothing the feathers of a hawk that sat on a perch beside him. Neither seemed much intent on matters of state. Emrys looked back, trying to find Gwilym again. It took him a few moments, for Gwilym was weaving in and out of the meinie from Lothian, exchanging comments here and there, taking a flagon to fill the wine-cup of the king. Emrys nodded sagely to himself. There, he thought, was the real power in Britain.

Emrys grew bored. He turned his face a little, so that he could secretly admire Boudicea whilst appearing to look at the council circle. His eyes lingered over the flawless profile of her face, the graceful curves of her body. She turned. Their eyes met and locked for a moment, but then Prasutagos made some comment, and she looked back at her husband.

Emrys shifted uncomfortably, remembering the soft warmth of her body folding about him in the darkness of Sabrina's Palace yesterday. That was what he wanted again, now, more than anything else, more even than he wanted Excalibur. No price was too high to return again to her embrace. And then he thought of the other occasions: a moment snatched in an empty chamber of his grandfather's fortress in Caermyrddin, the glory under the golden leaves of Afallach's autumn. What price could he pay? What currency was proper tender? Her face was turned away from him, but he could see the round shape of her shoulder under the Eicenni plaids, the curved line of her jaw and cheek, the cascade of ruddy hair down her back. The scent of rosemary and sage filled his memory as he thought of the day before, of their naked bodies locked in an embrace that sought to make of the two of them one entity. Emrys' eyelids pressed together as he remembered.

Whatever the price, O you gods, Emrys prayed silently, whatever the cost to me, I want Boudicea for my wife.

And it seemed to him that an image formed in the darkness behind his eyelids. It was the image of a woman's face. It was not Boudicea's; nor was it Morgana's. The face filled him with joy and dread at once, for it was a beautiful face, beautiful past mortal comprehension, but it looked sternly at him, as if it would chide him for his prayer.

155

A sharp noise made Emrys flinch. His eyes snapped open. It was as if cold water had been poured down his back. The vision drained away, like fine sand through a sieve. Slowly, the sounds and scents of Penfran returned, as if through a long tunnel.

Gwelydd, Archdruid of the Island of the Mighty, had risen from his seat on the dais, and had struck the stone floor for silence. The Great Council had begun.

XIX

Gwelydd adjusted his druid's robes, planted his oaken staff upon the ground in the decisive way Emrys had seen him do it in Afallach, surveyed the gathered nobility of the Island of the Mighty, and spoke to them in sonorous tones.

"Men and women of Britain," said the voice Emrys knew so well; he felt that, if he closed his eyes, he could imagine himself beneath the blossoms of Afallach once more. "Warriors and defenders of the Island of the Mighty, welcome you are to Penfran, hall of the High Kings in Lludd's Palace. You all know why we are here. Almost a hundred years ago now, High King Cassivelaunos swore to pay a yearly tribute to Rome. Emissaries are here already from Claudius, the great-grandson of Emperor Julius, demanding the renewal of the tribute. Do we pay that tribute, my friends, or do we defy Rome?"

Gwelydd returned to his seat. There was a moment's silence. Coroticos' eyes flickered for a moment, then he rose from his throne and descended the floor. Frowning, Emrys ran his eye over in the direction Coroticos had looked. Gwilym was there, his face impassive, sitting beside Cartimandua. Coroticos, meanwhile, had reached the central hearth. His fist was clenched, and he pounded the palm of his other hand to emphasize the point he was making.

"We already know," he said, "what the Romans want. This needs no debate. Nor is there any question as to who should be High King: I am king by right of our laws, Britonnic laws, not the law of some foreigner!"

Cymbeline was on his feet, red in the face, gesticulating wildly at his brother. But his words were lost, for the crowd had risen in an uproar at Coroticos' words, some jeering, some shouting their support. Gwelydd rose from his seat and struck the stone floor with his staff three times. The hubbub subsided.

"Let us choose one king!" cried someone; Emrys' eyes swept across the crowd to see who had spoken. But before he could locate him, another had risen from his seat, and was saying, "This is well spoken! How can we face Rome, divided against ourselves? Let us choose a High King, and then debate what we shall reply to Rome's ambassadors."

"Coroticos!" shouted a well-wisher. "Long live High King Coroticos!"

Immediately, noise swelled up from the crowd like the sea churned up by a tempest. "Coroticos!" cried some of the nobles. "Cymbeline!" cried others. Gwelydd was on his feet again, striking the floor with his staff, but he went unheeded for long moments. Coroticos and Cymbeline were facing each other in the open space before the dais, their faces inches apart, screaming into each other's faces. Coroticos' hand flew to his sword, and instantly half a dozen supporters jumped up to restrain him and his brother. Cymbeline shook off the men who were holding him, spat upon the ground at his brother's feet, and climbed the steps back up the dais. He held out his hands for silence.

"My friends!" he cried. Slowly, the noise lessened until it was no more than an angry buzz. "My friends," he repeated, "let us debate this issue like men of reason, with our hands upon our hearts, not upon our swords." Emrys thought about the guards on the door who had taken everybody's weapons. Something flashed in Boudicea's hand, and Emrys saw the short, keen blade of a hunting knife. Where, he wondered, had she hidden that? Prasutagos too was armed and, turning his eye this way and that, Emrys observed that hardly a hand in the hall was empty; nearly all held weapons.

Emrys caught his breath. He looked away from the council floor, between his knees. He felt light-headed, as if he had drunk too much. The image of the dragon came again into his head. Its head was curled round, and it was gnawing at its own entrails.

"Reason!" came Coroticos' voice. Emrys focused on him, and the vision faded like a dream. "There is little for reason to choose, for our choice is simple. The question is, do you, the valiant nobles of the Island of the Mighty, want to be free men, free to harvest your own grain and hunt your own boars, free to fly your own hawks in your own forests, or do you want to be vassals to a stammering fool, just because he wears the purple in a distant city?"

Cymbeline leaped down from the dais and all but shouldered his brother aside. "My brother speaks in ignorance!" he cried. "Emperor Claudius is a scholar. He has written histories. He is a man of reason. He will deal justly with us."

"Is this the message you wish to send back with these envoys from Rome?" demanded Coroticos. "Is this the message you will send to the Emperor who sits on his marble throne in Rome and broods on what peoples and lands far away he can enslave next? *Deal justly with us, mighty emperor, for we fear your greatness.* Will you crawl to him, base knaves, or will you stand before him and say, *I am a free Briton, like my father and my grandfathers before me, and I shall never submit to the yoke of another chieftain?*"

With a swirl of plaids, he resumed his seat amid great applause. A moment later, Gwelydd stood before the nobles of Britain. He did not speak at once, but surveyed the crowd, abiding their silence. He caught Emrys' eye, and Emrys thought there was a brief smile at the sight. Then he spoke.

"We have heard from Coroticos, may the gods bless a long life in him," said he. "But our choice is not so simple as it appears to be. We choose also between war and peace. Cymbeline's way is the way of peace and conciliation; Coroticos' that of war and vigilance. That is a difficult choice."

"What peace can there be under Rome's shadow?" asked a voice in the crowd.

"None!" returned Coroticos, rising from his throne. Cymbeline rose too and, once again, they faced each other, inches away, purple-complexioned.

"Let the Archdruid speak!" cried a voice; it was joined by another echoing his sentiment, and gradually, the uproar died.

Gwelydd did not speak at once, but held his hands out reflectively to the fire. "Cassivelaunos too challenged the Eagles," he reminisced, in an almost conversational tone, "and now they are back, wanting more. If we challenge them now, perhaps we shall, like Cassivelaunos, beat them now; but we cannot pursue them to Rome. We cannot wipe them out. They will come back, and we may never be free of their gaze again." Now he turned his back to the fire and paced forward so that his face was almost touching the faces of those in the front row. "The most important question we have to answer is, *can* we stand before Rome? The Eagles have proved themselves again and again. Our fathers knew Vercingetorix of Gaul. He was a proud man, and a mighty king of men. But he laid his sword at Caesar's feet. Gaul has fallen to Rome, and Germany, and lands more distant than those, Iberia, Egypt, Asia. The world bows before the Eagles."

"Death!" cried someone from Cartimandua's party. "Let us seek death before slavery! What counsel is this?"

"The counsel of a craven heart," answered Coroticos.

"The counsel of wisdom!" declared Gwelydd, and this time, when he struck the floor with his staff, it seemed that the voice of thunder spoke from above them, and would split the hall in twain. Gwelydd spun upon the crowds, and there was wrath in his eyes, imprinted upon his lips. "Do not cast away the wisdom of Afallach!" he boomed. "It is not given lightly!"

He ceased, and returned to the fire, and Emrys could see the tension in his shoulders, even through his robes. After a moment, he turned and spoke more thoughtfully. "Perhaps it is the gods' will," he suggested. "Perhaps we do ill to resist the wills of the gods. I grow old, and in my age, I should like to taste the fruits of peace, not the gall of war. I say, sue for peace. Let us pay the tribute now, and trade with Rome. Let us send ambassadors to Rome and learn from them, and one day, we shall be Rome's equal, and the Island of the Mighty will again rule an empire upon which the gods will smile!"

More thunderous applause accompanied Gwelydd's return to his seat. Cartimandua and Gwilym exchanged glances a moment, then Cartimandua hobbled to the centre of the floor. She stood for a moment without speaking, supporting herself with a stick, and her beady eye scanned the assembly, as Gwelydd's had done.

"Cartimandua!" a low voice from nearby Emrys said, as if the word meant *witch*. And the name was picked up, like a word of horror and dread, dredged up from the dark times before the gods brought form to the world: "Cartimandua! Cartimandua!"

"This is great wisdom that Gwelydd Archdruid speaks," Cartimandua said in a reedy voice. "He does well to remind us of the wills of the gods. I wonder, my lords and my ladies, kings and queens and nobles of the Island

160

of the Mighty, how much of his fear derives from the rumour that the Roman gods are mightier than ours?"

There was a deep rumbling of discontent at this remark, and Cartimandua held up her free hand for silence. "Let us admit it freely. Many of us quail because, it is said, these Caesars are gods. Julius is a god, and Augustus, his son, and Livia, Augustus' wife. What man can prevail when he contends with the gods? It is wise to heed such fears!" There were shouts of assent from the crowd. Cartimandua paused.

"Gods?" she asked at last. "When Julius came here, he walked upon the ground, as I do. Am *I* a goddess?" There was some laughter around the room at this. "Perhaps I *was* a goddess, when I was younger. Perhaps even the gods grow old!

"These gods of the Romans grow old too. They grow so old that they can die. Julius died, killed by his own best friend, and Augustus died, and Livia too. How then are they gods? Can a god be stabbed to death by a mortal? Pah! They are gods because their Senate voted them gods. The Senate and the people of Rome decreed that their emperors and their empress would be gods. And what kind of god would the people make? No greater than themselves, I reckon. These men, I think, are but men. They eat, they sleep, like us." She paused, and added reflectively, "They shit, as other men do." Laughter broke out in various places throughout the hall, but subsided quickly, and there were uneasy glances about the hall. Cartimandua had breached a taboo, but she had also made a joke, and no one, not the fiercest warrior present, wanted to challenge her.

Cartimandua went on: "Why then cannot they be defeated, as other men are? Compare these men to our Britons. The line of our High Kings is descended from Brutus, that Brutus derived his bloodline from the pious Aeneas, and that Aeneas was descended from Anchises and the goddess Aphrodite, whom the Romans call Venus. Our kings are nobly derived, then. Who voted to make Aphrodite a goddess? Not the Senate and the people of Rome. She was a goddess in the elder days, ere men could talk or vote. She is one of the Undying Ones. And her blood lives in the veins of our High Kings.

"Britons, I say, arise and fight! Vanquish Rome by the nobility of your blood and the might of your arms! Do not make our gods the slaves of the Senate and the people of Rome, as their gods are. Let us show them what power is in the gods of the Island of the Mighty!"

Cartimandua resumed her seat. Cymbeline was on his feet now, circling the fire like a predator watching his prey. Emrys watched Cartimandua. Beside her sat Gwilym, who looked for a moment at Cymbeline, then leaned over towards one of his retinue, whispering a message. The retainer rose, and walked through the crowds towards Rhydderch, leaned close, and whispered in his ear.

Emrys frowned. Could there be a conspiracy between his grandfather and Cameliard? For a moment, the vision of the dragon returned, and the hall seemed filled with its sulphurous stench. Then the vision was gone. But Gwilym's eye glinted. For a moment, it seemed to Emrys that his eye was golden, and divided in two by a slit of a pupil. Then the vision faded entirely, and Cymbeline had begun to speak.

"Smooth are the words of Queen Cartimandua of Cameliard," he said, purring. "Smooth and sweet. Most persuasively has she argued for war. And she is right." Cymbeline paused; this was unexpected, and he wanted to let the impact of his words be fully felt. Gwilym looked momentarily confused. "She is right," he repeated, when the buzz had died down. "Britain is a mighty kingdom, with noble kings supported by warriors of proven mettle, whose worth on the field of battle has been seen times beyond number.

"But Britain is more than a nation of warriors. Britain is an island beloved of the gods, where peace dwells, and art and poetry flourish, where smiths make fine torcs out of gold, as well as swords out of iron. We love good wine and ale, and good company and, though we fear not to smite our enemies, we had rather sit about the fire and tell stories of our kings and great heroes. There is much we can learn from these Romans—how to build roads, and palaces that touch the skies. There is much we can trade with these Romans—Cornish tin for Gaulish wine, our knowledge of the ways of the oak for their philosophy. My ancestors, Belin and Brennios, went to Rome, and made the Eagles bow to them. I say, let us go to Rome, but not as Belin and Brennios did—in peace, not in war. Let us ride our chariots along the roads, swifter than we can ride across the heath or along the drovers' paths that we know in this realm. I say, let us learn from these Romans. The tribute is a small price for the knowledge that we can gain from them. Let the Dragon learn from the Eagle, and our descendants will thank us for half a thousand years and more!"

Cymbeline finished. Emrys looked about him. He saw a number of heads nodding sagely at the High King's words. When he looked again, Cymbeline had returned to his throne, and Rhydderch was taking the floor.

"Sure, we thank his Majesty for his wise words," said Rhydderch. "Old do I wax, and little do I know of politicians and diplomacy. But when I was a boy, I too listened to the old tales, and something I know of them." Laughter ran around the council hall like a rill of running water through a high pasture.

"I know, as his Majesty does," Rhydderch went on, "of the other twins who ruled this mighty nation. I know of Belin and Brennios. They went to Rome bearing no olive branch, but swords and spears. In those times, too, Rome threatened these shores, and the brothers led an army and marched upon Rome. They were victorious." There was a rumbling of assent from the nobles, and Rhydderch warmed his hands at the council fire and let the rumble continue a moment before stilling it and continuing.

"I know, second," he said, "that when Caesar bent the knee of the world to him a hundred years ago, he could not subdue Britain, nor her High King, Cassivelaunos." A cheer went up from the crowd, but now Rhydderch did not pause, but plunged on with his speech.

"The past tells us what can happen now, and what may befall us in days to come, and I say, *Heed the past!* Rome spreads her wings over the whole world, but the shadow of its pinions need not fall upon the Island of the Mighty. I say, Britons, arise! Arm yourselves! Set your mighty arms and thews against these younglings! You are men of an ancient and dauntless nation. Resist those who would reduce you to dependent children. Refuse their demand for tribute and, if they dare to invade, cast them back into the sea. And when you have done that, follow them back to Rome, as Belin and

Brennios did many, many years ago, and take this stammering, drooling idiot of an emperor and smite off his pompous head. I have done!"

Rhydderch finished, and the hall was suddenly in an uproar. The nobles of Britain were upon their feet, and the din rose to the rafters. Emrys was shocked, for this was an aspect of Rhydderch's character that he had not suspected ere now. Emrys saw the ghost of a smile drift across his grandfather's lips, and then he returned to his seat. As he sat down, he saw him catch Gwilym's eye. Gwilym gave a slight, almost imperceptible nod. His eyes flashed, and Emrys thought he saw his pupils as serpentine slits in the gold once more.

Coroticos was on his feet again, his hand held up to still the noise. "Call the Roman ambassadors before us!" he cried, and the doors were thrown open.

XX

The ambassadors from Rome entered the hall. There were half a dozen of them, in the white robes Emrys had heard referred to as togas. One of them—he recognized Lucius—wore purple. A pair of them were soldiers, with gleaming breastplates and high plumed helmets. They strode through the hall, looking neither right nor left, and bowed before the dais. Lucius took a scroll of parchment from a leather case, flattened it out, and declaimed the words in a stentorian voice.

"Tiberius Claudius Drusus Nero Germanicus Caesar, by the Senate and the people of Rome Emperor, sends greetings to Cymbeline and Coroticos, of the house of Brutus, High Kings of the province of Britannia. He wishes to remind them of the tribute owed yearly to Rome, agreed between Julius, emperor and god, and Cassivelaunos, High King of Britannia. This tribute has been much neglected of late. Caesar wishes you to resume payment of the tribute, with arrears back to ten years, or else face the consequences."

There was silence in Penfran. The sound of a foot shifting echoed. Emrys' breath seemed loud in his ears. But again, he was feeling faint. Something seemed to be pressing on the sides of his head, like a gigantic vice. His hand reached out to the planking of the trestle, in an attempt to hold firm.

"What consequences, Gaius Lucius Ventidius?" asked Coroticos in a self-possessed voice.

Lucius dropped his hand, and the parchment snapped closed around his fingers. "Such matters are beyond the epistle I bear," he said. "And yet I am instructed by the Emperor to tell you that, if you refuse, he shall come with the legions and take it from you by force. These are the words of the Emperor."

Emrys' hand fluttered to his eyes. A grey film seemed to have risen between him and the world. His breathing was shallow, and he felt as if some force were plucking, gently but insistently, at his throat. The words of

Coroticos, raised in anger, came to him nevertheless as if down a long tunnel.

"We understand this well!" Coroticos cried out. "And we understand a great many things. The days of Rome's greatness are over. Julius, whom you call a god, was not able to take these islands from Cassivelaunos, for all his attempts. Not Augustus, nor Tiberius, nor Caligula even tried. And now the stammering fool whom you foolishly fashioned emperor has the effrontery to challenge the Island of the Mighty! Go back whence you came, and tell this historian, this theoretician, to go back to his books. Let him write his histories, for he will make none here, and if he comes to this island, even with the legions at his back, he shall find here an answer he shall not want to set down in one of his books!"

Emrys looked up. Coroticos was no longer himself, but the head of a great serpent, its scales as white as alabaster, its tongue flickering out at the eagle that confronted it. Another dragon, identical to the first, watched him from a distance.

Emrys shot to his feet, and cried out in a loud voice. All eyes in Penfran turned to him. Amazement, shock, deep embarrassment, shame: Emrys could read all this in their eyes, but do nothing to stop himself. The last thing he saw was Boudicea's eyes, and he read there fear and pity. Then a black veil came down between him and the world, and he knew no more.

* * *

He heard sounds before he saw aught: voices, distant and incoherent, like sounds heard underwater. He put a hand in front of him, as if he would swim up through the darkness towards the voices, but felt something or someone restrain him. He began to wonder if he was going to drown, though he was surprised to find that his heart was quite calm about this prospect.

The darkness melted away, and he found himself in a small room. The walls were hung with tapestries. There was an open window, through which he could see grey sky and hear a constant drizzle. He was reclining upon a bed, beside which was set a brazier. His shoulder felt very warm, but the rest of him tingled with an exciting coldness.

"He is returning to us," said a voice he knew—Boudicea's. Her face came into his view. It was followed, moments later, by her husband's and, surprisingly, Rhydderch's.

"Do not move," urged Boudicea.

"Boudicea," whispered Emrys. He frowned. "Why am I here?"

"We brought you here after . . . " She let the sentence trail away to nothing. She evidently did not know how to describe what had happened.

"After you made a fool of me and of all Cambrians." Rhydderch knew indeed how to describe the incident. "Damn fool boy! How you got into Penfran I'll never know. I don't even know why you came to Lundein with us, or why we let you. You should not be here."

"Who knows what moves a person like Emrys to be in one place or another," said another familiar voice—it belonged to Gwelydd. "It is not beyond credibility that the gods brought him here."

"Then the gods should have kept him out of the Council Chamber. He should have stayed outside the city. He should have stayed with his mother —it's what he's fittest for."

"I think that's going too far, Rhydderch, my friend." To Emrys' surprise, it was Prasutagos who spoke now in his defence. "I have seen little of your grandson, but I think he is fit for Afallach, for the druids. He may be a Seeing One."

"Seeing One? Faugh! He is an imbecile! How I have striven to forge an alliance with the High King, how I have striven to make the name of Cambria what it is! And to have it trampled in the mire now, on account of the rantings of an idiot boy! It is more than patience can bear!"

"Rhydderch of Cambria, still your tongue!" cried Gwelydd. "Whatever else he may be, your grandson is of your blood. And if he is indeed a Seeing One, his counsel will be worth far more than some petty alliances you have forged with your second-rate friends!"

Rhydderch was taken aback by Gwelydd's onslaught for a moment. Then he looked down at Emrys. There was something different in his eyes —was it fear? wondered Emrys.

Emrys struggled up onto his elbows. "I have never aimed to offend you, grandfather," he said. "But I cannot be other than I am."

Rhydderch said nothing. Then, ending the awkward silence, Gwelydd came forward. He had doffed his grand robes, and was clad simply in his white tunic. The hood was spread over his shoulders. He still carried his oaken staff. Two strides brought him to the side of Emrys' bed. Emrys looked up into his face. There was sternness in it. The features were hard, the lips pressed together. But behind the sternness, there was a gleam, a dancing light in the eyes.

"Emrys," he said, "what can you tell me about the words you uttered before the Great Council just now?"

Emrys pressed his eyes together, and thrust his mind backwards. He remembered the Romans, in red and white and violet, clustered before the dais, and Coroticos springing from his throne, his face contorted with wrath. Coroticos had the head of a serpent, Cymbeline another, and Romans were eagles. In his memory, the eagles seemed huge, the dragons tiny and quailing before the open beaks.

"I remember nothing," Emrys said. "I had a vision, a vision of two dragons and an eagle, but then all went dark, and I remember no more."

"Let me remind you of some of the things you uttered," said Gwelydd. "There were plenty of witnesses, and I have sifted the evidence of those who have the best memories. You said, 'The eagles fly on swift wing across the water, stooping upon all they see. But the dragons fight each other. From one another's throats they are plucked.'"

"That is obvious," said Emrys, sitting upright in the bed. "The eagles are Rome, the dragons are Cymbeline and Coroticos. They are so bent on fighting with each other, that the Romans will easily defeat them."

"That is as I thought," replied Gwelydd. "The rest seemed to be in an alien tongue, except that you said also, 'The she-wolf stands before the stag, but the eagle will bring them both down.' Can you explain that?"

Emrys thought hard. He caught sight of Boudicea, out of the corner of his eye. The she-wolf! Suddenly, he knew, and pain clutched at his heart. He fell backwards upon the bed. "I know nothing," he said, between clenched teeth.

168

"Think, Emrys," implored Gwelydd. "Who or what is the she-wolf? Who or what is the stag? Does the stag represent the druids?"

"Perhaps," said Emrys, though there was no doubt in his mind.

Gwelydd's face was working to restrain his passion. He looked away for a moment, and when he turned his face again towards Emrys, it was impassive once more. "Last of all," he said, "who is the hanged man?"

"The hanged man?"

"Yes. You talked of blood, and a man who is scourged and hanged and pierced with a spear."

"A triple death," said Emrys. Suddenly, he was calm. This seemed to him the most important of the prophecies he had uttered, but he knew not why. Quietly, he said, "The stag and the eagle will prostrate themselves before the hanged man."

"You remember!" whispered Gwelydd. "Go on."

"I remember nothing," said Emrys. "What did I say?"

"That the stag and the eagle will prostrate themselves before the hanged man." Gwelydd gave Emrys a moment to respond, but he did not. "Emrys, think. The god Lleu Llaw Gyffes died such a triple death. He was drowned, pierced by a spear, and hung upon a tree for three days, and then transformed into an eagle. Will the god Lleu fight for us against the Romans? Is that what your prophecy means?"

"Perhaps," replied Emrys miserably, though he was certain that that was not the proper explanation.

Rhydderch gave a contemptuous snort. "This witless boy knows nothing," he said. "He speaks in riddles because his mind is a mystery even unto himself. Why, he knows not even whose child he is!"

Rhydderch stomped from the room, the door crashing shut behind him. Prasutagos stayed a moment, peering with curiosity into Emrys' face.

"You should perhaps return to Afallach, boy," he said. "You might learn to know the ways of such things. A prophet is no use if he cannot interpret between the gods and the world." And he too left.

Silence hung in the room like a pall upon a bier. But at the last, Gwelydd spoke. "You will be glad to know," he said, "that some good has come of your words. A single High King has been chosen, though the choice goes against my will."

"Coroticos?"

"Even he." Gwelydd put a hand on Emrys' arm and gave it a comforting squeeze. "Rest," he said, "and give no thought to your grandfather's hasty words."

"You're not going to tell me that he really loves me, are you?"

"No," answered Gwelydd. "I don't think he does. But he is a great man nevertheless, and his greatness will be tried soon upon the field of battle. That is where he excels, not in loving his family."

"As usual, my friend, your words bring little comfort."

"The best of friends," answered Gwelydd, "bring truth, not comfort. Rest you well."

When Gwelydd was gone, Emrys was left alone with Boudicea, and she moved closer to the bedside.

"Who is the she-wolf, Emrys?" she asked.

"Such things are dark to me," answered Emrys slowly, refusing to meet her eyes. "I know nothing. My grandfather is right." And suddenly, tears that had been long suppressed came welling out of his eyes like an overflowing cistern, and he clutched Boudicea to him. "What is happening to me, Boudi?" he asked. "Why cannot I interpret these words? Why do I speak them? Why cannot I recall what I said? Was it even I who spoke? Boudicea, what am I to do?"

Boudicea plied kisses upon his forehead and the crown of his head. "Think nothing," she said. "Love me." She reached down and kissed him on the lips. It was long ere they parted.

"Let us run away," said Emrys. "Let us leave all these people behind. You can abandon your husband, I my grandfather. We can run anywhere—Orkney, Lyonesse, somewhere far away from war, and far away from politics, and far away from people who hate us. Let us live alone and together, as man and wife."

Boudicea held him at arm's length and stared into his eyes, a slight frown creasing her radiant brow. "Is this what you want?" she asked.

"Yes, more than anything!" cried Emrys. "I want you—I want your body, and your mind, and your soul. I want them all mine! I have never loved another woman, and never will. I want to possess you, and I want you to possess me wholly." He paused, reading her expression a little more deeply. "Is not this what you want also?" he asked.

Boudicea lowered her hands from his arms and turned a little away from him. Her profile was troubled.

"Is that not what you want, Boudicea?" asked Emrys. "Do you not want us to love one another, properly, as man and woman should do?"

"Yes." Boudicea looked back at Emrys. "Yes, I want that. But I want more than that. I want you to be my lover, Emrys, but I want you to be lord of my people also. And I want that because I don't think I could give up being sovereign of my people." She took up his hand once more. "I don't want to live far away from politics and war, Emrys, my love," she said. "I want to be right in the midst of all that. I want your love, but I want also to be a queen. I want the bards of future generations to sing of me in mead-halls, long after my grave is forgotten. Who would not want that?"

"Me," answered Emrys. "I do not want that, my queen and my love."

Boudicea leaned close, and kissed him softly on the lips once more. "My own dear one," she said, "we shall only be apart while my husband lives. But Prasutagos grows old. When he is dead, come to me, and join with me, and be my king." She got to her feet.

"Will you go now?" asked Emrys.

"I must," she replied. "The Great Council is disbanding. The Roman ambassadors went back to Gaul like whipped curs. Coroticos has given orders to all the under-kings to raise armies to throw against the Eagles when they return. The times of peace are over, Emrys. War sits on every hill, on every wall of this island. And I shall march with the armies, and I shall fight beside the High King."

"You?"

"And why should I not? I shall ride in my chariot, beautiful and terrible, and my people's hearts will grow greater because their lady rides with them, and the Romans will know fear in their hearts, for they like not to fight against women."

"And I?" wondered Emrys. "What shall I do?"

"Ride with us," urged Boudicea.

"No," decided Emrys. "All battle is vain until Excalibur is found. I must go to Caer Lloyw, and continue my search for the sword of kings."

"Then success be with you, Emrys of the prophetic voice," said Boudicea.

"And victory with you," replied Emrys; and once more they kissed and parted.

XXI

Caer Lloyw was built, a collection of wooden buildings bounded by a timber stockade, on the eastern bank of the River Sabrina. When Emrys came upon it, in the late afternoon of a day in mid-August, a breeze was blowing up the river valley from the sea, tugging at the smoke trails that rose from its smithies and bakeries, bringing with it the cleansing smell of the sea. Emrys touched his horse's flanks with his heels, and the hedgerows intervened between him and his goal.

The first thing Emrys did upon entering Caer Lloyw was to sell his horse, and he strode from the stable with coins in his purse, enough for a few weeks' lodging. But it would not be enough, he knew, to last long, and so he frequented the dark taverns of Caer Lloyw at nights, and sang songs that he invented at the promptings of his muse. And his stock of silver coins dwindled but slowly, while he spent his days searching the countryside for signs of Celliwig and the *Prydwen*.

One day, Emrys had wandered further than usual, and he sat upon some sandstone cliffs looking across the Sabrina to the coast of Cambria while he broke a small loaf of bread and guzzled water from a skin. The wind tugged his hair and the gulls overhead tipped their wings to swing over the estuary below. It was one of those moments: Emrys felt happy to be alive.

Down below, crawling over the dazzling blue of the estuary, Emrys caught sight of a triumvirate of fishing boats, returning with labour from their work. Emrys got to his feet and peered down the cliff. There, nestling against the foot of the cliff, was a tiny collection of huts—the village to which the fishermen were returning. Emrys regarded the fishing village thoughtfully for a few moments.

When he had finished his repast, Emrys found a way down the cliff, and scrambled through the wiry grass and great pools of purple sea-lavender. The sound of the waves breaking on the sandy shore grew louder as he descended, until it seemed to keep time with the beat of his heart. At length, he stood upon the beach even as the fishing boats put in.

Villagers rushed to help the fishermen unload their catch, and Emrys rushed with them. He heaved on the prow of one of the boats, until it rested high above the tide line, and then he helped unload the catch into the carts that would take them to market the next day. Afterwards, he sat among them, men and women together, and helped them mend the nets. He found his fingers able to the task, and he worked speedily.

"Who are you?" asked one of the fishermen.

"My name is Emrys," he answered. "I am a traveler, and new to these parts. My home is Caermyrddin, across the estuary in Cambria."

"It's far you are from home. What seek you in these parts?"

"I am a singer," answered Emrys, "and a teller of tales. I seek a roof over my head, and food in my belly. That is all—my needs are simple."

The fisherman did not answer at once. But at length, he said, "Tell us a tale as we mend our nets and the sun sinks over our day's labour."

Emrys thought for a few moments, and then he began to tell them stories. He told them stories about beautiful maidens of the sea who loved poor fishermen and led them to undersea kingdoms, and stories about the demons who live beneath the waves and lure unwary sailors to their deaths. He told them stories that made them laugh, or cry, or which froze the blood in their veins. And while he told them stories, they finished mending their nets, and built fires upon the beach, and roasted some of the fish they had caught upon the fires, and shared them with Emrys. After they had performed rites to Manawydan, the sea-god, a cask of ale was broached, and there was wrestling on the beach. Emrys did not take part, but he watched as the fisherman he had spoken to overcame one after another of the fishermen. He was twice the age of most of his opponents, but he bore them down relentlessly, bellowing with laughter as he did so. Some of the men set up a pair of sticks with a cross-bar, and then vaulted over it, adjusting the height each time to increase the difficulty. Emrys took part in the vaulting competition, and won it amid thunderous applause and hearty thumpings upon his back. Then one of the fishermen took out a fiddle, another a pipe, and they danced upon the sands beneath the stars while the surf rolled with a whispering voice up the beach.

"It's well you know the tales of the sea," observed a young woman, sitting near Emrys. She had a pretty face, Emrys reflected. She had drawn her knees up under her chin, and circled her arms about them, and her arms in the golden light from the fire were strong. "Why did you leave the net and the fish-hook for the harp and the tabor?"

"I did not leave the sea," replied Emrys, coming to sit closer to her. "My father was not a fisherman, nor even a mariner."

The young woman raised her eyebrows. "Then it's twice I am amazed by you, for your knowledge of the sea is as one who has spent much time upon it."

"I thank you," replied Emrys. "I seek only to utter truth."

For a long time, they each stared into the flickering flames of the fire. Then the woman said, "I am Gwyden; what name shall I call you?"

"I am Emrys, from Caermyrddin in Cambria."

"Welcome to Habren, Emrys of Caermyrddin," said Gwyden. She picked up a stick and poked at the embers of the fire with it. A few sticks dislodged, sending up sparks into the dark night, and the flames leaped a little higher. "Does your father live?" she asked.

Emrys hesitated. He looked out to sea. He could hear it rolling up the beach, but it was as black as ink, and invisible in the night. "I did not know my father. My mother lives."

"I am sorry," said Gwyden. Then she asked, "Is there a woman in your life?"

Emrys turned his head and examined her. Her face was quite lovely— her cheekbones cast delicate shadows over her smooth skin, and her eyes were dark, smouldering with a vivacity that she kept in check with a firm hand. He said, "My woman lives among the Eicenni."

"They must live far away," observed Gwyden, turning again to stare into the fire. "I have not heard of them."

"I have not been to their land myself," answered Emrys. "It lies on the very eastward edge of this kingdom, a country so low, so flat, that the sea threatens constantly to swallow it up."

"I should not like that," said Gwyden. "The cliffs, both here and across the water in Cambria, are beautiful. I would not like to live in a place that was flat."

"The sea is flat," Emrys pointed out.

Gwyden shrugged. "That is different. The face of the ocean changes from day to day. Sometimes the face is grey and angry, at others it sparkles as the sun strikes it. Sometimes, it rises in wrath against my people, giant hills made of water that overwhelm our boats and our menfolk. The sea is never the same."

"I see."

"Will you stay here long?" Gwyden asked.

"That depends," answered Emrys. "There is a thing I seek. Perhaps you can help me find it?"

"What is it?"

"A ship, an ancient ship. It would, perhaps, have been hidden in a cave, many, many years ago."

Gwyden frowned. "I have not heard of such a thing near here," she said, "but I know the caves, and not all of them have been explored by my people."

"Could you show me where these caves are?" asked Emrys.

"I could," replied Gwyden. "Next time the men sail out, and when my chores are done."

"I am indebted to you, Gwyden of Habren," said Emrys. She smiled, and stirred the fire once more.

* * *

The men did not sail the next day, nor the day after, and Gwyden was kept busy with many chores. But eventually, one grey dawn, the men pushed their boats out into the waves, and she was free. She and Emrys walked off down the coast, feeling the soft, cold sand between their toes, and scenting the salt in the air. She told him the names of the flowers that grew among the dunes, and pointed out the cormorants' nests perched on the cliffs. And for a while, Emrys forgot about Excalibur, and the Roman invasion, and war and the motives of mighty men. It was good to feel the salt breeze through his hair, and to talk with a woman who had no desire to be a queen.

The day grew hot, and it was pleasant, when they found a cave, to enter it and feel the cool air upon their skin. Emrys lit a torch, and the copper-coloured light dashed itself over the damp walls. As far back as the light reached, though, there was no *Prydwen*, not even any sign that men had been there before them.

"Why do you think this ship is here?" asked Gwyden. She had scrambled to the top of a large boulder, and was reaching down to help him up.

Emrys took her hand—it was slightly callused, he noticed, very unlike Boudicea's hands—and hauled himself up beside her. Holding forth the torch, he looked down into another chamber of the cave. The floor there was lower, and waterlogged. There was no telling how deep the water was.

"The ship was hidden in a place called Celliwig," answered Emrys. "I think that Caer Lloyw is Celliwig, and that the *Prydwen* must be nearby."

"Why would you find the ship? What is there in it for Emrys of Caermyrddin?"

Emrys handed her the torch and started to slide down the further side of the boulder. Over his shoulder, he said, "A clue to where a great treasure lies hidden."

"A great treasure?"

"Yes: Excalibur, the mighty sword lost many years ago by Cassivelaunos, High King of Britain."

Gwyden did not say anything more, but watched him as he reached the bottom. Emrys put a foot into the water. It froze him to the bone, and he shrank away at first. But then he ventured his foot once more.

"Just jump in," advised Gwyden, from above him. "The cold is a shock, at first, but you will soon be used to it." She paused a moment. "But what seek you to know?"

"How deep the water is," answered Emrys. "Perhaps the *Prydwen* is below this water." He put another foot into the water, and so moved forward, feeling carefully with his toes before putting any weight onto them. Soon, he was in the middle of the pool, and the water came up a little over his knees. He turned and came back, clambering up to join Gwyden.

"Is there another cave nearby?" he asked.

Gwyden nodded, and jumped down on the seaward side of the boulder. In a few moments, they were back in the open.

The day wore on, and they explored half a dozen more caves while the sun climbed in the sky. At length, in the heat of the afternoon, they came upon a pool of water separated from the sea by a curving arm of rocks. On the landward side, the cliffs rose in shaggy upheavals to a grassy crest, but when they stood beside the pool, the sea was not visible to them. They sat down and ate a simple meal of bread and cheese and dried fish.

"It is good of you to show me these places," observed Emrys.

"It is sometimes a relief," commented Gwyden, "to leave Habren for a while."

"You do not like your home?"

Gwyden shrugged. "I love my home," she said. "I love the ways of my people, and I love the ways of the sea. I love it when it is calm, and there is barely wind enough to move the vessels, and the sea is so blue that I cannot see where it ends and the sky begins. But I love it too when it is a deep green, like an old man thinking deep thoughts, or when it sparkles cheerfully with sunlight, or when it is grey and sullen, like a child jealous of its toys."

Emrys looked at her in surprise. "Gwyden!" he cried. "You are a poet!" Gwyden shook her head, but Emrys persisted. "No, Gwyden, you are—you see things with a poet's eye."

"It is but the sea," replied Gwyden. "And that I have thought on long, for I have lived beside it all my life."

"If you could but learn to rhyme and alliterate," mused Emrys, "you could sing such songs before all the kings of the Island of the Mighty!"

"Oh, I should not want to leave Habren—not for good."

"Do you never think of leaving?"

Gwyden thought the matter over for a few moments, while the surf rolled up the beach behind them. "Sometimes," she admitted. "Sometimes, the ways of fishermen seem too narrow. But I am who I am, and cannot be other."

"Do you not wish to see the world?" Emrys asked.

"I do not think I would find anything in it I could not find here in Habren," answered Gwyden. "My husband, whoever he will be, will be a fisherman from this village, a man honest and strong, smelling of the salt of his trade. These are the ways I know. The lives of all men and women seem too small sometimes, and they want to escape. But it is wisdom to say, *This is who I am!*"

"Yes," said Emrys slowly, "it is wisdom." He stared into the pool. The water was clear, and he could see a crab with ragged claws scuttling sideways in the shadow of a red rock. It seemed so perverse, Emrys reflected, that of all creatures in the world, the crab should decide to go sideways; and yet, he felt a curious kinship with the errant creature at that moment.

Gwyden smiled and nudged him playfully on the arm. "And who are you, Emrys of Caermyrddin?" she asked.

Emrys picked up a stone and tossed it into the pool, watching the ripples expand through the still waters. "I am one who is ever restless," he said. "What you say of your home sounds fine. Sometimes, I wish I were a fisherman. I have spoken with kings and princes, and fishermen are more honest, more direct, more alive, in many ways, than what the world regards as great men."

Neither of them spoke for a while. Then Gwyden said, "You could stay with us, Emrys of Caermyrddin. You could be a fisherman. My father could teach you the ways of the sea, and you could lead this life. You could lead it with me."

Emrys turned to look at her, and in that moment she seemed beautiful indeed. He thought of Boudicea, and of her body lying next to that of Prasutagos in the cold night of the eastern fens. She wanted to be a queen before she wanted to be his lover. He looked at Gwyden. Here was a woman who cared nothing for kingdoms. All she seemed to want was his love.

Emrys reached out and, taking her hand, kissed it. "You are a maiden fair beyond the beauty of princesses," he said, "and I receive your offer with love, and respect, and the highest regard. But there is that within me that could not be satisfied until my quest is achieved. Mine is a life of wandering, of search, of restlessness. I wish it were otherwise, but it is not."

Gwyden looked at him through narrow eyes. "Who are you, Emrys?" she asked. "Who is it stands in your shoes, and walks along your path?"

As if in answer, a chattering scream pierced the quietude. Looking up, they saw a small hawk, a merlin. It tilted a wing, choosing its own course through the wind. Even as they watched, the merlin spied a mourning dove, and stooped upon it like a thunderbolt. With a thump, the two birds came together. A few light feathers drifted earthwards, and then the merlin was gone, whither they could not tell.

Emrys looked back at Gwyden, and there was purpose in his eyes. "I am Merlin Emrys, the far-seeing one," he said, and he sounded almost surprised to hear himself saying it. "I am prophet and seer to kings," he went on, his voice becoming clearer and stronger. "It is I shall find Excalibur. I am Merlin the Kingmaker!"

XXII

Merlin stayed for several months in the village of Habren. Winter came, breathing with clammy breath over the margin of the sea, and Merlin hunkered down and ventured out seldom. But he resumed his search again with the spring. He explored the coastline with Gwyden, but then went further afield with Agor, her father, who taught him how to handle a boat and guide it through the pathless seas.

"It is the sun will tell you where you are in the daytime," Agor told him one afternoon, as they bobbed up and down in the fishing boat some miles down the coast, "but that is nothing. That you know already. But at night, keep your eye always on the Pole. The path to or from the Pole is a sure one, and never fails. Fixed it is, aye, and ever steady, unflinching even when the sea rises and falls like a fickle woman. You may trust the Pole Star, even if your most trusted friend betray you."

With Agor's boat, Merlin explored the coast on either bank. The coast of the Summer Country, west of Habren, was rocky and pocked with caves, and the search was a long one, and vain. Merlin crossed the estuary and explored the coast of southern Cambria, but the beaches were wide and sandy, and though there were caves, they were fewer. His search began to be a wearisome one to him, and he returned to Habren long after sunset, a gaunt figure with hollow eyes. One lonely afternoon, having climbed some cliffs in southern Cambria, he looked out over the sea and the coast, stretching away on either hand. He could see the fringe of the Summer Country before him. The wind lashed his hair, and it was a chill wind, for it brought with it the first hint of a squall. The lonely calls of the gulls, all around him, seemed to cast him far away from where he was; he thought, almost, that he could see himself, standing alone and distant, in a strange land.

"Manawydan, king of the waves," said Merlin, "guide me. Show me where I can find this vessel! If Belinos did not hide the ship in a cave, then my search is indeed in vain." He cast himself down upon a hillock and put his face into his hands. "Why did I ever think I could succeed, where all else have failed?" He was silent a few moments, his soul empty, his thoughts a vacuum.

"Boudicea," he said, "I have failed, but I will rejoin you, and at least fight beside you."

He rose, and clambered back down the cliffs. By the time he had pushed his boat into the bobbing waves, the stars were beginning to prick the velvet firmament, and he guided himself back to Habren by the sure light of the Pole Star.

* * *

The following morning, ere yet the sun had showed itself above the dark horizon, Merlin slung his harp over his shoulder, and his sword from his belt and stepped out of the hut in which he had dwelt the last few months. Gwyden was there, waiting for him, with her father.

She held out a package to him. It was sailcloth, bound with loose cords. "There is food," she said. "Bread and cheese, and some dried fish. It will nourish you on your journey."

"I shall not forget you, Agor and Gwyden of the folk of Manawydan," said Merlin, taking the bundle.

"Nor I you, Emrys with his eyes upon the stars," replied Gwyden.

"Remember the Pole Star," said Agor. "When all else has failed, the Pole is your sure friend."

Merlin reached out and embraced them each in turn; then he turned away from Habren, and climbed the shallow slope to the top of the cliffs.

He arrived in Caer Lloyw an hour before sunset but, to his amazement, found the gates barred, a crowd of people without. Some sat disconsolate upon the ground, others hammered ferociously on the gates. One woman was howling in distress, another hugged her small child and rocked back and forth, keening gently as she did so. Sprinkled throughout the crowd were warriors, but they were spent men, many with wounds, all with the look of the dead behind their eyes. For a moment, Merlin was taken aback, for he saw before him a mighty army overwhelmed by a machine, swift, remorseless, efficient, gleaming in the bitter sun.

"What news, friends?" asked Merlin.

One man, a warrior with a bandaged head, lifted his face to look at Merlin. One eye was under the bandage, the other shone with a dull light, like the last ember of last night's fire. "What news?" he repeated. "Can it be you have not heard? Ill, all's ill." He put his face in his hands, and would say no more for the moment.

"I have been in other climes, friend," said Merlin, "and know nothing of the great movements of the world. Why have these gates been barred so long ere nightfall?"

"The city prepares for a siege," replied another voice from the crowd.

There was a sickening sensation in the pit of Merlin's stomach. "Then it is certain," he said, "they have come at last." Turning to the warrior, he asked, "How long ago, and where?"

The warrior looked up again. "They landed at Durobrith, a little under a month ago. We fought them on the beach, but fell back, and they pressed us as far as the Medway. We thought the river would protect us—we prayed to its gods to shield us from our foes, but the gods of the Medway were deaf to our pleas!

"The Romans swam the river at night, and hamstrung our horses, so we could use no chariots in the battle. And there seemed no end to the Romans. No matter how many we slew, there seemed to be more and more and more to take their places! Then it was I was wounded, and sought to lead these folk to safety. But we must keep moving west, for the lord of this city will not open the gates to us. These are dire times, friend."

"Dire indeed," replied Merlin.

The fire in the man's good eye burned a little brighter, and he added, between clenched teeth: "I will return to the fight. It is but for a short while that I lead these folks, and once I have guided them to safety in Cornwall, I shall return to the battle-line."

"My friend, what can you hope to do?"

"Die," replied the other. "It would take but one stroke more. I shall hurl myself against the Romans, and I shall die. But I shall not live to see our round houses made square, our druids worshiping foreign gods."

Merlin knelt down beside him, and put a calming hand upon his shoulder. "My friend," he crooned, "it is enough you have done already. No coward are you, leading these folks out from danger. You have fought, and you are guiding others to safety. You have earned your rest."

His words were like a charm, chanted lowly, and the warrior closed his eyes and breathed deeply. Merlin watched him for a moment, his chest rising and falling without labour. Then he lifted the bandage and looked beneath. The wound was clean—he would never see out of that eye again, but it would not take infection. He had a long life ahead of him in Cornwall. Slowly, Merlin stood up. "What can you tell me of the High King?" he asked. "What is his hope?"

Another warrior spoke. "Little enough," he said. "When we left, Cymbeline was sent for, and he should have engaged the enemy by now."

"Where is Cymbeline?" asked Merlin.

"In Lundein. The last I heard, he held an army there."

"And his Majesty?"

"He withdraws to Mai Dun; but what can he do against that machine? Nothing can stop them. Line upon line upon line of shields, and nothing can get through, not spear, not sword, not chariot." He paused, and for a moment a grim smile pressed his lips together. "At first, they were afraid of us. They would not get out of their ships, but cowered within them, quaking in fear, for they think us a people of magic. But now they fear nothing. This is the end of our ways."

"Ways can change without losing wars," said Merlin. But are the Romans far off?"

"Nay; they come on, like the sea through a wall made of sand."

"Is . . . Prasutagos of the Eicenni with his Majesty?"

"Not that I know," replied the man. "It seems to me that the Eicenni were under Cymbeline's command, in Lundein." He smiled grimly again; and it seemed to Merlin that there was a renewed firmness to his jaw, a fire in his eyes. "Oh, but his wife, they say!"

"What do they say?"

"That she rides out to battle ahead of her husband, and she fights like ten men! If there is hope for the Britons against Rome, that hope dwells in the sword and shield of Boudicea of the Eicenni!"

"Long have I known it, friend," said Merlin, laying a hand on his shoulder. Indicating the sleeping warrior, he said, "You should change his bandages more frequently, but he will heal. Peace go with you, and with those in your charge." And Merlin vanished into the gloaming.

* * *

The journey to Mai Dun was at least seven days, and across the open countryside, for once he had passed Caer Ciren there was no direct road. It was a bare country he passed through, swept by wild winds and full of grey grass and heather. Merlin kept the Pole Star ever at his back through the trackless heath. From time to time, he came across a drover's road, or a trail worn by countless shepherds down the ages, some of whom he saw tending their sheep as he took his own course south. But paths made by others invariably intersected that he needed to take, and seldom ran parallel except for the barest few hours. Merlin was alone.

On the evening of the fourth day of his flight southwards, he was struggling along through the rough terrain, when suddenly he felt a prickling on his scalp. He paused, and looked around. The day had reached that point at which it hung on the brink, undecided as to whether it was day or night; and oddly, for the time of day, a mist had crept out of the ground to obscure things still worse.

Ahead of him, rising from the plain in the gathering darkness, Merlin saw several huge shapes, like crouching giants. His heart quailed as he looked upon them. But they did not move. After a few moments, he edged a little closer to them. They were massive stones, blue in the gloaming, reared up on their ends by ancient wrights, for what purpose now Merlin could only guess. Approaching more nearly, Merlin saw that they stood in two rings, like giant dancers, or old men gathered about a fire to tell sad stories.

"The Giants' Dance!" said Merlin aloud.

Of course! He had heard this place spoken of in Afallach. It was a sacred centre, as Afallach was, but of an ancient and forgotten people. With growing wonder, Merlin came forward and stood in the midst of the wide circle of stones. He reached out with infinite caution, and pressed his fingers lightly to one of them. There was strength in them, and robustness: the strength of the Britons of old, and of their gods. Merlin pressed his whole hand, palm and all, against them.

Suddenly, he saw the Giants' Dance on a gloomy winter morning. A crowd had gathered in its midst, their clothes coloured brightly. A noble crowd they were—great warriors and magnates, their armour glistening in the grey light, their cloaks flapping in the fitful breeze. Their clothes, though, were strange, and Merlin wondered if he were looking upon a host of foreign ambassadors. Their heads were turned down for, in their midst, one lay on a bier, the noblest among them. He was young, though, and he wore purple, and a crown was upon his chest, and a long sword, its edge hacked by many battles. Ranged about the dead figure were priests, or so they seemed, but their vestments were strange indeed, unlike anything Merlin had seen in Afallach. They all wore the same symbol, like a tree but stylized, formalized, and upon it hung a man.

At the head of the bier, weeping like a child, stood an old man with a seamed face and a large nose, hooked like a hawk's and, with a shock, Merlin recognized himself. Next to him, also weeping, stood a young woman, tall and of an elfin beauty, with hair as dark as night, blowing about her face.

The vision passed, and Merlin was alone and cold among the stones of the Giants' Dance. He looked over his shoulder. Many of the stones, he saw now, had been toppled over. There was a sadness that hung over all, like an epitaph for a mute past.

Merlin left the Giants' Dance with many a backwards look, and he slept that night in a hollow beneath a spreading oak tree.

* * *

He woke the following morning with a grumbling stomach, for he had run out of the dried fish that had been Gwyden's gift. It was easy enough to find streams, for the plains were woven with them, hiding between the shallow hills, but food was scarce, and his haste did not permit him to pause in his journey and hunt. He pulled his belt a little tighter, and went on.

All that day, Merlin made his way through the ankle-deep grass and heather of the Great Plain. In the early afternoon, he climbed what he thought was one last hill of the Great Plain and looked down upon a very different sight. A wide road cut through the countryside. On the near side was the plain, rising to where Merlin stood; beyond it was a dense forest of oaks and elms, their green heads bunched together as far as the eye reached.

The road was thick with wagons and people. The bellowing of the oxen, as their drivers beat them to move faster, or to move out of the ruts in which their wheels had stuck, came up to Merlin like the song of an alien people. The walkers, with packs on their backs and children in their arms, moved with heavy paces into the west. Merlin's eye turned to the east. The forest lay, fertile and innocent, in that direction too; there was no hint of the menace from which these refugees fled. But Merlin knew.

Merlin let himself gallop down the hillside to the road, calling out to the nearest of the refugees, "How far away are the Romans?"

The man looked up and shook his head wearily. "But two days' march," he said. "By this hour, they will have reached Caer Guinntwic. They will be in Sarum the day after tomorrow. The gods spare us!"

"May they do so, friend," replied Merlin, and for a while, he let the wretched rabble pass him, their heads bent towards the earth, their shoulders slouched. Merlin watched them for a while, then struck off westwards across country. He knew he could move faster that way than by road, under the present conditions.

Merlin's path now took him through the thick southern forests of the Summer Country, rich and green with their late spring vestments. Three days he plied thus westwards, until he came to the border between the Summer Country and Cornwall, and the forests began to thin and turn to moorlands. Then, at last, he turned due south and came, footsore and hungry, to Mai Dun at the sinking of the sun.

Mai Dun was built on a great flat kidney-shaped hill. The hill was stepped for defensive purposes, and its perimeter was enclosed by stout ramparts. At the eastern end was a wide circular courtyard, where stood the citadel, winter residence of Magos, king of the Summer Country. At the western end was the township of Mai Dun. Merlin was approaching it from the north, and before long, he came upon the road he had seen earlier and further east. He joined the press of people passing through the entrance, and soon found himself in the wide courtyard within.

"Blow the horns!" came a voice—it was the captain of the guard on the gate. "The sun is setting, and we must close the gates!" There was fear in his voice; he had heard how far off the Romans were too.

"How can I close them?" cried another voice. "The people press; how can we shut them out?"

"Coroticos has not yet returned from viewing the enemy," added another.

"His Majesty knows the password," said the captain. "I have my orders. Shut the gates, and bar them fast!"

The guards set about it, putting their shoulders behind the oak, and slowly, to a pitiful wailing from without, the gates were shut and the bar dropped into place.

Merlin turned to look at the scene within the courtyard of Mai Dun, and the sight smote him in the breast, so that he could not move for a moment.

"Move along, there," said a guard from behind him, pushing him as gently as might be with the shaft of his spear. Merlin stumbled forward.

All around him were the wretched faces of the Island of the Mighty, hollow-cheeked, with dark rings about their eyes. They sat upon the ground, their heads between their knees, or their faces turned upwards to implore some passerby for food. Some moaned for their wounds, others for their slain husbands or children. Merlin moved through them like one passing among the departed souls of the Otherworld, and his soul wept for them.

"Emrys!" came a voice. Merlin looked up, but could see no one he knew. The voice came again, and suddenly, there was Cathbhad before him, and he found himself locked in an embrace, and weeping upon the shoulder of his old friend.

XXIII

At length, Merlin took a moment to look at the bard. Cathbhad was dressed more like a warrior than a poet, with Cambrian plaids upon him and an iron-rimmed helmet. A shield was slung over his shoulder, and a short, plain-hilted sword hung from his belt. "Emrys, what do you here?" he demanded.

"I am here to stand or fall beside my people," answered Emrys. "But you, my friend: what is this transformation? This is not my friend of old: where is the harp, and the sickle, that you were wont to carry?"

"This is a time for swords, not sickles," answered Cathbhad. "When the Romans are driven out, there may be a time for such tools once more. But in the meantime, we must fight. My harp is up yonder"—he pointed—"in the citadel, and I shall sing satires upon the Romans ere battle is joined. But when the moment comes, it is my sword, not my harp, that will protect me and slay invaders." He hesitated. "Your quest," he said, more quietly, "it has brought no reward?"

"Given time," answered Merlin, "I might have achieved the thing I sought, but no, I have met with no success. Where Excalibur might be hidden is as dark a mystery to me as it ever was. Is Boudicea here?"

"Nay, but have you not heard?" Merlin looked blankly at him. Cathbhad's brow darkened. "Coroticos met and engaged the Romans at Durobrith, and Boudicea fought alongside him, bringing with her many warriors from Eicenniawn. And she fought valiantly: I saw her stained to the elbows with Roman blood. But long it could not last, and as the day waned, the Romans threw us back, and we withdrew. Then Boudicea was recalled to Lundein by her husband."

"Then she is in Lundein?"

"Stay awhile, little hawk, for the tale is not done yet. She went to Lundein, taking what men remained to her for the defence of the city, while we retreated westwards, expecting a check to the Roman advance. They could not leave Lundein unsacked—Coroticos knew they would have to deal with

Cymbeline, and this would leave us time to regroup. But they came on, past the Medway. They passed Lundein, and pressed on through Logris."

"Leaving Cymbeline on their flank?" said Merlin in amazement.

"No." The syllable was bitter, like bad wine. Cathbhad's mouth was pressed into a tight line, the corners turned down, his nostrils a little flared. "No," he said again, "though we did not learn until yesterday what had happened."

"What passed?" said Merlin. "Do not keep me in ignorance!"

"Cymbeline promised us reinforcements at the Medway, but they did not arrive. They did not arrive because Cymbeline surrendered Lundein to the Romans. The Eagles fly over Lludd's Palace. It is a word almost too bitter to say."

Emrys gave a gasp. He felt as if his blood had turned to water. "Is there truth in any man?" he whispered.

Cathbhad reached out to steady the young man. "Boudicea's word went not with this betrayal, you may be sure," he said; "her path was chosen for her. It would have fed your heart to see her throw herself against those shield-walls, time and again. No, this is her husband's doing, and Cymbeline's. Now Cymbeline is on his way to Rome, and Prasutagos is king of the Eicenni—not the lord merely, but the king. Claudius' strategy is to divide the Island of the Mighty into many tiny kingdoms, each of which will be easier to rule than all of us at once."

"And so it has come to this," breathed Merlin: "the last stand of the Island of the Mighty."

"The High King has gone forth to view the enemy forces, and he is expected at any moment," said Cathbhad. "We are yet enough to do our enemy hurt, perhaps a hurt enough to help a negotiated peace."

Merlin looked about him at the refugees huddled in the courtyard. A fitful wind was blowing chilly in from the east, and he gave a shudder for a moment.

No, he thought, there is nothing to come of this battle but death.

"But come," said Cathbhad, "your grandfather and uncle are in the citadel, awaiting the High King's word."

"I fear I shall find no welcome from them," said Merlin.

"But come anyway," said Cathbhad, "for you are a prince of the Island of the Mighty too."

At that moment, horns sounded from outside the gates: Britonnic horns. Warriors parted the crowds that thronged about the gates, and a chariot trundled through, the horses' flanks flecked with sweat. Coroticos leaped down from it, and strode with a purpose towards the citadel, crying, "The Romans come on! We must look to our defence! Lords and princes, time-honoured warriors of the Island of the Mighty, to me!" And he bounded up the stone steps and into the citadel, the lords of Britain following after.

* * *

Merlin followed with the rest, though his soul was heavy, and fain would he have stayed away—it was in his heart to fly, to turn his back on Mai Dun and return to the fishing folk of Habren, among whom he had found such welcome. He thought of kind old Agor, and his solid, salty wisdom; he thought of Gwyden, his daughter, and the simple pleasure of exploring the coastline with her. He could find his way back, and never think on matters of state again. Somewhere, someone was bound to be untouched by the invasion.

But then a vision came unbidden into his mind. He saw the fishing boats, drawn up on the beach as he had seen them many times in the last few weeks. But these were like skeletons, their dark ribs jagged and exposed to the sky. Rainwater had gathered in them, and seabirds had made their nests upon the prows. The houses of Habren, climbing up the sides of the coombe, were roofless.

Merlin went with the nobles of Britain into the citadel, although fear clung to his soul like mud to a traveler's cloak.

The Great Hall of Mai Dun was packed with Britonnic nobles. There was hardly space to move at all. Merlin and Cathbhad pushed their way through the throng, until they stood with the Cambrians. Rhydderch acknowledged Cathbhad with a nod, and then his eyes fell upon Merlin. He raised his eyebrows.

"From whence have you come?" he asked.

191

Merlin averted his eyes. "I have been seeking a thing," he said, "but now I am come back, to fight beside my people."

Rhydderch snorted through his nose. "Did you find it, this thing you sought?" he asked. But before Merlin could answer, a clamour rose from the throng as the High King mounted the dais. He unfastened his cloak and threw it aside. His knuckles were white around the pommel of his sword.

"I return to you at this dark hour," he said, "with news that is not news, for that the Romans come on, you need hardly be told. That they are a mighty foe, you know already. You may not know that their ranks have been replenished with fresh soldiers, so that the army is as great as ever it was before now—perhaps greater."

"This is cold comfort!" laughed one fellow towards the front of the crowd. A chorus of laughter echoed him.

Coroticos let a laugh play briefly over his lips. "It is not to bring comfort that the High King has returned to his people," he said. "There is none in my news, if it is a life long and full of eventless days that you seek. But I seek something else, and I say: the stronger the enemy, the greater our glory! When your grandsons' grandsons listen to songs of this age, it is our names that will ring in their ears. If you wished to live a life without pain, you should have been born elsewhere. But you are Britons, and we Britons are never content with our own horizons. We must struggle after that which lies beyond them.

"I come now to offer you a choice. For this battle is hopeless. We can fight, but we will be overcome—if not now, shortly. The choice is this: fight and fall with me here, the last stand of the Island of the Mighty, or leave this place and make peace with the Romans. My course is plain to me. Your choice is still open. Only this would I add: that if you leave, take not your weapons. We shall need them."

There was a buzz of discontented conversation, and then a voice spoke up: "What if we leave, and you win?"

"Then I will be overjoyed," said Coroticos. "But fear no reprisals. It is my friends who stay with me to fight, but it is also my friends who will walk out to their families—and my friends they shall remain, friends and subjects both."

Merlin stared at him intently. There was a change in this man, a change that cut deep. It was a few brief months since last he had beheld the High King, but now his face was impressed with cares. He seemed a dozen years older, and a dozen centuries wiser.

The din of agitated conversation was building. It felt as if someone were drumming upon Merlin's head. Then, all at once, it ceased. Coroticos held his arms wide for silence.

"The gates," he said, "shall stand open for one more hour; no blame shall attach to any man or his retinue, if they choose to leave during that time. If you stay, stay for certain death, but for undying fame; for your name will be a theme for future ages, and bards from this day until the end of days shall sing of your last and most glorious hour!"

With that, he left the Great Hall to view the defences, and thought no more about those who would desert him.

* * *

"What will you do, grandfather?" asked Merlin, turning to Rhydderch.

Rhydderch turned his eyes upon Merlin. They were steady, yet there was some immense power behind them. They reminded Merlin of a dam that was about to burst. "I shall fight and die," said the king of Cambria. "And you?"

"The same," answered Merlin.

"Father," said Grwhyr, who was standing nearby, "Emrys is a good fighter, if he fight defensively. I have seen what he can do."

Rhydderch's eyes narrowed. He turned slowly to face his son. "Grwhyr," he said, "you are my son, and I have always been proud of you. But now we must say farewell."

Grwhyr grasped the hilt of his sword. "We can say farewell tomorrow, when we ride to face the Romans," he said. "Tonight, we shall feast together, one last time."

"No," said Rhydderch, with great effort. His voice was beginning to crack. "I am an old man, and should I live beyond tomorrow's sunset, I should not have many years left to rule the Cambrians anyway. But you are

193

still young. It is your shield must defend Cambria, your sword that must lead your people."

"Father, no!" cried Grwhyr.

"My son," said Rhydderch, "I will not be countermanded in this. It is my command to you as your father, and as your king." He reached up, and removed his crown. A circle remained indented in his hair, like the image of kingship. "Take this of me," he said, offering it to Grwhyr, and holding it as if it were a heavy weight. "Tomorrow night, when the sun sets, and you are fifty leagues from this place of slaughter, place it upon your head and take with it all the responsibilities of kingship."

"The king will not fly the battle!" Grwhyr said with vehemence.

"He shall not," replied his father, "for the king remains here, while his son flies hence; and tomorrow at sunset, the king will lie dead upon the field, while his son, the king, rides to the defence of his own people."

"I would rather die beside you, father," said Grwhyr.

Rhydderch smiled, taking his son's hands and placing the crown in them. "I know," he said. "You were no king if you did not desire this; but you were no king if you did not also desire to protect your people. I am old, but I am not too old to learn new things. And I have learned that there is a kind of courage that is different from that which dares wounds, and even death. It is that kind of courage I wish to see in my son now." Rhydderch reached out, took Grwhyr's face in his hands, and kissed him upon either cheek. "Go now," he said, "and ready those who would not stay. We shall yet meet again, in the Land of Youth beyond the grave, and there we shall tell long tales of our deeds upon the field of battle!"

Grwhyr looked long at his father. Tears welled in his eyes and forged glistening paths down his cheeks. He said no further word, but dropped to his knee, kissed his father's ring, rose again to his feet, turned, and was gone.

Rhydderch turned to Merlin. "Let me see your sword," he said.

Merlin drew it. It stuck a little in the sheath. He handed it to Rhydderch, who examined it for a moment. There were brownish patches along the blade, and its whole length was tarnished to near-blackness. The edge was hacked, but the dents were dull, and the hilt rattled slightly.

"With this sword," said Rhydderch, "you may die among heroes, but never acquit yourself as one, and few Romans will regret setting themselves before you." He handed it back. "Cathbhad, take this prince of Cambria to the armoury, and there fit him with arms that become the grandson of the king of Cambria."

"Grandfather!" exclaimed Merlin, dropping to one knee and pressing his lips to Rhydderch's hand.

"Go!" said Rhydderch, retracting his hand. "I know not what good you may do our cause, but I would not deny you the chance to prove yourself. Go, get yourself proper arms." Merlin turned to go, but Rhydderch called him back a moment. "And, Emrys," he said, "try to make no prophecies on the field of battle!"

Cathbhad led Merlin out of the Great Hall and across the inner courtyard to the armoury. It was already full, seething with men grabbing whatever weapon they could reach. Cathbhad pushed through the crowd and called to the Captain Armourer: "What arms for the grandson of the king of Cambria?"

"Little enough!" replied the burly man. "But I shall see what I can find."

He disappeared and, after a moment, returned with a tall helm, ribbed with iron and rising to a blunted point at the top, and a keen-edged sword the length of Merlin's forearm. Merlin slipped the new sheath onto his belt and re-girded it, swinging the sword through the air a few times before sliding it home. He slipped his left arm through the leather hoop and grasped the wooden handle of the shield the armourer handed him. It was oval in shape, but narrowed somewhat in the middle. It was light, made of three-ply, and rimmed with bronze. Merlin thanked the armourer—who could not spare the moment to listen—and turned away.

"Come," said Cathbhad, "let us to the king."

A herald, sent by Coroticos, stood outside the armoury, calling out in a strident voice: "Be it known that the High King commands all able-bodied men and boys to report at once to the armoury! No man is to be impressed! Every man who fights does so with a free heart; be it proclaimed throughout the host that Britons shall never be slaves! But those who will not fight must leave Mai Dun at once."

They hurried past him and through the gate into the outer courtyard, then up a flight of steps to the top of the palisades. A moment later, they stood with Coroticos and his nobles, beneath the fluttering scarlet dragon, standard of the High Kings of Britain. There were heaps of pellets, little grey stones, piled here and there against the stockade. From the platform over the gatehouse, it was possible to see a wide prospect of rolling hills and thinly-wooded slopes.

An old warrior, grizzled and thick in the chest and arms, was talking: "That's where they will set up camp—out of range of slingshots. But if they bring their ballista, we are certainly within *its* range. We were at Hod Hill."

Merlin turned his attention to Coroticos.

"We may endure no siege," the High King was saying, "since we have had no opportunity to provision this fortress, and the refugees who have fled before the Romans add to this burden. No. Our only hope is to issue from the gates at once, abandon Mai Dun, and fight one last time, to the death, beneath its walls. This is no hope of victory in life, my friends. Our victory is to have stood at all."

The nobles of the Island of the Mighty were silent. As one creature, they turned their eyes to the east. and Merlin looked with them. The road, still choked with refugees, stretched out to the horizon; and there, faint but pale against the deepening blue of the sky, was a tiny cloud, the dust kicked up by the marching boots of the oncoming legions. As they watched, the sinking sun glinted on something metallic.

"And now," said Coroticos, "let us feast. We do not have the provender to withstand a siege of even a week, so let us eat, friends, as was our wont of old, and then let us rest. For tomorrow, we shall fight together, heroes whom the gods themselves could not muster!"

Coroticos' officers drained away from the platform slowly, but Merlin remained, his eyes riveted on the growing threat from the east.

"You are the prophet," said a voice. Merlin turned and saw that he was not alone: Coroticos had remained. "You are the Seeing One. I remember you from the Great Council, and Gwelydd told me about you."

"At your service, Majesty," replied Merlin.

Coroticos breathed a deep sigh. The Roman army was now visible for what it was: a great mass of martial humanity, banded with steel and half-concealed within the dust that their own boots had thrown up.

"I might have needed a prophet," said Coroticos. "But at this moment, you are not the only one able to see the future."

For a while, they watched the oncoming Eagles together.

"Eat well, prophet," said Coroticos and, clapping him in friendly-fashion upon the shoulder, went down from the platform. But Merlin remained behind, while the Romans came on and the darkness of the last night of the Island of the Mighty descended upon the land.

XXIV

The creeping grey light of dawn grew about Mai Dun. It could not be called sunrise, for there was no moment at which light broke out over the Great Plain. The light seeped into the night, like damp through the planking of a ship. The clouds overhead were thick, the light reluctant, the air damp and cold.

The Romans were ready for battle. They were drawn up in three cohorts, massive red blocks, as if huge squares had been quarried out of the plain, exposing scarlet rocks beneath. To the south, halfway up the gentle forested hill, one cohort stood at the ready, three hundred yards from the eaves of the forest. To the north stood another cohort on the crest of another low hill. The third cohort stood in the valley between them.

A stiff breeze billowed out of the south, bringing with it the faintest tang of sea-salt. It occurred to Merlin that Mai Dun was built close to the sea—the stone pellets that had been brought hither so laboriously must have come from the beach.

"Look." The old warrior who had spoken of Hod Hill the night before pointed. "The ballistae. What did I tell you?"

"They are out of sling range," lamented Coroticos. But he brightened almost at once. "We shall have to get nearer to them."

"Or bring them nearer to us," suggested the old warrior with a grin through his grizzled beard.

Coroticos smiled slowly. "Let us try it," he said. "At the Medway, they hamstrung our horses. Here, they have had no opportunity to do that. Let them taste the edges of our swords, brandished from atop our chariots. That is a dish they have not sampled yet in Britain. Come, to horse!"

A shout went up from the men on the platform, and Coroticos descended quickly, his cloak billowing out behind him, his nobles filing after him, their swords out already and brandished over their heads. From the courtyard below came the sound of a harp, then Cathbhad's voice, loud and clear, rose on the cold air:

Ravens gnawing men's throats,
Blood bursting in the fierce fray,
Sinews splitting, blades biting,
Bodies broken, deeds of war!
Morning monstrous, death day dawning!
No man lacking at Coroticos' back,
Go forth, Men of Britain, go forth!
Battle breaks out, sword unsheathed,
Red host limp with horror
Before the wrath of the Britons!
Open the gates and issue forth,
Proud men of Britain,
Lords of the Island of the Mighty!

Another terrific roar went up from the Britonnic host as oaken beams were drawn and the stout gates thrown open wide. Merlin peered eastwards, towards the Roman host. The commanding officer of the Romans had been moving towards the front of his army, his chariot drawn by a pair of stunning white horses, olive branches held high.

"Vespasian," muttered the old warrior, as if the man's name was a bitter taste in his mouth. "Does he wish to parley? No need of that now!"

A whip flickered over the backs of Coroticos' horses. Coroticos cried out, "Men of Britain, brothers in life and death, follow me!"

The chariots filed out of Mai Dun, winding their way down the defensive ditches and assembling at the foot of the hill. Coroticos gave an order, and they rumbled forward, picking up speed until they hurtled towards the Roman host like water through the breach in a dam, two or three abreast, but fanning out as they crossed the wide plain eastward of the fortress. The earth shook with the beating of the hoofs, the air rang with the battle-cries of the Britons and the rattle of their wheels. The gap between the hosts narrowed, the Britons charging in a shallow V-shape, like a flight of geese. The noise rose like the roar of a tempest.

From within the Roman host, a horn blared. There was a movement, like a millwheel stirring sluggishly at first under the impetus of water, and then picking up speed, cog against cog, stone tooth sliding closely in beside

199

its mate. Hundreds of arms jerked backwards together. Another movement, a single movement made by hundreds of Roman arms in unison, and instantly, the air was full of spears. They arced up towards the heavens—the skies ruled by their god Apollo—and a thousand keen points flashed for a moment before turning slowly downwards. It looked like the wrath of the gods visited upon a mortal world.

No sooner was the first flight of spears in the air than the second followed. The Britons' charge went on, but the slower chariots on the edges faltered. A moment later, the spears drove into the onrushing host. They hit simultaneously, like a single hammer blow. Horses pitched to earth, dragging down healthy beasts running beside them, all along the front row. It was as if a great wave had found itself checked by a submerged shelf of rock, and had disintegrated. The chariots went catapulting over the carcasses of the fallen horses, breaking into fragments on the turf beyond, and scattering the human inhabitants over the earth. Merlin winced, turning his face from the carnage. The sharp screams of the horses and the bellowing of wounded men rent the air, like the wind tearing down masts and rigging from an imperiled ship.

The Britonnic host was already in disarray when the second flight of spears plunged into them. But miraculously, Coroticos was unscathed, his chariot flying as if Manawydan's team drew it. One after another, chariots emerged from the wreckage, and began to pick up speed once more.

The Romans closed ranks with a mighty clash. Their shields, blocks of scarlet and gold, stretched in an impenetrable wall across the shallow valley.

The wall began to move.

At that moment, the Britonnic chariots met the oncoming Romans with the sound of empires falling. Hoofs rose and fell upon leather shields and steel helmets. The grey light flashed on the blades of Roman swords as they stabbed upwards. The Britons poured into the Roman host, like a waterfall plunging into a pool.

But still, the Romans were moving—moving over their enemies, crushing them beneath the heels of a thousand boots.

Coroticos was still mounted in his chariot, and his blade was smeared with blood as he swung this way and that. But looking up, and seeing that so few of his shield-companions remained, he waved towards the fortress with his sword. Drops of blood trailed from it as he did so, flung like garbage back at the host that had donated them. The chariots turned, disentangling themselves from the cohort, and began the retreat towards Mai Dun.

Trumpets shouted again, their brazen voices cracking like whips over the field of battle. The Roman cohort came to a complete stop. There came a new sound: hoof beats again, but faster than those of the chariots. Cavalry were emerging from behind the Roman cohort, and quickly bearing down upon the fleeing Britons. Their swords were out—longer in the blade than their counterparts carried by the infantry—and they slashed with economical movements as they caught up with the chariots. One after another, charioteer and warrior tumbled to the turf and, leaderless, the horses slowed and veered away.

They were but two hundred yards from the gate now, and along the palisades, men with slingshots waited anxiously, their weapons loaded already.

Merlin closed his eyes for a moment. The dreadful noise of dying men and horses echoed in his ears. He stopped them with his fingers, but the noise would not go away. He shook his head.

Another sound: the whir of stones loosed from slingshots, slashing through the air with deadly accuracy towards the Roman cavalry. Merlin opened his eyes. Several Romans were down already, unmoving on the green earth. Another one turned slowly backwards over his horse's saddle. His armour rang on his body, his helmet bounced away from him down the slope, but he was still alive. He started to crawl away. Another stone struck him on the back of the head, and he lay still, his hand clawing the earth in the direction of his friends. A few horses cantered aimlessly about the field. Down below, the gates shut with a bang, and the beam was dropped back into its place. Slowly, like the end of a rainstorm, the pattering of the rocks ceased. Coroticos had returned.

* * *

The field between the Roman host and the beginning of the defensive ditches of Mai Dun was strewn with the dead and wounded. Their groans filled the air, and the stench of blood rose to the battlements of the fortress in an obscene miasma. The cohort against which Coroticos had thrown his charge had reformed, not very far from where it had first stood, but a little further south. There was some activity behind the cohort, and a squeaking noise, like the wheels of a heavy chariot, drifted up to the platform.

At a noise from behind him, Merlin turned, and saw Coroticos spring up the last step onto the platform. He had wiped his face, but his chest and arms were spattered with blood, and he was panting hard.

"What news?" he asked.

The old warrior from Hod Hill pointed. "Look," he said.

Teams of legionnaires were pushing forward four great machines of wood. Each had an elongated body, with slender arms stretched out on either side. A great square panel, like a shield but open in the centre, supported the wheels, which were making the squeaking sound Merlin had heard earlier.

"Ballistae," said the warrior.

"Ballistae!" repeated someone, his voice rising in pitch. "They are using ballistae!"

"Andraste!" cried another, calling upon the goddess of victory. "Save us!"

Behind the ballistae, a line of soldiers marched up and stood to attention, waiting, unmoving. Their line was perfectly straight.

"How do they do it?" breathed a voice. Merlin turned. Cathbhad had joined him. "How is it possible to force thinking men into such straight lines?"

A trumpet sounded, and the Roman line broke. For a few moments, the soldiers fussed around the machines. Then silence and stillness returned. The legionnaires stood to attention around the ballistae. Each ballista looked identical to its neighbour, each legionnaire stood in an identical posture and in an identical position.

The trumpet again, and four economical movements. Four dull sounds, metal striking thick wood, a dull sound carried from a distance on the heavy air.

Something screamed through the air close to Merlin's head. Out of the corner of his eye, he saw a Britonnic warrior carried ten yards through the air, a monstrous arrow protruding from his chest. At the same time, the whole battlement shook to the sound of splintering wood, and an iron arrowhead, the size of Merlin's hand from wrist to fingertips, protruded from the shattered palisade a dozen yards away from him. In his shock, he could not move.

The Romans busied themselves about their ballistae again. Once more came the dreadful sound of metal on wood, and the slicing sound of the bolts screaming through the air. Merlin watched as one post, wrenched from its position in the stockade, shuddered free of the battlements and tumbled into the courtyard below. A man screamed. Merlin turned. A warrior, who had been crouching behind the wall, now slumped over a spreading pool of his own blood. The arrow-head that had pinned him to the wall poked obscenely from the middle of his chest. Merlin clutched at his throat. His body was trembling all over.

"Emrys!" came an urgent voice. "This way!" Merlin looked around. It was Cathbhad. Crouching, he followed the bard north along the battlement. When they had gone twenty yards or so, Cathbhad ventured himself above the top of the stockade. "They are targeting the gatehouse," he observed. "Probably, they will clear the platform of our men, and send an assault against the gate."

Indeed, a small division of soldiers had moved up, and was standing in perfect ranks behind the ballistae. On a trumpet's brazen command, they raised their shields over their heads, or thrust them outwards and locked them with their neighbours' shields. They had formed four tight little groups, the shields locked on every side and over the top.

Someone on the battlements laughed harshly. "They look like tortoises!" he said. Others joined in the laughter.

But the veteran from Hod Hill was silent. "I have seen these tortoises," he said, "and I do not laugh."

Still, the great bolts loosed from the ballistae crashed into the top of the gatehouse, splitting the pine-logs from which it was built, reducing the platform where the High King of the Island of the Mighty had so recently stood to splintered and bloody wreckage. A few Britonnic bodies lay ungainly amid the debris, but no living soul remained with them.

Another trumpet sounded, and the tortoises began to move. For the flicker of a second, Merlin could see four sandaled feet below the lower lips of the front shields, then again, and again, as the tortoises crawled across the carnage-strewn plain. They paused as they reached the beginning of the defensive ditches, but then they came on steadily, threading along the path that the chariots had so recently taken, inching along the line of the ditches rather than trying to make the climb.

Up above them, Britons raced for the piles of stones. Slings whirled through the air, and stones hissed towards the enemy, but they pattered uselessly on the leather shields, like summer rain on the roof of the hall of a mighty king. On came the tortoises, regardless. Merlin watched, his knuckles whitening on the edge of the stockade.

For a long time, as the Roman formations crept closer, both sides exchanged missiles. The ballista bolts crashed into the gatehouse, reducing the platform to nothing, cracking and splintering the tops of the gates. The bolts that missed the gatehouse altogether hurtled over their heads and into the fortress, killing or destroying down below as surely as on the top. The groans of the wounded came now from within Mai Dun as well as without. And all the time, Britons on the stockade sent down a shower of stones upon the advancing tortoises. A cheer went up as one Roman broke formation and somersaulted backwards down a ditch. A dozen stones immediately pelted him, and he lay still. But yet, the tortoise whose shell they had breached advanced steadily along the narrow path, until it was yards away from the gate.

The Britons became frenzied now. Stones rattled like hail from the shields of the Romans. Merlin was astonished to see how much the piles had been reduced, when there lay but one dead Roman along the way.

Merlin sniffed the air. Something was burning. He stole a quick glance over the edge of the battlement. The leading tortoise had reached the gates, and they had lit a fire at its foot. Already, black smoke was curling up across the face of the gate.

Merlin exchanged glances with Cathbhad. The bard looked grim, his face bathed in shadow. When he looked up, Merlin saw emptiness in his eyes.

"Cathbhad," he said, reaching out to take the other's hand.

"Little hawk," said Cathbhad. "I think I am ready to die."

Another voice called out to them. Merlin looked around. It was Caled, one of his grandfather's warriors. "Come—the Cambrians will fight beside their High King!"

Cathbhad turned to Merlin. "Little hawk," he said earnestly, "I have loved you as a father loves his son. Farewell! May we meet again someday, at the feast beyond the grave!"

They embraced a moment, and then dashed off after Caled.

XXV

Merlin and Cathbhad followed Caled down from the palisade, and through the courtyard. It was littered with twisted shapes—those who had fallen to ballista bolts, wooden beams wrenched from their moorings, bits of rope. Merlin saw the wretched dragon standard of the house of Pendragon, rolling across the grassy floor in the sluggish breeze. Behind them, a steady column of smoke was rising from the gatehouse, filling the air with its acrid stink. The wailing of women and the shrill shouting of men came from all directions, though few were actually visible—most had fled beyond the reach of the Romans' weapons.

They were halfway across the courtyard, when Merlin heard a hissing behind him, like the rough breath of a venomous snake. He turned. A ballista bolt slammed into the ground beside him. He felt the earth shake, as if the gods of the underworld were wrangling over a lost soul. Merlin was caught off-balance for a moment, and dropped to one knee. Cathbhad hesitated, but Caled was dashing ahead of him toward the gate that led from the citadel into the town of Mai Dun. Merlin sprang to his feet and sprinted after them.

At the gate, they picked up a few more followers, other Cambrians whom Caled had summoned. Caled hauled open the gate, and they piled through.

It was a very commonplace scene that greeted them: an open space of green, dotted with round huts, their thatched roofs rising in shallow points like wide-brimmed hats, their wattled walls daubed and whitewashed. Between them wove dirt tracks. Pens with beasts in them, ducks and geese waddling unconcernedly about. But there was something lurid about it. The township waited, pensive, as if expecting the fall of some thunderbolt. And it was utterly devoid of people.

The Cambrians flooded through the township, running along the main thoroughfare like the incoming tide along narrow river banks. They flew between the byres and forges, past the inn and through the marketplace. At last, they laid eyes on their destination: at the western end of the town, a great crowd of menfolk had gathered, brandishing swords, spears, mattocks, pitchforks, anything that lay readily to hand and could be used to reap the life from a man. In the midst of them, mounted upon a hayrick, stood Coroticos.

"This is our hour of glory, men!" he cried, as they drew close. "The west gate is unknown to the Romans, else they would be besieging it too. They are not. So we shall issue out of this gate, and creep through the forest to the south of the fortress. We shall assail their southern flank from the cover of the forest, whence they least expect attack. O! my dear hearts! I do not ask you to fight for your country, for what is that? These hills and trees will still be here, long after we have finished our natural lives. I do not ask you to fight for your king, for he is but a man, even as you are. I do not ask you to fight for wife and child, though they deserve defence. I ask you to fight because it is right to do so. I ask you to fight because an invasion by foreign men should not go unchecked. I ask you to fight because this day should be remembered as long as harp is heard in hall!" A mighty cheer went up from the host. "Come, my brave lads! Let us go, and may the Romans drink shame like water hereafter when this day is named!"

The gates were thrown open and, like a pent-up river through a sluice, the Britons poured out through them. Merlin looked left and right at a landscape that seemed untouched by war: to the north, hills swept into the distance, dotted here and there with spinneys; to the south lay the naked eaves of the autumnal forest. Merlin plunged in among the trees.

The forest was mainly beech and elm, and there was a rich smell of humus on the heavy air. The undergrowth and the deep carpet of gold and brown leaves rustled as the men picked their way through, but they did not make so much noise that the enemy would be disturbed. They forged on through the trackless wood.

On the edge of the forest, as they gathered for the final stint of their journey, Merlin saw an apple tree. It was an old tree, for its branches drooped as its kind do when in advanced years, so that they touched the leafy ground on the further side. The bole was split in two near the base, and while one stem hunched over like an old crone brewing, the other grew more or less straight. Small brown apples lay scattered around its base, and Merlin caught a whiff of rottenness on the air. A song came to him, borne upon the current of the past, and he hummed it quietly as the army of Coroticos gathered around their leader.

> Sweet apple-tree, with blossoms red,
>
> The ground beneath you stained with blood,
>
> Hide me from sight, among your branches,
>
> Sweet apple-tree, that grows in a glade.

But there were no blossoms on the apple-tree now. It offered no hiding-place. Merlin shivered. The year had grown old.

Merlin looked towards Coroticos. The army had nearly gathered by now. Rhydderch was ready, his knuckles white upon the ash-haft of his spear. Beside him, on either side, stood Cathbhad and Caled, both eager for the fray, like hounds who have spotted their quarry but are held in check. All around him, Merlin saw gathering the nobles of Britain, nostrils widened, lips pulled back from their teeth. They were ready to fight; they were ready to die.

"It will be spears first," said Coroticos, and his words were repeated in whispers all the way to the back of the host. "The Romans will be within easy range. Twenty paces, stop, cast your spears, then draw your swords and dash into the legion before they have time to cast their own javelins."

Merlin had no spear. Quietly, he slid his sword out of its sheath in readiness, adjusted his grip upon the shield. He caught Cathbhad's eye.

"This will be a good song!" he said.

The whispering had ceased. Coroticos glanced back over his army. He raised his arm. All eyes were riveted upon it.

Down it came. The army broke cover.

So intent were the Romans upon the gatehouse that they did not, indeed, see the emergence of the Britons from the forest. The cohort they faced was not the same one against which Coroticos had thrown his chariot charge earlier in the day. These were fresh, awaiting orders. It seemed that the Roman intention had been to draw the Britons out between the hills, and then crush them between the two cohorts they had positioned on either side.

Nineteen paces, twenty. The front ranks of Britons stopped. Their arms came back like the undertow before the mightiest of waves. Then, in a moment, the air was thick with spears. Drawing their swords, they leaped at the enemy like salmon up a waterfall. The battle cry went up.

The Romans heard it, but no order to turn about had been given, and when the volley of spears crashed into their midst like deadly rain, most of the casualties were transfixed between the shoulder-blades.

Merlin was running now, his step springing over the grass. Behind him, the next group of Britons cast their spears. They rained upon the Romans in a wide area. Legionnaires in the front row flew backwards, borne over by the course of the Britonnic spears; others further back fell also. Tattered gaps were appearing in the Roman wall, as if the mortar had grown weak with lack of use.

Finally, Roman trumpets sang piercing notes over the army. The shields began to move into place, but it was a ragged movement, utterly lacking in the precision he had seen against the chariots. More spears crashed into the Romans, and Merlin saw booted feet kick at the sky.

The front rank of Britonnic footmen surged over the front line of Romans. The deadly tide flowed right over them, and overwhelmed them utterly. They hurtled into the next rank like a wave against a cliff. Swords swung, and the noise shook the earth.

Merlin found himself faced by a Roman soldier. The man's eyes were grim. He thrust at Merlin, not with his sword, but with his shield. Merlin felt the blow, and staggered backwards. The soldier advanced upon him, thrusting out his sword. The blade was parallel to the ground, so that it might more easily slide between an enemy's ribs. Merlin parried the lunge, and the man checked his forward movement, but too late. The point of Merlin's sword pierced his chest, and his whole body twitched as he dropped to his knees.

In dread, Merlin withdrew his sword. The man was not dead, but was clutching at his chest. By a fluke, Merlin's sword had slipped between two of the steel segments that made up the man's armour. Now he looked up at Merlin, and the two regarded each other in fear and horror for a moment. Then the man slumped to the earth, his eyes still open, reflecting the wrack of the heavens, whence now his soul fluttered. His blood was smeared over the tip of Merlin's sword.

Merlin's head felt light, as if he had drunk too much mead, and he almost felt as if he would fall to the ground. In a moment, though, his horror was replaced by rage. He hurled himself at the Romans, his sword singing. Legionnaires fell before him, one after another, and he leaped over their falling bodies, plunging after the next victim in his wrath.

Suddenly, there were no more Romans to kill, and Merlin paused, like a boat cast high upon a shore by a mad wave. His sword dripped.

The Romans were running away, down the hill, a rabble now, and their trumpets were calling out desperately. The mill was broken, the wheel flung in pieces over the ground.

Merlin looked around. He was twenty yards ahead of the Britonnic host, and his grandfather and Coroticos were staring at him with wide eyes. Behind him, three Romans were stretched out upon the earth, dead as stones, in a more or less straight line—the men he had killed after the Britons had ceased their advance.

Merlin felt his stomach twitch, and he vomited its contents upon the bloodstained turf.

"Emrys!" called Cathbhad. "Come back—we must retreat to the forest! It is the order of the High King!"

Merlin looked both ways. The Romans were already reforming, their shields locked in a wall, and he and the other Britons were within range of their pila. The Britons were falling back towards the forest. He ran with them, over the bodies of fallen Romans—no Britons, just these foreigners in foreign gear.

But then the host froze, and Merlin almost collided with the man before him.

While the Britons had striven with the cohort of Roman infantry, the cavalry had left their positions and mounted the hill. Now they were arranged in a double line before the forest, and they were perfectly blocking the Britons' retreat.

* * *

"This is it!" cried a man somewhere in the host. "This is the end!" His voice was shrill, on the verge of hysteria.

Coroticos' eyes flashed at the offending warrior. "The end of what?" he demanded. "Your life would end anyway, sooner or later. Only glory lasts for ever! Look at them—look! These Romans are not like us. They cannot act for themselves. They must follow their trumpets and their drums, and march in straight lines, one beside another. They are not like us. You kill a Roman, and you break a part of a great machine; but kill a Briton, and you kill a warrior, you kill a man, who has lived like a man. We have lived as warriors for many years now—and the hour has come that we have long known must be. Let us show these cogs and wheels what it is to be a man!"

A cheer went up from the host, and they rallied around their commander.

"Now," called Coroticos, "each man take up a spear—there are plenty about us on the ground. We have one cast each—make it count!"

Another cheer, and the Britons assembled, spears poised and ready. The Roman ranks were coming on, the tramp of their boots like corn ground between wheels of granite. At the top of the slope, the cavalry sat as still as mountains. Half a mile away, the ballistae were hurling rocks at the gatehouse. Even as Merlin watched, the timbers fell in a shower of sparks, sending a huge black billow of smoke up to the sky. The tortoises broke up and Romans rushed into the fortress of Mai Dun.

"Now!" yelled Coroticos, and the Britons let loose their spears. Merlin flung his with all his might, following its path through the air eagerly. He lost it almost at once, for it was like one drop of water flung into rapids. The Roman wall flickered as gaps appeared, but still it came on.

"And now, for glory, and everlasting fame, charge, sons of Brutus! Charge!"

Coroticos' voice rose to a battle-cry, and the Britons rushed down the incline towards the oncoming legion. The hosts met, and the shield-wall buckled inwards. The Britons surged into the midst of the legion, and the heavens shook to hear the clamour of weapons and harsh voices. Merlin saw his grandfather swing at a legionnaire's face as it peered above the massive square shield. The helmet sprang away from the bottom half of the man's head, and he sank backwards. Cathbhad threw himself against another soldier, shoving the Roman's shield with his own. Both of them went down to the turf. The pommel of Cathbhad's sword was raised, and fell once. Then he was up, and running for his next foe.

Merlin swung and slashed while the battle raged all around him. He had learned to avoid the shield when it was thrust at him, and duck under the blade, thrusting upwards at each adversary. But for every one that fell to his wrath, another appeared to take his place, and another, and another.

"Emrys!" came a voice. Merlin took a step back, and looked sideways. It was Cathbhad, blood frothing on his lips. With an economical thrust of his short sword, a legionnaire took Cathbhad in the stomach. The bard folded in the middle, and the Roman stepped over him, drawing his sword easily from the body.

Merlin screamed in fury, and leaped towards the body of his friend. He swung his sword at the Roman who had felled him. It rang upon the back of his helmet, and the Roman whirled to the earth. But Merlin could not reach his friend, for another Roman stood over him. Out came the shield—Merlin stepped backwards. Out came the sword, and Merlin ducked, thrusting upwards. The Roman stepped backwards, and Merlin swung at his leg. He felt a sickening crunch, and the legionnaire collapsed, crying out. Merlin's sword plunged into his throat.

In a moment, Cathbhad was in Merlin's arms. The eyes opened, and the lips moved. "Fly, little hawk," they said. "It is for you to sing this song."

Merlin looked up, his eyes awash. The Romans were coming on in two flanks, grinding the Britons between them. The Britons ran, like water draining from a punctured bucket, but blood was flowing in all directions, drenching the ground, dripping down the leather shields.

Cathbhad gave a long sigh, and the light went from his eyes. Not far off, Merlin heard another voice, and he looked towards it.

His grandfather, Rhydderch, king of Cambria, stood upon a heap of slain men, his sword flashing in his hand. He was singing, in a stern voice, a fierce song in an ancient tongue. But even while Merlin watched, a javelin

took him in the shoulder. Rhydderch stepped backwards, and a Roman behind him thrust a sword into him so that the point emerged from his chest.

For a moment, all seemed quiet to Merlin. His own eyes and those of
his grandfather met, and locked, and spoke softly. Then Rhydderch's rolled
upwards, and the body that had once housed his great spirit slid to the
ground.

The Roman army moved on, squeezing the Britons so that blood flowed
in a torrent down the hillside. The Britons fled from the scene of the battle
and, at last, the cavalry moved, descending upon them swiftly and cutting
them down even as they ran.

XXVI

For the briefest of moments, the sun peered from behind the clouds, shedding its lurid crimson light over the carnage, and then sank. Blue pools of shadow began to form. On the flat top of the northern of the two hills outside Mai Dun, away from the forest and away from the field of the fallen, the Roman legion pitched their tents and posted pickets. Campfires sprang up, flickering in perfectly straight lines between the ruler-edged lines of tents, and the sentries walked with measured paces a precise distance before turning and marching back.

Several details, like small hosts of fireflies, clambered down the hill, torches in hand, to begin the work of disposing of the dead. Brusque commands were exchanged in a tongue that those hills had not heard ere that night. The Romans they laid side by side in mass graves, the Britons they laid face-up in long rows—far longer than the graves. The moon broke out from behind the clouds, and was reflected back by the still, dull eyes of the fallen.

Merlin stirred, and opened his eyes. In the dim light, he could see the frozen face of Cathbhad, lying next to his own. The bard's features were blank, completely smoothed out. The tension had left them altogether. But he did not look restful. He looked strange, alien, empty, like a sack from which the contents have been poured. Merlin reached out—sharp stabs of pain exploded in his shoulder as he did so—and touched his friend's face. He wiped blood away from the corner of his mouth. It was cold. With much labour and pain, Merlin struggled into a sitting position, rubbing his bruised shoulder. He seemed to be otherwise unwounded.

How long was it since he had blacked out? He gazed around at the dim, obscene world of twisted wreckage and blood around him. It had been late afternoon when he had seen his grandfather . . .

His grandfather. The king of Cambria was dead. He would never hear his voice again, never see him sit on his throne, or laugh aloud in the feast-hall. Merlin felt a great emptiness yawning within him. Where had they all gone? Where was the horse, snorting and stamping in the cold evening? Where the rider? Where the giver of gold? Where was the hall-friend, where the pleasures of the feast? Merlin broke down and wept, sobbing so that his shoulders heaved. He put his face in his hands and curled up like a child in the womb, trembling all over.

At the sound of a voice, Merlin looked up.

A detail of Roman soldiers was approaching. Their swords were sheathed, they bore no shields or helmets, and they carried torches. Merlin sprang to his feet.

"Stay!" cried a voice, in Brythonic. "Do not fear!"

A man stepped forward from among the Roman soldiers. He was dressed in the clothes of a Roman civilian. His hair was close-cropped, and he wore no beard. There was a faint smell of civet about him.

"My name is Decius Agrippa," said the civilian. "I am interpreter for the Second Legion Augustans under Legate Titus Flavius Vespasian. Who are you?"

"Merlin Emrys," replied Merlin, in a choking voice, "grandson to Rhydderch, king of Cambria."

The man's eyes widened; for a moment, a fire burned behind them. Merlin studied him carefully, but oddly, he saw no treachery, no guile. Decius Agrippa said, "The battle is over, and no one will kill you or try to hurt you; but the legate has great need of your services."

"Why should I help the man who has killed my grandfather and my shield-friends?" asked Merlin suspiciously.

Decius Agrippa paused a moment. Then he said, very quietly, "You have no motive at all. If you do not wish to help us, you are nevertheless free to go."

"You could force me, if you wished to do so," observed Merlin.

"Yes," replied Agrippa. "Rome has many slaves, but the emperor seems to dislike that, and does not wish for any more." He gave a wry smile. "Indeed, he has made quite a name for himself among his former slaves. Will you help us?"

Merlin looked intently at Decius Agrippa. His mind explored the young Roman's, and there he found much ambition. But there was no deceit in this matter. In this matter, he was entirely honest, so far as Merlin could tell. "What would you have me do?" he asked.

"I would rather let the legate tell you that himself," answered Decius Agrippa. He held a hand out to Merlin. After a moment, Merlin took it in cautious friendship. Then Agrippa dropped it, clapped him on the shoulder, and turned to lead him away. Together, they picked their way through the fallen towards the hill on which the encampment had been made.

* * *

Legate Titus Flavius Vespasian was in his tent with his staff officers. A map was spread upon a table. The legate was in his early thirties, with a round, genial face and slightly curling hair, already receding from his brow. His eyes, which had seen service on many fronts already, were hardened by experience, and yet not devoid of honesty. Merlin watched him closely as he and Decius Agrippa entered the tent and stood, waiting, beside the flap. He saw that every officer in the tent was older than Vespasian, had seen more battles than he, had killed more men on the field than he. And yet Merlin saw also that these men would obey his orders, and he knew that, after this day's work, their respect for him had grown enormously.

Vespasian dismissed his officers, and his Greek slave poured him a cup of wine. He greeted Decius Agrippa, and they spoke together in Latin for a few minutes without regarding Merlin much.

Merlin looked around with interest. It was an austere life these Romans led, he reflected. A cot, over which was thrown a red blanket, was one of the legate's few possessions in the tent. A brazier, wrought from Cyprian copper, stood in one corner, a scarlet rug bought in one of the marketplaces of Rome lay on the ground, a couple of chairs were drawn up to the table, but no one sat upon them. Otherwise, the tent was devoid of furnishings. The sword that was hanging beside the entrance had a bone handle and a massive wooden pommel. A gold stud on the end of the pommel completed it. The scabbard was of black leather, with gold-work around the lip and the tip.

Decius Agrippa finished speaking to Vespasian, and then brought Merlin forward. Vespasian studied Merlin for a moment with interested eyes. Then he spoke, in Brythonic, but with a thick accent. "I hope," he said haltingly, "that you will excuse me if I speak through an interpreter. I know Greek, Hebrew, and German, but not yet Brythonic." Merlin nodded, and Vespasian spoke rapidly in Latin to Decius Agrippa.

"His Excellency commends you, on behalf of all Britons, for the valour with which you fought this day. You have been worthy opponents, brave and resourceful. He salutes you."

Merlin looked to Vespasian, who inclined his head formally. He returned the gesture.

"The legate wishes to inter the chieftains of your great army with proper honours," Decius Agrippa went on, "according to the custom of your people." Agrippa listened for a moment, while Vespasian added some more to this. "The legate also wishes to know," Agrippa continued, "if you would be willing to identify these chieftains. He particularly wishes to know if Caractacus lies among the slain. Will you help us in this?" Merlin did not speak at first, thrown by the Roman pronunciation of the High King's name. Agrippa asked Vespasian a question, and the commander replied in a few terse phrases. He watched Merlin curiously. Merlin avoided his gaze. Agrippa said, "The legate assures me that you will be set free in exchange for this invaluable service."

"I shall do it," answered Merlin. He would indeed like to know the whereabouts of Coroticos himself, he reflected.

Agrippa conveyed Merlin's words to the legate, who nodded. Vespasian spoke to his slave, who filled another cup with wine. The legate handed it to Merlin.

"Britons and Romans," he said, in his thick accent, "we will be friends, I think."

Merlin's brow creased. Something had happened when the commander had passed him the wine cup. For a moment, he had seen not the Roman legate, but a man in imperial purple, oak leaves about his head.

"Hail to thee, legate of the Second Legion Augustan," said Merlin, "that shall be emperor hereafter!" Vespasian looked as if his blood had just turned to stone, and he backed away from Merlin. But Merlin went on: "Look to the son of your loins, emperor, who languishes in sickness; but the son of the emperor will not be cured, except by the Son of Man!"

Vespasian turned to Agrippa and spoke rapidly. Agrippa said, "The legate wishes you to repeat what you said."

Merlin blinked. "What did I say?" he asked.

"Come now!" snapped Agrippa. His brow was clouded. "You *must* know what you said!"

Merlin shook his head. Agrippa conveyed a few thoughts to the legate in short phrases. Silence hung about the tent for a moment, then Vespasian spoke again to Agrippa, who said, "I have told the legate what I can recall of your words, which have struck him with amazement. He wishes to know more."

Merlin sighed. "I am but the tool of my gods," he said, "and they do not obey me. I can seldom recall what words I have spoken when I prophesy."

"You called His Excellency emperor, and referred to the healing of his son by a son of men?"

Merlin thought for a moment. "These words are dark to me. Has the emperor a son who is sick?"

"The legate has a son, who is in good health, and with his mother in Rome," answered Agrippa. "He is not of an age to be separated from his mother at this time." Agrippa stepped closer, and spoke quietly, but with urgency. "But His Excellency is not the emperor. The emperor too dwells at this time in Rome. Why would you cast the purple on him thus?"

"Sometimes," explained Merlin, "I see what has not yet come to pass, but which might. This is perhaps the future."

Agrippa spoke to Vespasian; Vespasian replied, and Agrippa said, "If you know anything about the health of the legate's son, please tell us."

"I fear I have nothing to say," replied Merlin. He closed his eyes a moment. His mind reached out, stretched its fingers through the great Empire of the Romans. But he saw nothing more. "I cannot help the legate. I am sorry."

Agrippa and Vespasian exchanged a few more remarks in Latin; at last, Agrippa said, "The legate wishes you to begin your work now."

Merlin finished the wine and, bowing his head briefly to the legate, returned the cup with thanks to the slave. A moment later, he found himself surrounded by legionnaires, all bearing torches into the dark field.

* * *

A day passed in the sifting of the slain, while the sun sailed across the sky behind its veil of clouds. To Merlin, it was a day of bitterness, of weeping. Here were the noblest of the Island of the Mighty, their faces in the mud, clawing at the earth, or their eyes turned to the mourning heavens. Merlin looked into each face, and each one sent daggers into his heart.

When the sun had once more sunk behind the silhouette of Mai Dun, and torches had been lit so that leaping orange light was all around, Merlin found himself looking down into a shallow grave in which reposed the bodies of thirty-eight chieftains. Rhydderch lay there, his hands folded across his chest, and Cathbhad. Merlin wept.

A command in Latin and a coordinated rattle of arms told Merlin that the legate had arrived. Decius Agrippa was with him. Vespasian joined Merlin and peered with curiosity down into the grave. The faces of his enemies returned the stare, their features frozen. Vespasian put his hand on Merlin's shoulder.

"Thank you," he said in his heavily accented Brythonic. "I know this was not a pleasant task. I thank you." He spoke to Agrippa, who said to Merlin: "My commander wishes to know if King Caractacus is among these slain."

"He is not," replied Merlin.

There was an exchange between the two Romans, and then Agrippa said, "The legate wishes to know if there are any rituals attending the inhumation of these brave chieftains that you can administer."

Merlin took a deep breath. What he wanted to do was jump in beside them and pull the earth over his head. At length, he said, "Let each be buried with a tankard of ale, a joint of meat, and his weapons, that their places at the banquet beyond the grave may be honourable."

219

"My commander allows the tankard and the meat," said Agrippa, after a quick exchange of comments with the legate. "All weapons are to be confiscated, and so he cannot allow that."

Merlin closed his eyes. Once again, his soul put forth its fingers, stretching them out to the soldiers and officers surrounding him, and to the vast Empire that had grown up around seven hills in the sunny south. He saw plain-faced farmers on sun-drenched slopes pushing the plough through the fertile earth, wily politicians lurking in the narrow alleyways of cities, nurses tending their babies and, in the midst of it all, an aging emperor scratching away at a roll of parchment with a quill. He had spent his life writing histories, and now he had made some of his own. Merlin sent out his soul to them all, and felt its fingers brushing past their bodies, deep into their lungs, and up, through their throats and past their tongues and lips. His own fingers tingled, as if they were on fire, and he felt the fire in his own chest. Merlin took a deep breath, and opened his eyes.

"His Excellency is most generous to his subject," he said in perfect Latin. "Might I now be allowed to leave in peace?"

Agrippa's and Vespasian's eyes grew round. "Why did you not tell us that you could speak Latin?" demanded Vespasian.

"I did not know I could until this moment," replied Merlin. He smiled wryly. "My gods are good to me," he said.

Merlin slid his sword out of its sheath and presented the hilt to Vespasian, who took it wordlessly. Then he bowed to the grave containing his grandfather and best friend, turned, and began to leave. But before he had gone ten paces, Vespasian's voice stopped him.

"You are a prophet," said Vespasian. "Will you not stay with us, that our conquest of Britannia might be as devoid of violence as can be managed? A man of your skills could stop the flow of much blood."

Merlin indicated the grave. "These men could have helped you to rule the Island of the Mighty without *any* shedding of blood," he said. "They died rather than deliver Britain up to slavery. It is my curse that I too did not fall. But my place is with my people, and I cannot help you."

"Go in peace then, Merlinus Ambrosius," said Vespasian, "and may your gods prosper your ways."

Merlin inclined his head briefly, turned, and vanished into the night.

* * *

The weather began to close in as Merlin plied his way across the Great Plain. Overhead, the clouds loured, heavy with winter rains. All around him, the grass was flattened by the muscular winds that winter brought in. When Merlin reached the solemn ring of stones once more, the Giants' Dance, it was a sombre day of iron-coloured clouds, with light, wet snow driving into his face from the north. He strode into the midst of the giant monoliths and placed himself at the altar-stone, leaning forward over it, his mind immersed in thought.

Merlin had eaten little since leaving Mai Dun, and so his face had lost the softness of youth. It was hardened with age, and by many years of the world compressed into a few short months. His brows hung dark over eyes that glinted coldly as they stared into the north, past the Great Plain, past the world, into what lay beyond.

How long did Merlin remain there, with the snows blowing about him and the gigantic stones of the Ancient Ones surrounding him? Even in his later, and remarkable days, when he had been councilor to many kings, he could never say. Time seemed to have no meaning. The world seemed to move about him. He felt a power tremble in his sinews, and flow out through his fingers and into every corner of the realm. He saw the defeat of his people. He saw scarlet-clad soldiers tramping along razor-straight roads into the furthest reaches of Britannia. He saw square houses of square-pointed stone stand in straight lines where heroes had once gathered around the circular hearth. He saw the line of Brutus driven into the hills, to live in hunger and fear.

But he saw far more than that. For there was more to sing than defeat. Coroticos was alive: that he had known already, but now he saw him, his head bandaged, but his eyes open, and authority returning to him as he gathered the scattered remnants of the lords of Britain to him. It would not always go as the Romans wished. There would be an opposition.

"Show me more, Argante!" breathed Merlin, and he pushed the fingers of his mind further outwards. And he saw the Romans leave the Island of the Mighty, and he saw a city rise from the hills and valleys of Britain, silver its walls, and rising to the clouds, and in the hall a king such as the world had never seen, or would ever see again.

And in his hands was Excalibur.

The vision ceased, and Merlin felt the coldness seep back into his bones. He was on the Great Plain once more, surrounded by the Giants' Dance. He felt something, a small weight against his thigh, and he wondered what it was. There was a small, hard object in his belt-pouch, and he drew it forth curiously. It was the small figure of the merlin, given him by Gwelydd when he had left Afallach. He marveled for a moment that it had remained with him through so many moments of danger and anguish. His fingers closed tightly about it, and he nodded, once.

There was no track through the Great Plain, but Merlin struck out with boldness, as if his feet had found a highway. Merlin put the Giant's Dance and Mai Dun behind him, and strode resolutely into the north.

The End of Book One
The Matter of Britain

This is not a work of historical fiction. This is not an attempt to tell the story of Merlin "as it really was." If there really was a Merlin at all, he lived in the sixth century, not the first (where I place him) or the fifth (where most historians place Arthur), and his name was Myrddin. Some poems, attributed to this Myrddin, have survived, and I used some of these for my Merlin's prophetic speeches, and some of the symbolic detail of the narrative, particularly the apple trees.

It's fair to ask, then, exactly what it is I am doing. My aim is to tell the kind of story that would have been told in the Middle Ages, using more modern novelistic techniques for depicting scene and character. Traditional writers—Geoffrey Chaucer, the anonymous author of *Sir Gawain and the Green Knight*, Chrétien de Troyes—used a variety of sources to arrive at what they considered the most authentic—they would have said *authoritative*—version of a story. I have synthesized a variety of sources into something I believe is internally consistent and entertaining. I haven't tried to recover the historical Merlin, but the Merlin of medieval legend.

The first source for most writers of Arthurian novels is Geoffrey of Monmouth. His *History of the Kings of Britain*, written in about 1136, tells the story of all the kings of Britain from Brutus to the hapless Cadwallader. Merlin appears in one episode, in which he reveals that he had no father, having been engendered by a spirit; later, he enables Arthur's father to seduce Igerna, and so beget the Once and Future King.

Geoffrey's story was not original. He took it from *The History of the Britons*, once thought to have been written by a monk named Nennius. In this version of the story, the boy without a father is called Ambrosius or, in Welsh, Emrys. This and other medieval stories about Merlin were anthologized in a book that is, alas, out of print at the time of writing, called *The Romance of Merlin: An Anthology* (edited by Peter Goodrich, Garland, 1990).

In the early thirteenth century, an author named Robert de Boron melded together the stories of Merlin and the Holy Grail in a trilogy of poems called *Joseph of Arimathea, Merlin,* and *Perceval* (*Merlin and the Grail,* translated by Nigel Bryant, Brewer, 2001). According to Robert, the devils, after the Resurrection, decided to engender an Antichrist. Selecting a virtuous woman, one of the demons seduced her and the result was Merlin. His demonic paternity gave him the gift of prophecy. But the woman was a very pious person, and confessed her encounter to a priest, who consequently baptized Merlin, so that now his supernatural powers were harnessed for good, not evil. It is Robert de Boron who recounts the tale of Merlin's prophetic laugh at seeing a man buying leather to patch his shoes. The man, of course, dies before he reaches home with the leather. It seems like a bit of a sick joke to us in the twenty-first century, but Merlin's laughter is not belittling—it's more of an ironic, almost despairing laugh, that comes about because his prophetic powers help him to see the sorrow of life and death more keenly than others.

The standard scholarly history of the legend of Merlin is A. O. H. Jarman's *The Legend of Merlin* (University of Wales Press, 1970), and there are excellent, and sometimes very detailed chapters in *Arthurian Literature in the Middle Ages* (edited by R. S. Loomis, Clarendon, 1959) and *The Arthur of the Welsh* (edited by Rachel Bromwich and others, University of Wales Press, 1991). A splendid book on Merlin, from which I took many details, and which is largely persuasive in identifying a historical Merlin, is Nikolai Tolstoy's *The Quest for Merlin* (Sceptre, 1985).

No one knows much about the druids, except that they practised human sacrifice, and that oak trees were sacred to them. I have therefore invented most of the details about them. I took the description of the battle of Mai Dun from historical sources, though of course I have embroidered them somewhat. The description of Roman military tactics is quite accurate, since I couldn't invent anything better (or more terrifying) than that.

So many people, having read J. R. R. Tolkien's *The Lord of the Rings,* eagerly scurry off to their local bookshops to buy other fantasy novels, and are surprised that none of them come quite up to scratch. I would suggest that, although many modern Arthurian novels are excellent—Mary Stewart'-

s Merlin Trilogy, for example—the best place to go for further information, if you have enjoyed this novel, is to the medieval sources I have listed here. Happy reading!

* * *

No author works alone, and the help I have received from others is profound. First of all, I would like to thank my family for all the inconvenience that they have had to put up with. I know it was disturbing for Kit and Jack that I got up so early in the morning to work on the manuscript, and I know that my wife, Adrianne, has found it most inconvenient that I should spend so long in front of a computer, especially when she was herself working so hard on her doctorate. Will and Nick have on innumerable occasions woken up early, and crept upstairs into my lap, where they have again fallen asleep as I type. I hope that the results are worth what my family has had to endure.

In addition, I'd like to thank Adrianne for being the best proof-reader and friend any man could have; my son, Kit, who read the manuscript and offered the kind of invaluable comments that could only come from a fourteen-year-old boy; Di Francis, former colleague and fantasy author, who offered me many suggestions about marketing and rewriting my manuscript; and my former students, friends and colleagues at Missouri Valley College, who read and suggested, over many beers, many revisions: Nate Williams, Harry Carrell, Jim Crozier, Loren Gruber, and Emilee Murphree. Since they have all done what they can to save *The Hawk and the Wolf* from error, any flaws that remain are my own.

* * *

I'm honoured to have the opportunity of publishing a new edition of *The Hawk and the Wolf*, a little before the publication of its sequel, *The Hawk and the Cup*. It has given me the opportunity of correcting a few minor continuity and typographical errors, and including a glossary and pronunciation guide. I'd like to thank everyone who has bought and read *The*

Hawk and the Wolf since its publication in October 2008, and especially those whose helpful comments have enabled me to produce a slightly better novel. My thanks go especially to my new colleagues and students at Wyoming Catholic College in Lander, Wyoming, and, of course, to my family—Adrianne, Kit (now nineteen), Jack, Will and Nick.

Lander Wyoming
December 31, 2009

Glossary of Rare, Archaic, and Foreign Words, and Proper Names Appearing in *The Hawk and the Wolf*

ABER ALAW: Town near Afallach on Ynys Mon

ABER: River mouth (Welsh)

ADDANC: (Ah-THANK) Type of dragon created by Morgana

AFALLACH: (AH-vuh-LAK) The principle stronghold of the druids on Ynys Mon

AGOR: A fisherman of Habren, father of Gwyden

ALBANACT: Second son of Brutus, founder of Albany; guardian of the Bridle of Gwynn

ALBANY: One of the Seven Kingdoms of Britain, founded by Albanact, son of Brutus

ALED: An acolyte in Afallach; a maker of ink

ALUN: Servant in the household of Rhydderch

ANGHARAD: (ang-HA-rad) One of the Morforwyn, devoted to love and springtime

ANNWN: (AH-noon) The Otherworld, the realm of Morgana

ANNWYL: (uh-NOO-ul) A ship of ancient legend

ARAWN: (uh-RAWN) One of the Morforwyn, consort of Argante; he forged Excalibur

ARCHDRUID: Chief druid (q.v.)

ARGANTE: (ar-GAN-tay) One of the Morforwyn, consort of Arawn; she wrought the sheath for Excalibur

AVALON: The hidden realm of the Ladies of the Lake, those Morforwyn who survived the war against Morgana

BADISOMAGOS: Founder of the Summer Country and guardian of the Harp of Teirtu

BALOR: One of the Morforwyn, consort of Morgana; he fashioned the Siege Perilous or Dangerous Throne

BELGABARAD: (BEL-guh-BA-rad) Former High King of Britain, a lover of music but unfitted for kingship; he stole the Harp of Teirtu from the king of the Summer Country, but in turn lost it to Morgana

BELI: Father of Lludd

BELIN: Previous High King of Britain; twin brother of Brennios; together, they fought against and defeated Rome

BELINOS: (bu-LEE-nus) Friend of Cassivelaunos and king of the Summer Country

BELTANE: The spring festival of the druids, held on the first day of May

BOTHIE: A hut or small cottage

BOUDICEA: daughter of Cydwelli of Dinas Morfan

BRAN: Surnamed "the Blessed;" former high King of Britain; disappeared trying to rescue the Cauldron of Garanhir from the Addanc.

BRENNIOS: Previous High King of Britain; twin brother of Belin; together, they fought against and defeated Rome

BRUTUS: First high King of Britain, grandson of Aeneas

CAER CIREN: A Britonnic city fifteen miles southeast of Caer Lloyw

CAER GUINNTWIC: A small city in southern Logris

CAER LLOYW: (KAIR HLOI-oo) City in the Summer Country

CAER LUEL: A city in the north-west corner of Cameliard

CAER SIDDI: (KAIR SEE-thee) Morgana's fortress in Annwn

CAER: Castle (Welsh)

CAERMYRDDIN: (ker-MER-thin) principal southern fortress of Rhydderch

CALED: A member of Rhydderch's warband

CAMBER: Eldest son of Brutus, founder of Cambria; guardian of the Cauldron of Garanhir

CAMBRIA: The two peninsulae west of the River Sabrina (modern Severn), a land of mountains and valleys

CAMELIARD: (kuh-MEL-yard) One of the seven kingdoms of Britain, north of Logris and south of Albany

CAMELUS: Founder of Cameliard and guardian of the Veil of Gold

CARTIMANDUA: (kar-ti-MAN-du-ah) Queen of Cameliard

CASSIVELAUNOS: (Kas-i-veh-LAU-nus) previous High king of Britain, the last to bear Excalibur

CATHBHAD: (KATH-vad) Bard to Rhydderch of Cambria

CELLIWIG: The resting-place of the Prydwen

CERETICIAUN BAY: (KE-ruh-TIK-yawn) The wide bay between the two great peninsulae of Cambria

CERNGWYN: Prince of the stags of Afallach

CERVINE: Of deer or the deer family

CLYTWYN: (KLUT-win) One of Rhydderch's councilors

CONLA: Ancient king of Albany, who lost the Bridle of Gwynn

COOMBE: A narrow valley

CORDELIA: Daughter of Leir and, for a time, High Queen of Britain

CORINEUS: Lieutenant of Brutus; responsible for killing Gogmagog, chief of the giants in Britain

COROTICOS: Son of High King Tenvantios; twin brother of Cymbeline

CYMBELINE: (CUM-buh-lin) Son of Tenvantios; twin brother of Coroticos

CYNAR: (CUH-nar) Erstwhile king of the Summer Country

CYNFARCH: (KUN-vark) Lord of Caer Luel in Gwelydd's youth

DECIUS AGRIPPA: Interpreter for Vespasian, attached to the Second Legion Augustans

DERGAN: Druid of Afallach, who teaches memory

DIGON: One of Rhydderch's councilors

DINAS ERYRI: (DEE-nus e-ROOR-ee) The palace of Bran the Blessed, situation on top of Mount Eryri, the tallest mountain peak in Cambria

DINAS: Fortress (Welsh)

DRUID: A pagan priest of ancient Britain

DUN GUINNION: Principal fortress of Albany, built on the River Dubglas

DUN: dark (English); fort (Welsh)

DUROBRITH: City on the south coast of Logris

EFNISSYEN: (ev-NIS-yen) Evil brother of Bran the Blessed

EICENNIAWN: A region in the east of Logris, chiefly fenland, ruled by Prasutagos

EIRIN: (AIR-in) The large island west of Britain

ELIUD: Ancient High King of Britain

EMRYS: Gandson of Rhydderch, son of Viviane and somebody else

ENLLI: (EN-hlee) The northern peninsula of Cambria

EYAS: An eagle's nest

FERREX: Former High King of Britain; fought a civil war against his brother, Porrex.

GAIUS CALIGULA

GARANHIR: (guh-RAN-heer) One of the seven male Morforwyn, god of feasting and revelry, creator of the Cauldron of Plenty

GEASA: Plural of *geis*

GEIS: A fate declared upon one person by another (Irish)

GIANTS' DANCE: A stone circle located on the plains of the Summer Country

GLEDE: A burning coal, an ember

GLEIN: (glane) River dividing Logris from Cameliard

GOGMAGOG: Chief of the giants of Albion, slain by Corineus

GORSEDD ARBERTH: (GOR-seth AR-berth) The Hill of Arberth, site of one of Rhydderch's minor courts

GRWHYR: (GREW-heer) Son of Rhydderch

GUIDGEN: (GWID-gun) Druid of Afallach, teacher of philosophy

GUITHELIN: (GWI-thuh-lin) Twenty-fourth High King of Britain

GWEIR: Ancient king of Cameliard, who lost the Veil of Gold, one of the Seven Treasures of Britain

GWELYDD: (GWEL-ith) Archdruid of Ynys Mon

GWENDDOLAU: (gwen-THO-lai) Former king of Camgria; father of Rhydderch and great-grandfather of Emrys

GWENDOLYN: Daughter of Corineus, and husband of Locrin; after his death, High Queen for a time

GWERN: One of the boys in Rhydderch's court at Caermyrddin

GWILYM: Friend of Rhydderch's

GWYDEN: Goodwife of Habren, daughter of Agor

GWYNN: One of the Mororwyn, a tamer of beasts; he fashioned the Bridle of Gwynn, which was said to tame the beasts that wore it

HABREN: Fishing village at the estuary of the River Sabrina, on the northern coast of Cornwall

HERIT: Servant of Morgana

HOD HILL: Hill fort in southern Logris

IBAR: Druid of Afallach, teacher of prophecy

IMOGEN: Wife of Brutus and first High Queen of Britain

IOLO: (YO-lo) An acolyte in Afallach

IORWERTH: (YOR-werth) Druid of Afallach, teacher of rhetoric

JULIUS CAESAR

LEIR: In ancient times, a High King of Britain who, in his old age, attempted to divide his kingdom between his daughters. He was survived by one daughter, Cordelia

LLEU LLAW GYFFES: (hloo hlah guffis) The Britonnic god of light

LLUDD: (HLEETH) Former High King of Britain, son of Beli the Great, builder of the great walls and mighty buildings of Dun Lludd, or Lundein

LLYGAT: (HLUH-gat) Druid of ancient times, who possessed and learned to control the Sight

LLYWARCH: (HLUH-wark) An old man living in Aber Alaw

LOCRIN: Second High King of Britain, youngest son of Brutus and husband of Gwendolyn, after whom Logris is named

LOUVRE: A ventilating tower or hole

LUCIUS: Gaius Lucius Ventidius, emissary of Claudius Caesar to Britain

LUNDEIN: (LUN-deen) Principal city and fortress of Logris; principal court of the High Kings of Britain

LYONESSE: (LEE-uh-NESS) Archipelago between the southern coast of Britain and Benwick; founded as one of the minor kingdoms of Britain by Brutus' friend, Thera

MAGOS: King of the Summer Country

MAI DUN: A fortress near the south coast of Britain, within the borders of the Summer Country

MANAWYDAN: [MAN-uh-WUH-dun] One of the Morforwyn; famed for his love of the sea; built the Chariot of Manawydan

MARCIA: In ancient times, regent of Britain during the minority of her son, Silicios

MEDWAY: River in the south-east corner of Logris

MEINIE: A group of followers, attendants, or courtiers

MERLIN: A small falcon, with bluish wings and a reddish hood

MESSALINA: Wife of Claudius Caesar, empress of Rome; a woman of proverbially loose sexual conduct

MORDRAIG: Ancient ship of Britonnic legend

MORFORWYN: (mor-VOR-win) The gods and goddesses of the Britons. They were fourteen in all, seven men and seven women.

MORGANA: One of the Morforwyn, the fourteen gods and goddesses who fashioned the realms of Albion, Eirin, and Benwick in the time before the arrival of Brutus and the Trojans; she rebelled against the other Morforwyn.

MORGANNAWG: (mor-GAH-nog) Kingdom situated within Cambria, on the south coast.

ORKINNES: Founder of the kingdom of Orkney, guardian of the Chariot of Manawydan

ORKNEY: The archipelago kingdom north of Albany

PEN: Head (Welsh)

PENFRAN: (pen-VRAN) The great hall in Lludd's palace in Lundein

PILA: Plural of *pilum*

PILUM: The spear used by a Roman legionnaire. It was designed to bend upon impact, rendering it useless to an enemy

PORREX: Former High King of Britain; fought a civil war against his brother, Ferrex.

PRASUTAGOS: (PRAS-oo-TAH-gus) Duke, later king of Eicenniawn and aged husband of Boudicea

PRYDWEN: (PRUD-wen) Ship belonging to Cassivelaunos, in which Belinos took Excalibur before the battle with Julius Caesar

QUILLIONS: The crossguard on a sword's hilt, which protects the bearer's hand

RHIANNON: (ree-AH-non) One of the Morforwyn, she invented all the speeches of the birds and beasts, and was the poet of the Morforwyn. She cast her spells about the Cauldron of Garanhir, imparting the gift of poetry to those who drunk or ate from it

RHUFAWN: (ri-VAWN) Druid of Afallach, principally important for dying

RHYDDERCH: (RU-therk) king of Cambria, son of Gwenddolau and grandfather of Emrys

SABRINA: One of the major rivers of Britain, marking the border between Logris and Cambria; takes its name from Sabrina, the lover of Locrin, son of Brutus

SAMHAIN: (SAH-wen) The festival of the druids that marks the beginning of winter, celebrated on the last day of October

SAMITE: A heavy silken fabric

SARUM: Hill fort in southern Logris

SILICIOS: (suh-LEEK-yos) Twenty-fifth High King of Britain; son of Marcia

SPARROWHAWK: A type of small hawk, flown in the Middle Ages by priests

SPINNEY: A small wood or thicket

TEIRTU: (TAIR-too) One of the Morforwyn; he fashioned a wonderful harp to accompany the voice of Rhiannon, his consort

TENVANTIOS: (ten-VANT-yos) High King of Britain; father of Coroticos and Cymbeline

THAMES: (temz) River flowing through Lundein

THEWS: Muscle or sinew; hence, strength

TIBERIUS CAESAR

TIERCEL: A male hawk, about one third smaller than the female

TORC: A rigid circular neck ring

TRYBRUIT: (truh-BROO-it) River in Cambria, bordering Morgannawg to the west

TYLWETH: One of the local goddesses of Britain, not properly one of the Morforwyn; she is a water spirit, one of the race like the Greek naiads, created by Tyronoe

TYRONOE: (tuh-RON-way) One of the female Morforwyn, the goddess of lakes and rivers

VESPASIAN: Titus Flavius Vespasian, Legate of the Second Legion Augustans; in later events, Emperor of Rome

VIVIANE: Daughter of Rhydderch; mother of Emrys

WAIN: Cart

WATTLE: A wooden latticework of wooden stakes which, daubed with a mixture of clay and sand, formed the walls of many poorer medieval buildings.

WYSG: (oo-IZG) River in Cambria, bordering Morgannawg on the east

YNYS MON: (I-nis MON) Modern Anglesey, the home of the druids

YNYS: Island (Welsh)

About the Author

Mark Adderley was born in the railway town of Crewe, England. Like many of his contemporaries, he grew up devouring the novels of C. S. Lewis and, later, Ian Fleming and J. R. R. Tolkien. It wasn't until he was studying at the University of Wales, however, that he discovered the passion for the Arthurian legend that has now lasted . . . well, a very long time.

During his studies in Wales, Mark also met an American woman, Adrianne, whom he married. Moving to America, he got, in not very rapid succession, four children and a PhD in medieval literature from the University of South Florida. He has lived in Florida, Georgia, Montana, and Missouri, and now teaches writing and humanities at Wyoming Catholic College in Lander, Wyoming.

The Hawk and the Cup
The Matter of Britain: Book Two

The Island of the Mighty has been defeated. The shadow of the Eagle lies across the land. The Britons are a broken and defeated people. But hope lives in one man and one woman. The man is Merlin, Seer of the Island of the Mighty, whose quest for the ancient sword, Excalibur, kindles hope that the royal bloodline of Britain will one day be restored. The woman is the fiery-tempered red-haired beauty Boudicea, whose destiny it is to strike fear into the hearts of her Roman oppressors, and bring fire and blood to the cities raised by these foreign invaders.

This sequel to *The Hawk and the Wolf* continues the tales of Merlin and Boudicea, but paints a vivid tapestry of a defeated land, torn by betrayal and deceit, by political and religious factions. It is a land of war, a land of passion, a land of savagery; but it is also a land where, beyond all hope, can be found the one miraculous treasure that can restore peace to the land and fulfill the purposes of the gods of old.

The Grail.

The Hawk and the Huntress
The Matter of Britain: Book Three

Her home and family destroyed by Saxon invaders, young Nymve of the Cornawfi pursues her enemies relentlessly, bow in hand. She has nothing left; but the mysterious stranger who saves her life tells her that she is the possessor of a strange and daunting power that will enable her to influence kings and change the destinies of nations, a power he calls the Sight.

Set in an age hundreds of years after *The Hawk and the Cup*, *The Hawk and the Huntress* depicts the turmoil left in the Island of the Mighty when the Romans leave, and the Saxon barbarians invade. Seers and kings, warriors and goddesses abound in this exciting and violent novel. And at the centre of it all is Nymve, huntress and horse-tamer, prophetess and advisor to the High Kings of the Island of the Mighty.

Made in the USA
Charleston, SC
01 September 2010